Joolz Denby is an award-~~~~  word artist and illustrator. F~~~~ the CWA award for New Cr~~~~ 'Billie Morgan' saw her sho~~~~ She has performed at count~~~~ rary music festivals, and lite~~~~ ...hen not travelling, she lives in Bradford in a house stuffed with cats, musicians, and curios. She is a sporadic gardener, a practising tattooist, and an obsessive reader who never quite manages to get enough sleep. For more info, go to **www.joolzdenby.co.uk**

by Joolz Denby

novels
Stone Baby
Corazon
Billie Morgan
Borrowed Light
The Curious Mystery...

poetry
Mad, Bad & Dangerous To Know
Emotional Terrorism
The Pride of Lions
Errors of the Spirit
Pray For Us Sinners

Wild Thing

Joolz Denby

ISBN: 978-0-9567786-2-8

Typeset by Steve at Ignite.
www.facebook.com/ignitebooks

Printed and bound in the UK
by MPG Books Group,
Bodmin and King's Lynn

Dedication

Dedicated to anyone who ever loved a wild thing.

My thanks and respect to the Goddess, as ever.

Acknowledgements

I would like to thank Steve Pottinger for his unceasing support and hard work - without him this book would not have happened.

Prologue

Metatron

'My Beautiful Blonde'
© 2006 Velvet Shank: Eliot/Graves/Lingard/Johansson

She smokes black Sobranie at midnight
Her hair is silver with tipped moonlight
Her nails sharp tinted with blood
Her lips feel like velvet dust

Bridge: *I'm on fire I'm in flames*
When she looks at me my world will crumble
When she looks at me my world will fall
When she stares into my innocent soul I'll know

Chorus: *You're my beautiful Blonde (repeat).*

She smokes black Sobranie at midnight
I miss your lips your sweet acid kiss
I miss the way we walked together
I miss the way we used to fuck

Bridge

Chorus

She smokes Black Sobranie at midnight
The only woman to scar my soul
She lived fast within my kingdom
I could have given you the world, my world, my world

Chorus *(repeat to fade).*

Once upon a time, long ago and far away, I had everything you're supposed to want. All the stuff they tell you about on the telly and in the celeb mags, the lifestyle you're supposed to die for. I had a good job at a major record company, a bijou loft apartment in London, the parties, the clothes, the gorgeous rock-star boyfriend, the cocaine, the champagne, the permanent guest-list at the kind of clubs that pissed-up silicone-sculpted glamour-models are paparazzi'd leaving with a Premier League footballer in tow and without their knickers. The Brit Awards. AAA passes to everything from Unsigned Bands Night at some tiny, hip club to The Pyramid Stage at Glastonbury and The Stones Honest-To-God-Final-Goodbye concert at Wembley - all four nights. I had invites to everything; the *OK!* wedding of a whippet-sized chart-topping popstrelle and her thicko backing-dancer fiancé, the openings of the hottest new bars, clubs, galleries, boutiques; oh, you name it, I turned it down because I couldn't be arsed. Or I went, and made out like I was bored stiff, which mostly, I was, celeb culture not being all that, in actuality.

All of it. I had all of it, and more. Jesus, the tales I could tell - not that anyone would believe me because they wouldn't be about how great it all was and what fascinating and worthwhile people boy-bands, pop-whores and rock musicians are. Or MPs, newscasters, actors and celebrity chefs either, for that matter. Those stories wouldn't toe the party line, boost the media profile, you see. Ha! Christ, far from it - like, remember that MP, the one who was on the box all the time saying how Britain should return to a state of decency and Christian principles? Him with the blond hair and fat red face? Yeah - you know. I once saw him at a party stark naked on all fours on a dining table, coked off his tits, eating - well, yeah, not the entrées anyway. People were cheering him on while they shook bottles of Moet and sprayed him and his - dinner - with them. Cool, eh? Right.

Once upon a time, I'd never have named the names - it was a point of honour. But honour is an expensive luxury when so much is at stake. Oh, God - I never, ever wanted this, I didn't, I prided myself on being discreet, being dependable, being the sealed repository of so many, many secrets. But sometimes, like they say, you have to do what you have to do. I've got someone else to think of now, not just myself. Yeah, yeah, maybe I'm just being over-sensitive, the likes of those tossers get theirs one way or another whatever - but I bet they never thought it would come from the likes of me. I'm a weapon, now, and I've pulled the trigger, pressed the button, loosed the arrow. It's all chaos, now.

Jesus, it's so cold here, freezing. I'm freezing. What the fuck have I done? What possessed me to bring it all to this? God in heaven, what have I done? I thought I was right, you know? I was so convinced, so completely sure I was right, I thought I was doing the decent thing, being stand-up, a real heroine. But it's such a mess, such a fucking mess.

And Wild Thing is out there. On the frost-silvered black hillside. I know what he'll look like; I've watched him so many times before. He'll be a dark shape cut out of the icy ground and the sharp diamond glitter of the freezing stars; sinuous, silent, full of power; a shadow moving this way like thunder creeping over the horizon. You'd never spot him if you didn't know how to look for him. But I know. I know.

He's on his way home.

He loves me.

Book One

Michael, The Archangel.

'The Edge . . . There is no honest way to explain it because the only people who really know where it is are the ones who have gone over . . .'

Hunter S. Thompson

One

When I moved back home to Bradford it rained for three weeks solid. Everyday the sky hung overhead, blossoming grey like diluted ink laid on wet blotting paper, silver veils of rain drawing across the city like the sequinned dupatta of a Bollywood queen, the glorious amber of the intricate sandstone buildings soaked to a dull and dirty mud colour.

OK, I thought, let's see who breaks first. I admit I was wavering by day fourteen or so, but Bradford doesn't rate the weak so I stuck it out, bought a pair of pink paisley patterned wellies and an outsize umbrella and, when no-one was looking, stuck two fingers up at the sky. I knew what was going on; this was the prodigal's return, Northern style. I'd left when I was seventeen, putting those same two fingers up at my family and the whole world. I packed my little bag with what I considered a college girl's necessities - Clearasil, cheap perfume, spare knickers, my hoard of Miner's make-up, a tangle of trash-glitter jewellery - and hitched to London, to do English at the good university I'd got into without any trouble and the blank amazement of my family, all by my lonesome. No tearful mummy and proud daddy with the Volvo full of their darling girl's possessions for me; no brand-new college scarf from dear old Auntie Marge as a good luck gift, oh no. I was on my own. That was made abundantly clear to me by my dear brother.

I wasn't ever coming back. I promised myself that as I shivered in the passenger seat of a decent-enough fella's company saloon, while he worried about the skinny girl huddled in his nice motor, a plum-black bruise shutting her left eye in a congested knot and a split lip making smiling difficult - if I'd wanted to smile, which I didn't. Not then. It was too painful and not because of my swollen mouth.

Those bruises were my brother's parting gift, you see. Allen's little *memento mori*, his response to my refusal to play the part of a dutiful daughter and obedient sister, as he played the wholly imaginary part of a loving brother and our mother did a bravura performance as a heartbroken widow. Keeping up appearances. Not disgracing the family. Nobody's business but our own. The rug nailed firmly in place over the truth. Allen's wiped his memory clean of the actual past nowadays and expects me to do the same, but guess what? No deal. Not that it matters, to be honest, I never see them, write to them or phone; no Christmas cards, birthday kisses, nothing. They return the favour. I suppose I divorced them, if you like, but if so, it was by mutual consent. I never was good at sticking to the party line and all that and unless it's Allen's way, it's no way, as they say. So be it.

We were what they like to call a nice, middle-class family, the heavy, gelid bandages of respectability forming us into a shape acceptable to society. To suburbia, if you like. We lived in a so-called 'good' part of Bradford (i.e. no corner shops, cloth houses or tatterdemalion rows of curry houses - no *coloureds* as my mother still persists in calling Black or Asian people). It was a white enclave of slightly-better-than-Barratt houses and neatly kept B&Q gardens. My late father, the bastard, was a head teacher at Ravenscliffe Middle School and my dear old mum a housewife who could, and often did, spend entire mornings on her knees polishing the kitchen lino. Brother Allen is five years older than me and built like a brick shithouse, echoing in his maleness mums's thickset, mono-bosom physique. Earthy, heavy. Naturally, Allen - never Al, by the way - played rugby and drank like a fish. Mum and Allen are dark brunets with hazel eyes set a tad bit too close together to be really attractive. My father was stocky, brown hair fringing a balding pate; he shaved twice a day but always had a blue chin and his small, deep-set brown eyes were like chips of obsidian.

Me, though - oh dear. I'm blonde, my thick yellow hair reaching nearly to my waist in an uncut static plume which I keep in an untidy braid. It's faded a bit now, getting silvery, but it's still genuine, unbleached and authentic blonde. Rare, these days, so they say. I am tall, skinny and wiry, with long attenuated limbs and no tits or arse to speak of. You can count my ribs and the knobs of my spine but I eat like a pony with worms. My eyes are the clear, bright sky-blue of the Viking North. My skin is ivory-white; in winter, without the sun to give me a paper-brown tan and warm me up, I am so pale as to be faintly 'illuminous' as they say in Bradford, meaning luminous. I like illuminous better; it's prettier and as I'm not exactly an oil painting, being snub-nosed, lumpy-cheekboned, slanty-eyed and angular, I need all the prettiness I can gather to my bony chest.

In fact, truth be told, I apparently resemble almost uncannily Bob Hansen, the local odd-job fella and garden maintenance chap. My actual dad. My mother's - what? Lover? Shag? Stud? Bit on the side? None of these descriptions gel with my lifelong image of mum as the dowdy, stolid background to our family's own personal mini-true-life-drama-soap-opera thing. But whatever you could - and father did - call mum, her time with Bob was her once in a lifetime moment of complete and utter madness; her one, and only, rebellion. Everyone has one, and in mum's case she got a lasting souvenir of it - me. Not that Bob knew about having an illegitimate daughter, or I ever knew him, my illegitimate dad. He'd moved on years before I was old enough to know why the family treated me as they did. I did try to find him later, when I was older, and I succeeded; but I was six months too late, he was dead. Both of them are dead - Bob, and Denis, my so-called father, the man who gave me his name, Wynter. I'm Anne-Louise Wynter. Annie Wynter. Pleased to meet you; and for those who might remember me from the Big Smoke Days, yes indeedy, you are correct, it's Annie Wynter the Snow Queen. Minus the snow, though, and the blow, and the Jack and the Stoli. Minus the designer threads. Minus Johnny. Clean as real winter snow, in fact, and as good as white spun gold. You don't believe me? Well, it's a stone fact, lover, and no mistake. I am a new woman.

But to get back briefly to my family - excuse me if I laugh. Mr. Wynter, as I thought of him, though in public I was obliged to call him 'father'; not 'dad' or 'daddy' - too intimate, that, too bloody familiar - was what is sometimes called a strong disciplinarian. A good Catholic, a pillar of the Church and so strict that he eventually got asked to re-sign from his school for caning a dysfunctional little brute who whacked a young female English teacher round the head with a chair, sending her to Casualty with a broken cheekbone and concussion. Corporal punishment was no longer the acceptable face of school care, to father's chagrin. The kid should have been counselled, tutored in anger-management, possibly, eventually, excluded; you should have heard what father thought of *that*.

Anyway, there were too many rumours father enjoyed belabouring the mini-thug's arse with a garden bamboo more than he should have. Well, yeah - I could have told them he would have, I expect he got no end of a kick from it. He always did when he smacked me or mum around. Had to lock himself in the bathroom with one of his totter-ing stack of porno mags and get it out of his system after every savage, silent struggle round the living room. He was always careful though, as he punched mum or me in the sides and back - no facial bruising, that's a dead give-away, Allen should have taken note - not to knock over the collection of devotional German porcelain he was so proud of. Our Lady, strangely blonde and buxom for a Jewess, watching me from glazed china-blue eyes; Our Lord hanging from his pottery tree, the expression on his smooth Aryan face a saccharine simulacra of sympathy.

I was the excuse, you see, the reason that allowed father to do what he wanted to do so badly. I was the trigger that let him justify venting his rage and frustration at being stuck rotting alive in a backwater provincial hole - as he thought of Bradford - and being forced to run a fifth-rate baby-sitting service for inbred, retarded estate scum disguised as a school, and him with the good Cambridge degree, boo-hoo. He was a young man with a bright future, as they say, until he met mum at a Catholic Youth Alliance dance and her then shapely curves, entrancing perfume ('Tabu'), Revlon red lips and shining dark hair done all à la mode bewitched him and forced him to fuck her unprotected like a good son of the Faith until she fell for our Allen - her fault, naturally - and they had a classic shotgun wedding.

Boom-bang-bang. His dream of a life of glittering advancement collapsed like a pricked balloon. Then oddly enough, some cold and barren years after he stopped desiring her and started hating and tormenting her, mum eventually turned to the winning charm (I'm making this up, because of course, I wasn't there and have no idea if my blood-dad was charming or just available) of Bob, the local rake, if you'll pardon the gardening pun.

I was the final body blow, the bitter icing on the rancid cake of Mr. Wynter's failure, the by-blow foisted on him by a callous whore. He made sure I knew my place, him and Allen, the true son, the golden boy.

Oddly, given father was a teacher and could well have put me off learning for life, school was my saviour (rather than Our Lord, as it goes). I was a bright student, because it took my mind off what I had to go home to; I was reasonably popular because I made sure I was. I perfectly created the image of a willing, pleasant, trouble-free pupil, always happy to stay behind and help out with the Art Club, or the Chess Club or the Girl's Brigade or absolutely bloody anything that meant I could shorten my time with the family. I got good grades. I got excellent reports. No one ever saw me wincing as the bruises ached or pulled. No-one ever knew I was a cutter.

Yes, indeed. The teenage girl's best friend is all too often a razor-blade, the sharp solution to pain relief; nothing eases mental pain like that icy slice of physical hurt that *you* control, *you* apply like a plaster made of broken glass to the thudding hurt of your wounded heart. I don't expect many understand how it works, but if you've ever done it - you'll remember the feel of that bright, familiar intensity and hear that fibrous sound as the edge parts your skin and the flash of feeling hits your body with a wave of adrenalin. I was a cutter. Not a massive one with arms like chopped liver, but discreet, private. I did it purely for myself, for my own relief. I grew out of it eventually. Sort of.

I was a big mess with a bright smile and long sleeves, even in summer.

Anyway, Father died in a car crash when I was just eighteen. Two days after my birthday, in fact, and a couple of months before I headed off to the place at North London University I had fought for and won. Father had scoffed long and hard at that; hardly Cambridge, after all. But good enough for the likes of me, and I need not think he'd

8

be topping up my grant money. Whatever. He went head on into the river at that bad curve on the way into Bingley at the stroke of twelve one rainy night. Died instantaneously, they said, but they always say that, don't they? A classic drunk driver. He drank, too, as you might imagine; naturally drugs were the devil's candy, the terminal ruination of a morally corrupted society, but industrial quantities of Johnny Walker Red Label are a real man's pleasure, like the prostitutes he frequented and told mum about in alcohol-stinking wire-tight ratcheting whispers as they lay side by side in their icy marriage bed like enemy soldiers forced to take cover together in a fox-hole. I could hear it though, in my little bedroom next to theirs, the walls being paper-thin in those houses; I think he knew I could, too, because sometimes he said things that betrayed him. It was a threesome, only instead of sex with a pair of bored street-walkers it was two shivering women listening against their wills to him puke out his sins, to receive the unholy malediction of his confession; it was a kind of spiritual rape.

I knew all about sex by the time I was twelve. All about it. Every suck, fuck and tug. He never laid a lustful finger on me but he didn't have to. He fucked my head. I was a physical virgin until I was eighteen - yeah, that old - but I was as familiar with the techniques of lust as if I were a forty-year old professional courtesan.

But we never spoke of any of this in public. That was unthinkable. Even after he died and the charade of us being a loving, devastated family began. Even mum, who you'd think would have been ecstatic at her liberation and run away to join the Merry Widow Brigade, folded in on herself and continued to be the perfect wife, in death as she was in life, bound to the consuming rage of a brutal and self-obsessed man. Allen just became father. It was uncanny. The night of the funeral he backhanded me for saying I wasn't sorry father was dead. Smack, and the taste of blood in my mouth again. *'He was a wonderful man and a credit to his profession, you little bitch - you should be grateful he took you in and didn't send you to an orphanage like any other man would have, I should make you stay here and care for our mother, instead of letting you go gallivanting off to bloody college . . .'* Etc, etc, on and on, while mum sobbed tonelessly like a leaky tap and said nothing. Just like she always had.

I realised then that getting out of Bradford was not merely a jaunt, but a matter of survival.

Two

London, eh? The Great Wen, the Metrollops, the biggest shill of all. Sometimes, when I get out of my car having driven fifteen minutes out of Bradford and fetched up in some gorgeous bit of russet and purple moorland, each autumn fern embroidered with ice-pearl sequinned curlicues of frost, the sky the melting, tender blue of the Blessed Virgin's cloak, the air crystalline and singing with the high, silver note of rubbed glass, I do wonder how I stuck the Big Smoke so long.

I never intended to come home, I'll make that clear straightaway. Even after I finished college and everyone expected me to return with my useless bloody degree I didn't, but instead continued to struggle into the music industry like a besotted moth battering itself against a fluorescent tube. I thought about it, about giving up and going back many times, like when I was half-dead with homesickness, hunger and exhaustion, lying shivering in my doss bag on the floorboards of some scabies-ridden squat, or especially when I trudged the streets looking for temporary work, or attempted to get some money from London's infamously harsh dole offices.

Someone told me once they'd worked for the dole in London, and had been instructed by their superiors to ensure that those claimants coming from outside the city were made to go back and starve in the provinces by any means possible, rather than litter up London with more transient trash. Insult them, the boss had said, cut their money off for any and every reason, abuse them and make their lives a hell of humiliation and shame. Right-oh, this

11

fella had said, and handed in his resignation after a week of seeing the boss had actually meant it, good-style.

The first time I went to Tavistock Square dole office, for example, and waited my turn in the damp stinking fug of misery and stoic hopelessness, clutching my numbered ticket in my ratty Goth-queen lace-mittened hand, chewing at last night's black nail polish and thinking of food, lovely, greasy nosh and lots of it, the civil servant who interviewed me called me a whore and a disease and told me to go back to the stinking slum I'd crawled out from, pronto. That was just the start of an unending brutalisation that saw young men, pushed past bearing, throw themselves at the screens dividing the scum - us - from the decent types - them, and bounce off the Plexiglass weeping. That saw old people ripped into by mealy-mouthed girls in ill-fitting blue suits, that saw lone young mothers abandon their toddlers in Archway Towers Office because they no longer had the dosh to feed two mouths always open like baby birds. It was as near to hell as I can imagine.

But I wasn't going to go back to Bradford, no way. Not even when Allen and mum moved down to Chichester when Allen got his much-vaunted job in IT after marrying that snivelling slice of permatanned Leeds strawhead anorexia, Judi. No, even though I was then finally technically free to return to Bradford, I didn't.

After all, I had the legendary London lifestyle. By age thirty-five I'd done well, dragged myself up by my concho'd bootstraps, up from the gutter to a position in the music industry most women would think enviable. I got there by sheer hard work, slogging it out in student bars, then becoming social secretary for the student's union (the 'union' part being a joke, you understand) and after that, in clubs, then venues, then up and up and up through carefully cultivated contacts, favours done and owed, secrets kept. I had the kind of blind, demented determination and ambition that comes from knowing *exactly* how far you'll fall back down if you fail. And I never fail. I never let myself fail. I was far too terrified for that. My life was fully mapped out, fully one hundred and ten percent sorted.

So, I had the flat - sorry, loft apartment - which was bijou to the point of actual claustrophobia and cost an arm and a leg. There was the social life - work related and drug related - and the job, personal secretarial assistant to Vinny Fallon, head of A&R at GMC Records. That's Artistes and Repertoire in case you ever wondered. We looked after the meat market. Yeah, so, GMC, *Global Music Corporation,* that should tell you all you need to know about what sort of music company we were. But I'd always liked music, I was always humming some tag of a song and unlike some in the music industry, I listened to my tottering stacks of CDs for pleasure. And I loved the shoddy glamour of showbiz. Suited me down to the ground; I could play the fast track, as I thought, and not have to wear a bloody suit myself. I wasn't going to remain a secretary, no way. I did all my work and Vinny's, too, I knew his job better than he ever could and his good standing in the company was wholly my doing. He knew it, and was very free with the bribes and sweeteners.

So I strolled into the Tower, as our offices were called, in my wildly expensive but worth every penny R. Soles custom-made cowboy boots, perfect black Italian faux-biker jacket and exquisitely knackered Levis, and was considered by the jovial executives to be an asset to the decor. I snorted coke at lunchtimes, drank Jack Daniels or Stoli iced and straight up by night, and had a few pipes of good mellow weed every bedtime to smooth me out before hitting the futons. I had my hair done at Daniel Galvin by the man himself and a spa day once a month with my girlfriends at The Sanctuary. We usually chose the Detox Seaweed Body

Wrap in the belief it would help get the shit we'd consumed for the previous twenty-seven days out of our systems. Then that night we'd go to Heaven, the Town And Country, or The Marquee and stick it all back in ourselves again. I was a long skinny blonde with a pitbull attitude, great people skills from the years I'd spent hustling and cadging round the squats of North London and I ran useless, spineless, gormless, well-connected Vinny's micro-empire single handed.

I also had Alec. My boyfriend, partner, co-habitee, call it what you want. We'd hooked up early on, when I'd first joined the company. He was tall, emaciated, Irish and wore long voluminous black overcoats. I used to joke that naked, we looked like two strands of cooked spaghetti. He never laughed; people think all the Irish are naturally hilarious, but it's a stupid racial stereotype, as mindless as all the rest. Alec was from just outside Belfast. A Protestant. Humour wasn't really his thing. He was an in-house graphic artist, doing album covers for various bands including Bradford's finest, Ultimate Angel - who were Vinny's (my) pet project at the time. That's how we met. I didn't like his first offering for the band's third album, *Carcinomicon*. The difficult third album. Like the difficult second album, but worse. Anyway, Alec had mindlessly churned out something corporate and bland, which he admitted after I'd chewed his ear for a while on the phone. He sounded so crestfallen and his accent was so cute and Undertones-ey, I offered him to come see the band that Saturday. He did, we became lovers, and two months later we moved in together.

The first six months of our relationship was fun; we shagged ourselves blind as you do until you're out of baby oil and desire, and ran all over the city like nutters; or at least, come to think of it, I ran and Alec followed me like a muttering scarecrow shadow. Looking back, I don't think he enjoyed it much, he did it because that's what you're sup-posed to do if you're from Belfast (or any other provincial city) and you've managed to become a Proper Artist Living In London. Something to big up for your sad little mates back home. *Last night me and the bird went to the Te&C to see the Angel, yeah, backstage, course, oh tons of coke, booze - and the women, fuckin' hell, tits out all over, skirts up their arses, like a fuckin' strip show, beggin' for it, offerin' blow-jobs for passes, oh yeah, honest, not a word of a lie - not that I'd - y'know - what with Herself in tow but I could've, oh yeah . . .*

Then, after we'd been together, properly living together for two years, I fell pregnant. At first, I couldn't believe it; it seemed impossible somehow, not something I'd ever seen myself doing, becoming - a mother, *a mother*, me? No, it was . . . Frankly, it was fucking ludicrous and it didn't fit in with my Grand Plan one little bit. I tested and re-tested myself, watching that plastic stick crank out blue crosses until I was forced to accept the fact that I was up the duff. Two and a half months or so gone, to my dizzy, frantic reck-oning. Panic flooded through me like an icy-hot wave, feverish and shivering. There was something growing inside me, I was making another human being in my completely flat and normal-looking belly. Throwing the last positive test into the corporate waste bin in the corporate Ladies, I took the afternoon off pleading a forgotten dental appointment - no-one cared. It was Friday anyway, no-one worked on Friday afternoon in our business.

I walked through the iron-grey streets and stinking vertiginous alleys contemplating my fate. Obviously, I had to get rid of it. I'd book the appointment on the coming Monday. I couldn't have a baby, the very idea was a joke - me, with my lifestyle? Ha bloody ha. I think not. Why, the people I hung with would think me mad to even consider it. I drifted up to Oxford Street for no particular reason;

perhaps I'd nip into Selfridges or Liberty's and buy some desperately expensive perfume, as a gesture of defiance. Something heavy and musky, something no self-respecting mother would wear. Yeah, why not? My mind skittered over the thought of the actual abortion like a skater creaking and grinding on thin ice; the details I'd heard from my night-time pals stuttered in my head. I knew exactly what happened, I'd been served the gory elaborations many times - the suction, the pain, the humiliation. There were even clinics of choice, discussed as if they were the latest sushi bar, marks being given to the ones that didn't cost and arm and a leg and didn't subtly - or not so subtly - make you feel like a whore and a murdering bitch. Not nice. But, so what? If they could hack it, I certainly could. It wasn't like I had a choice.

As I walked on, hands thrust into the pockets of my jacket, London seemed awash to the gunnels with hugely pregnant women breasting the swell of the shopping and sightseeing crowds like galleons in full sail, their faces heiratic and sealed, inward-looking. Women pushed funky buggies stacked with kids and shopping, or window-shopped Hamley's with mesmerised toddlers floating round them on kiddie-reins like tethered buoys. It was a like a plague of Madonnas, an epidemic of fecundity. It was disquieting, uncomfortable - didn't they care they had no life anymore? Weren't they bothered about giving up their lives to a red-faced brat screaming in a too-big Paddington duffle-coat about sweets? They must be mad, I reckoned, bonkers.

I stopped at a coffee bar and ordered a double espresso. I didn't have to be careful what I ate and drank because shortly, I wouldn't be knocked up anyway. I lit a fag, one of my signature Black Sobranie, and took a deep drag.

It tasted like shit, and my gorge rose. Stubbing it out quickly, I drank a sip of bitter coffee. At the next table, a woman with a baby in her arms smiled at me, thinking, I suppose, I'd put the cigarette out from courtesy. Because of her baby.

Her baby.

The woman bent and kissed the sleeping baby's head. Just brushed her lips against its perfect chocolate-brown forehead that creased slightly like fine silk. Its eyelashes were so curled as to almost form a roll, and its lips perfectly and exquisitely pink.

My baby would be as fair as this little one was dark, I thought. My baby . . .

Something rose up and bloomed in my heart like a dark flower, a thousand petals expanding into every part of my being.

And the bravado and panic that had driven me ebbed slowly to be replaced by a trickling inrush of an intense and painfully tender joy; sheer joy, a kind of bliss as I fell in love with the little thing in my womb. With my baby, my child. As I watched that mother and her child I knew that this baby, my child, would be the one creature in the world that I could love unconditionally and who would love me back the same. Who would fill the roaring void that my upbringing had riven in my spirit. I would be whole, at last. It was a revelation, a vision. I began to make plans, to put aside all the petulance that had made me take test after test, the voice that said *'what about your lifestyle, gigs, that razzle-dazzle free and footloose tango you've worked so hard for?'*

I looked at my life and it seemed like a adolescent fantasy gone well past its sell-by date; it'd been fun, but now - well - now I had bigger things to do. I allowed myself, for the first time in my life, to dream of love. Not the thing I had with Alec, but proper, real, love. I knew it would make me vulnerable, put a chink in my carefully constructed carapace of hard-nosed tough-bitch armour, but I didn't care. It would be worth it. Throwing caution (and a good twenty-five quid) to the winds, I got a taxi home rather than scrabble about in the Tube. Alec, a daddy - how weird was that? God, he'd be thrilled. Only last week he'd said how his brother had two little'uns already and him not twenty-two, *he* wasn't firing blanks at any rate, and their sister was on her third, ready to pop any day. Their mammy was in heaven with the grandkids.

I cooked my best dinner - steak, salad with my own special dressing and buttered new potatoes, followed by Belgian Chocolate Haagen-Daz - and uncorked a bottle of choice burgundy I'd been given as a bribe by an agent. I lit candles, got my best at-home kit on. Then I told Alec.

At first I thought he hadn't heard. He kept chewing his sirloin and forking more salad onto his plate. I repeated what I'd said. Nothing.

'Did you hear me love? I'm . . .'

'Yeah, I heard.'

I was puzzled. Maybe it was such a shock he couldn't take it in. 'Well, whaddya think? Are you - are you pleased, I mean . . .'

He pushed his plate away and got up. Picking his coat up from where it lay on the sofa, he walked the step to the front door. Then he turned and looked at me, his face dead white and a red splotch high on each sharp cheekbone. Chill radiated from him like a frosty fume.

'This has got nothin' ter do with me, d'y'hear? I didn't want this,' he said in a dead, toneless voice. 'You'll have ter deal with it yourself. I'm off out, Babylon Red are on at the Astoria, don't know when I'll be back. Don't wait up.'

The finality in his voice was like a physical blow.

'Alec, Alec, for fuck's sake, you can't . . .'

He didn't come home that night, or the next. His mobile was turned off and he didn't reply to any of the increasingly frantic texts I sent him. On the Sunday he appeared as if nothing had happened and when I tried to talk to him about it all, he went to bed saying he needed an early night, he had a big job starting tomorrow with The Hellions cover.

He didn't shout, rant or row with me. He didn't say anything. It was a taboo subject. If I said anything, or he caught me retching in the tiny, damp smelling bathroom, he looked disgusted and went out. Desperate for some moral support, I told work, and all my friends; I told them he was thrilled but didn't want to talk about it because his family thought that bad luck. You know, the Irish. Very superstitious. No-one questioned it, even though Alec was a Belfast Proddy not a staunch village Catholic from County Clare or wherever; no-one I knew knew anything about the reality of Ireland or wanted to, it was all *The Quiet Man* and *Finnegan's* bloody *Wake* to them, bejaysus begorrah.

Alone in my strange new world, I browsed Mothercare and bought cute little outfits for Lump, as I called it, waiting for Alec to come round; he was panicking, I thought, just a bit scared but in a little while, when I really began to show and he saw it was reality he'd accept it and see how it would be the making of us and everything would be OK. It would. It would.

I wanted it to be alright with Alec because I was so happy; not in the way I used to be happy - with that hot scratchy high from getting a new outfit, pulling off a little office coup or getting passes for some blow-out concert. This was a kind of enfolding warmth that left me staring out of the window a smile blooming on my lips as I felt the narcotic peace of detachment and fulfilment, a fulfilment I'd never dreamed of, never saw myself as ever wanting before, crept through me. I began to think the unthinkable; if Alec didn't come round, I - well, I'd just go it alone. Not that it would come to that, but if it did . . . It'd be me and

Lump, just the two of us. I'd manage. Hadn't I always?

Two days after I started making plans for my new life, I developed influenza. Not a cold, but proper, real, killing flu. Four days after that, sick as a dog, with a temperature of 103 and all alone in the flat as Alec had gone to a music convention in Birmingham despite my begging him to stay, I lost the baby. I lost my baby.

I was in hospital when Alec finally got back. I hadn't bothered calling him, nor did I ask the nurses to. I'd called a married pal of mine, Jenni, who'd run round with her husband and got me to Casualty, she'd seen what was happening straightaway, having been there herself; she'd wanted to call Alec, but I'd said no, no, don't bother. I expect she thought we were splitting up, that's what you'd think, right?

But we didn't. Not for quite a long while.

Alec looked after me sketchily in a cool, disinterested fashion and said nothing about the loss of my child. My child, not his. He fetched and carried ungraciously while I convalesced and fielded calls from my friends when they found out about the miscarriage. They all thought he was too distraught to talk about it, that he was a typical bloke, unable to cope with emotions; they tsk'd and heaved knowing sighs; men, you couldn't invent 'em, eh?

In time, I recovered. I returned to work, twice as efficient, twice as energetic, twice as up for anything that distracted me from my solitary mourning. Alec and I continued as if the whole thing had never happened, but the remaining time was a long gradual slide into bickering and sniping because, really, we hated each other, now I look back. It wasn't huge flaming rows, *that* I could have dealt with, it was all nit-picking about who should take the bin-bags out, who should load the washer, who should clean the bog. Sex ceased. Cuddles ceased. Everything ceased after I got home from a weekend away at a festival to find him fucking my so-called best mate Marie. In our bed. I pulled her off him - he always was lazy - by the hair extensions and slapped her face. Hard. As she squealed and struggled into her nasty red lace Ann Summers thong, Alec told me to leave her alone, it wasn't fair, she was delicate, unlike me, she was a proper woman not a fucking bitch always trying to break a guy's balls and destroy his life, and she was someone he cared about very much and had done for over a year. How about that, you fucking bitch, over a fucking year.

He cared about her, Jesus. What a fool that man was. Don't men ever realise they can say anything in that situation - except that? Say you were just shagging her, lads, say it was meaningless, she put it on a plate and temptation got the better of you, say you'll never do it again, but never say you care, or that you love her. That's the end of everything. Women can stand just about anything except you loving someone else, and in mine and Alec's case, it was all the excuse I needed.

I threw all his possessions out of the front window and booked a week off work, during which I wept until I couldn't breathe, eat or sleep. I didn't weep because of a broken heart over Alec, but because I'd wasted so long in a pointless, dead relationship and because I hated the humiliation of being betrayed - and for such a long time. As he saw it, I discovered, I'd ruined his life, got myself pregnant just to trap him and he'd stood by me until he couldn't bear it anymore and he'd run to the comfort of a real woman, not a hard cunt like me. Marie informed me of all this one night over the phone in a spiteful pissed-up hissy-fit when her insecurity got the better of her. I imagine Alec, knowing him as I did, had been comparing us and despite his version of our break-up, and him being so hard done to and all, had still managed to give the poor silly cow the distinct impression she didn't quite measure up. I knew this because he'd done it to me in regard to his previous girlfriend and doubtless he'd done it to her too. It was a control device he enjoyed. But I couldn't be arsed to explain that to poor old Marie, so I put the phone down without saying anything. I had bigger things on my mind than her pitiful, gin-fuelled rantings.

Alec, I didn't miss.

But my baby, my baby; oh, my whole fucked-up self ached like shattered bones for my child. I was amazed at how much I mourned my dead baby, how much my physical body seemed to become a concentrated point of longing for the child now lost. I don't think a day has gone past when I haven't grieved. But it was a done deal. I had no choice but to go on, to keep walking.

What it did do, though, was leave me wide open to John-Paul Eliot, Johnny X, the undisputed Big New Thing; front man of Velvet Shank. Oh yes, *that* Johnny X, the famous one, the real deal who graced the covers of every music mag going and shambled through the gossip rags like a beautiful disaster – but that was later, much later. When I met my Johnny, he was merely a mention in the little band round-ups of the *NME*. Our London talent scout – named Tonto by the office for good reason – had name checked Velvet Shank along with half-a-dozen other bands as one of his latest maybe-perhaps-could-be-possibilities. That's all. Just a whisper, just a flicker of a serpent's tongue.

Ah, Johnny. The crack in my armour, the vulnerability I had welcomed for my child, had never closed, and it was quite big enough for Johnny to slide through and into my heart. Beautiful, irresistible, barking mad Johnny-Boy whose undoubted stage charisma and husky vocal talents combined with his sexy, intense looks and 'mysterious' (oh, please) stage-name earned him the press moniker of 'The Italian Stallion' though in fact, he was from Clapham and the nearest he'd got to Italy was a cup of cappuccino, heavy on the sugar. Johnny liked sweet things - any sort of sweet thing. When naturally skinny (no celeb pies-and-purging binges for our Johnny, unlike some) Johnny took his shirt off to reveal his smooth, perfect chest, his tight abs, gender-bender pierced belly-button and a hint of pubic hair, young girls wet themselves and straight men got surly and sucked in their guts. When Johnny ran his hands up and down the mic stand in his carefully unconscious way, moaned in his surprisingly deep voice about what he wanted and looked up from under his heavy fall of dead-straight shining dark-bronze fringe with those chocolate eyes, gay men panted like dogs and grown women undid their top buttons and sighed. Johnny was sex. Johnny was pure rock 'n' roll. Johnny was the music industry's Indie bad boy whore, a major potential source of cash on the hoof, a genuine Star in the making. If he played the game, of course, if he and the band *'made with the grey matter and waxed us some hot ones'* as Vinny was wont to say, like the incomparable dick he was.

But all I knew of Johnny before we met came from Tonto. *That Velvet Shank's frontman's a bit fuckin' tall for a singer, it aint natcheral, they're usually shortarses wiv Napoleon complexes, innit?* So I thought Johnny was just another tedious, anorexic wannabe-rocker, until I met him; another skinny motherfucker on the make. One of hundreds of similar boys all willing to - as one such singer once memorably said - wank a tramp off if that's what it took to be famous.

Until he finally sidled into my office amid his tumbling litter of fellow band-members, and I fell in love.

First and last and always, as the old Sisters Of Mercy track goes. That's Johnny, for me.

Three

Have you ever been in love? I mean *really*, not just fancying someone chronic and going on a three-month vehicular shagfest round the lay-bys of Yorkshire, or being comfortable with a great person you like a lot but who if you admit it - which you won't because there are, like, security issues involved; *your* security - deep down inside, bores the pants off you. No, I mean that terrible agonising moment when you know, genuinely know at a cellular level, that this is the person you want to marry, have kids with and adore for ever and ever, amen.

Well, I did, and at one and the same moment I knew I was royally and permanently fucked. I think I gasped out loud, I know I thought I was going to throw up and momentarily wondered how early the menopause could happen because I'd broken out in a hot sweat under my artfully distressed vintage Ramones T.

It was so simple. Everything big and grown-up and terrible always is. In slouches my Johnny, all six foot of surly, pouty youth. I look up, annoyed, as his musicians yaw and fidget round my Scandinavian open plan desk area. I ask him, elaborately bored, if he and the band, like, want anything and he says *'you, you're beautiful'.*

Collapse of musos into fits of giggles, collapse of me as his eyes lock onto mine and he doesn't smile. Yeah, it was that easy. Take note, boys and remember, if you want something or someone, go for it. Johnny did and he got - me.

Not a bargain. Now, this may all sound dead romantic and swooney but in fact it was crap because I was thirty-six and he was twenty. Just twenty. So what, you may ask?

24

It's a modern world, anything is possible, what the hell. Well, let's put it this way; what could a thirty-something rock chick, stylish perhaps if I say so myself, but not a looker, with major emotional baggage ever really be to a gorgeous young rock star with a massive future and seriously pretty girls crawling all over him 24/7 like a rash? Answers on a postcard, please and the first person to correctly surmise 'sod all' gets Cliff Richards' entire back catalogue on CD.

But for whatever reason, and I was never fully sure why, he wanted me and he had me. Maybe he liked older chicks, some guys really do. Same as some guys love short girls, or tall girls or have a thing for girls in specs. It's just how their chemistry is. Women are the same, how many of us fall over and over for Heathcliff? He said he loved me, really and truly loved me, and you know what? I believe he did. It's not self-delusion, wishful thinking because I loved him so much, because you see, he didn't have to say it. He didn't. I'd have done anything for him anyway, whatever he said - or didn't say. Love like I felt, well, you don't expect a return. If you get it, great, if you don't - your fate is on you and that's an end of it, no escape, nothing you can do. You love. That's it. Bang-bang, you're - dead.

Johnny was so perfectly what I'd always dreamed of in a man. And he was a man, despite his youth. He was more of a man than Alec ever had been or would be, more of a man than the wannabe-rockers and saddo ageing wild-boys that peopled rock-world like the greying comb-over of a has-been football manager. Johnny was sweet, attentive, adorable, thoughtful, romantic and sensual to a degree I'd never found in any other man, before or since. I had never had sex like it; I didn't think sex like that really existed, except in fabulously romantic films about gypsies and chocolate shops. Desire didn't wear off like it had with Alec and all my other blokes, settling down to a comfy leg-over every few weeks, it blossomed and grew as we fed it, our bodies creating rituals and intricacies that became more and more intense as time passed. To hold him or be held by him afterwards, his slim, silky, sweet-smelling body coiled around me, the wiry strength of his long arms and legs relaxed, his face sleepy and hazed with pleasure was a joy that never palled, never became less exquisitely tender. Johnny loved to cuddle like he loved sex, because he wasn't hung up about physical things and he loved women, both sexually and generally. He was the youngest in his big Catholic family and the only boy in his generation; his mother, sisters, cousins, grannies and aunties had spoiled him rotten and adored him unconditionally from the cradle. He was, as a female journalist once wrote of him, 'woman-friendly' and he was certainly the only Englishman I ever knew who could pay a compliment and not disguise it in an insult, make it sound like it had been dragged out of him by wild horses, or give the impression he was after something. Johnny just said whatever nice thing came into his pretty, feline head, and he liked to make women happy. He knew how to make a woman love him, not in a cruel, selfish way but simply because he enjoyed being loved and loving in return; easy, simple, pleasurable. Like the cat he so resembled, Johnny loved to be petted. Johnny, you see, was Love itself.

Sure, he wasn't perfect, he was physical, human and very far from a saint. He was often chaotically mercurial, moody, and he could be properly nasty in a row - he was a handful when he was in a temper - but he was an artist, a singer, they're all basket-cases. Sure, he took drugs and drank - who doesn't? - but in those days he kept it within reasonable bounds and he never went onstage or into the studio stoned, which in our business was the height of dedication and self-discipline. So for all his so-called faults, my

26

Johnny was ten times nicer than he was nasty, unlike some others I knew only too well. I was used to musicians, I understood how much it cost them to do the thing they did and how they lived on their nerves, strung out taut and agonising as they waited for a gig, or made something new. That was my world, Johnny was a little king in that world and I knew how to look after him. Maybe that was it; he never had to explain himself to me. I just loved him.

Johnny pulled every heartstring, pressed every button, rang every bell. Was there something maternal mixed in with the phenomenal sex and the emotional rollercoaster? Was there something that called up the lost and the dead from inside my broken heart and made me give him all the love I'd stashed away until sometimes just loving him made me weep with the sweet pain and pleasure of it? Yeah, yeah, and yeah. All of that and more. Every woman feels that heady mixture of mother-love and passion, fierce protectiveness and aching tenderness when she really falls in love - love is a mixed-up thing at the best of times and like pulling the wings off a butterfly to see how they work, if you over-analyse love it will never fly again. So I didn't. I just went with it, blind and with a kind of ecstatic faith that everything would be, miraculously, OK, as it hadn't been for me and my child. Hail, Mary, full of grace - pray for us sinners now and at the hour of our little death.

Because as much as I adored him, he brought out every possible insecurity which had lurked, muttering, in the darkest corners of my poor, bewildered brain. How could he possibly want me? I was so unattractively, bonily, titlessly skinny; I was no longer young, and had never been a looker; he could have anyone, anyone - why me? Sure, he said I was beautiful, he loved me, he respected me but - he couldn't possibly mean it, could he? In this world, in this society, handsome young artists didn't date women like me, they went with beautiful models or glamour girls with perfect skin and - and - oh, it nagged and nagged at me, but there was no rational (to me) explanation. That he might simply have liked me didn't seem to compute. I was walking a tightrope, blindfold over an abyss; so I just held my breath and walked because what else could I do?

I loved Johnny to insanity, you see. Really, to the point of craziness. And he wanted love so much, so much. You couldn't love him enough; in fact, I don't suppose anyone ever could. It's axiomatic that front men crave love like an addict craves the needle, otherwise they wouldn't be up there night after night soliciting it from the punters; but with Johnny, he gave as much as he took, which is not so usual.

He was a joy - and ultimately, unavailable. I knew from the off I couldn't keep him, fight against it as I might; he was a wild thing. You couldn't keep the kestrel or the fox you found hurt and nursed back to health, you had to set them free again because they weren't pets, weren't tame, and neither was Johnny. He was my Wild Thing - I called him that in our lovers' talk and we'd sing that silly old Troggs cover together and laugh our heads off.

Wild thing
you make my heart sing
you make everything

groovy

Hilarious; but in this case, true. Johnny did make everything groovy, but he was his own man. The band always came first, always would come first. Under that charm there was solid self-interest. Johnny came first to Johnny. In that he was pure artist, one hundred percent frontman.

28

At first, I didn't care. Then as the months went on and turned into a year, eighteen months, two years and we were one of the couples people envied, slightly taboo, slightly daring due to the age gap but always crazy in love, I wanted more than the three nights a week he could spare me from band practice, then the no nights when he was in the studio and the no weeks when he toured. I came to realise my time with him was drawing to a close and I couldn't bear it. I cried and fretted and built scenarios; I killed the joy of what I had by ripping myself to bits about what I wouldn't have. In the future. When my beautiful wild boy was gone.

The pain of that inevitability was horrible and I couldn't control it. I turned into a compulsive wretch, always watching for signs of the inevitable end, the rope breaking, abyss opening under my stumbling feet. I'd give about anything for those days back, now, I'd do - yeah, right. I'd do the same all over again. We are what we are, in the end. We can try to improve if we have self-knowledge and strong wills, but inevitably, the clay returns to its original mud at the first shower of rain.

He was good about it, or as good as a young man could be. It bored him, all the weeping and gnashing of teeth. God knows it bored me a lot of the time - and I was under a lot of stress at work which didn't help. Stress never comes when you can cope with it, does it? Vinny was being moved sideways, which meant his job was up for grabs. I knew I could do it - Christ, I'd been doing it for long enough and everyone knew it. I applied.

Then one evening when I trudged home from the Tube, I found two letters waiting for me on the shelf by the communal front door to the flats. One from GMC, one from Johnny.

Four

Dear Annie,

firstly, we would like to thank you for your application for the position of A&R executive and to let you know how much we value the terrific contribution to the company you've made over the years.

However, we cannot at this time offer you the position. Instead, we would like to offer you a salary increase should you decide - and we hope you will! - to continue to work in the department alongside our new appointee, Marty Brigham, who we're sure you remember from that great band, Do It By Numbers. Marty will need your expertise as he settles in and we are prepared to offer an increase commensurate with the added workload. We also thought you might like your workspace upgraded, in keeping with our new look for the company's working environments globally, so just let us know your choices from the brochures we'll be sending you!

Yours sincerely

Bob D. Willerby
Executive Personnel Manager, GMC UK

Hi Annie

not good at this stuff but I suppose you can guess what I'm writing to you for. Yes we're off to America in fact I'll be gone when you get this. Its a long tour and I don't know when I'll be back so I just think theres no point in you having false hopes or anything its time to call it a day. Its been proper amazing a wild ride I want you to know that. This is really hard but I have to go. You know I wont ever love anyone like I love you I never will, never. You are so special but we always knew it couldn't last what with our ages and everything like you said we just weren't lucky that way. If you'd been my age I'd never have let you go, ever, you know that. I love you, My Lady. I love you so much. But this is it. The real deal. Like I always said I got to follow my star and all that and this is our big chance. I know you will understand its all we talked about come true. I'll never forget all youve done for me and the band we couldn't have done it without you. You are a really great great person. Take good care of yourself My Lady, my Blonde and maybe well meet again one day over the rainbow like we always said yeah? Really sorry I couldnt see you before I went but its been such a hassle getting things organised and everything I know you will understand coz were rock n roll you and me arent we yeah?

Your own always-loving-you My Lady

Johnny (Wild Thing) xxxx

Two pieces of paper. That was all it took. Two pieces of paper and my life tore into hot, bloody, agonising shreds.

I just sat there, at the crummy little breakfast-nook Formica fold-out fucking table and stared at the letters lying neatly side by side in front of me in front of the cork mat with the condiments on it. Naturally, I dialled Johnny's mobile twenty, thirty, fifty times but always got his answer phone. Oh, that Orange bitch - *'welcome to Orange Answerphone . . .'* Jeez, fuck her, whoever she is. I hate her. I texted. The same thing over and over. *i love u i love u dont do this please dont johnny please.* I got nothing back. I felt as if he had disappeared into the night sky, dissolved into the great bloody beyond. If he had died, I could have understood him no longer being in the World and I could have grieved, recovered. But he was out there, somewhere, and I would never see him again. It ripped at me like an animal's claws, dirty and blunt but tearing, tearing. Time passed, but I wasn't aware of it. I got colder and colder but I didn't care. Thoughts swam randomly through my head like fire-rimmed ashes from a bonfire flying up into the night and fluttering away; *he's gone - the bastards - my heart is breaking - a new colour scheme for the office whoop di fuckin' do - Johnny no no no - they can stuff their - Johnny no no - oh Johnny I love you I love you don't - my life is over my life is over my life . . .*

I came to around midnight, as I recall. Virtually fell off the chair, stiff as a board and freezing right through. I thought I'd choke with the pain of it and that's a fact; even now it twinges when I remember it. I love it when they say a broken heart isn't physical, not real pain, don't you? Man, only someone who never really had one could think that. It was like someone smashed my chest in with a brick, repeatedly. I couldn't breathe. I couldn't eat, drink or be sodding merry. My world collapsed in on itself in dead cold cinders and dross, then plummeted into the abyss.

Dramatic, eh? It was a bit, to be honest. I can make jokes now - feeble ones maybe - but then I thought the end had come. I mean, the real end, the end of my life, of my existence. Really. Without Johnny, living had no salt, no savour. Without his bright presence I could only see the endless days stretching out like Death's beckoning hand, a honky-tonk busted carousel of the same old same old, until I'd wake up aged God-knows-what and look in the dirty mirror to see a raddled sterile party-whore well past her sell-by date picking the eye-black out of the corners of her rheumy eyes while last night's still-drunk fuck struggled to get away as fast as he could clamber into his Calvins.

So given this bleak view of my possible future, did I calm down, give myself a sensible talking to and take up Buddhism? No. I did what I did best - or worst. Fuck it, I thought with what remained of my dazed and confused brain cells, if that's how it's going to be, no child, no Johnny, bring it *on*. I don't care. I couldn't give a rat's fart. What does it matter now, anyway? Now the light of my life is gone, better to go out in a blaze of glory, you know? Yeah, that's how fucked up I was, and I had no one to tell me otherwise - all my so-called friends were cut from the same shoddy cloth, the stuff that looks OK in the blinding dazzle of amphetamines and alcohol, but wouldn't stand up to the cool silvery light of a Northern winter morning. They said a few meaningless half-phrases about *what a shame, ooh, the bastard aren't all men pigs* then chopped a line to 'buck me up'.

So, I took shed loads of cocaine, drank like a fish with a drink problem and went out into the endless tawdry London debauch every night dressed way beyond my means in unsuitable and ruinously expensive glittery rags and tatters that barely covered my increasingly bony chest and arse. Food was a bore. I could hardly choke down a yoghurt. I crawled into work in the mornings and took more cocaine. I snarled at my new boss - the sap - and had the office done in egg-yolk yellow and pistachio for a laugh.

Then, one night at the after-show knees-up for Ultimate Angel's *Winter Tour* gig at the Astoria, the runaway train finally crashed.

Oddly, I remember exactly what I was wearing. Funny, isn't it, what sticks in your mind? It's always been like that for me - I remember the clothes I had on, or the chorus of a pop song, or the smell of someone's cologne - everything else I forget, but some jagged little spur will lodge in my rag-bag mind.

It was an unforgivingly turquoise Paragon Syndicate Baby Doll chiffon top stitched with iridescent black sequins and artfully ripped to revealing tatters over a made-to-be-seen matching push-up bra (tits out lasses, we're on the pull), super-skin-tight Guru Sisters black-wash jeans revealing a hint of Maitresse Noir black silk-satin key-hole knickers if you cared to look (yes, I had sunk that low) and of course, a pair of my precious cowboy boots - the black ones with silver leather appliqués of roses. I had long black glass Smith & Co. chandelier earrings on and I reeked of something decadent from Diptyque. There was a matching candle probably still burning in my flat. I'd put heavy iridiscent greeny-black eye-shadow on in the latest style, and that weird mascara that has a white base-coat so that when you put the black top-coat on, your eyelashes look like big fat clumpy tarantula's legs. With the slashes of shimmering bronzer bisecting my cheeks, the creeping slick of nudey-pink vinyl-shine lipgloss that was gradually smearing my gob into a sticky plastic nightmare, and my hair straightened flat as a fairly stiff board I fancied I looked hot, moody and glamorous. Young, even. No, I did, really.

Of course, in reality - and I mean proper reality, not cocaine reality - I looked fucking ridiculous; mutton tricked out as teen. But that's coke for you, great for building false confidence. Oh bollocks, this is mortifying even now, but there we go, you can't undo the done deal.

So; throughout the gig, I'd been having major eye-contact with a guitarist from a band I knew slightly, and who had supported Johnny a couple of times. He was young, very skinny and had a long, pale, bony face and equally long designer-hacked hair and cool clothes; in my pals' opinion, he was a major hottie and, given that, mysteriously unaccompanied. I think his name was Dave. Or Steve, or - I can't (won't) remember. I suppose I could find out easily enough, his band became quite well-known for a short while before plummeting into the usual oblivion, but I'm not going to.

Anyway, at the party in the stinky, disintegrating naffness of the Astoria's Keith Moon Bar, he bought me a Stoli and we flirted, as I fondly thought, like characters from *Dangerous Liaisons*. I probably simpered. I know I did that Meaningful Looks From Under Your (Spider's Legs) Eyelashes thing, to my eternal shame. He moved closer and ran his finger up and down my bare arm. I smiled, knowingly. Fuck Johnny, fuck him - see? I could pull anyone I chose. I didn't need Mr. Johnny Bastard Eliot. Johnny fucking X. No, I did not. I pouted, and shook my hair. Somewhere in an Alternate Reality, bats flew at that dry, whispery rattle and wolves howled as a Pale Rider smiled.

'So, wanna come back to mine? Or shall we go to yours for a, yeah, huh huh, nightcap?' smirked my Prince Charmless, as well he might.

'Oh, I dunno' I prattled, making him wait for it (oh God, but there we are, that's what I thought).

'Hey, no need to play the innocent, yeah? We all know you like a bit of action, darlin'. I mean . . .'

I paused, puzzled. *We all know* . . . Even in my fuddled state I realised all was not exactly well.

'What does that mean?' I bridled unsteadily.

He laughed out loud. 'You know, come on - you wuz bangin' Johnny from the Shank, wuzn't yer? You older chicks, yer red-hot, yeah? Older chicks'll do anyfing, they ain't like young birds, all neurotic an' that. Older chicks, they know wot they want, an' they go get it, innit? An' you got contacts, aint yer? Yer in the know, like. We all reckon that's how the Shank done so good, aint it? Wot wiv you 'elpin' him I mean, gettin' him stuff. I reckon Johnny dropped proper lucky, scorin' a bird like you, we all did - wot a fuckin' player that Johnny, eh? Wot a bad boy, him. 'Ere - I wuz finkin', you should come along to one of our gigs, see wot you fink, we could come to an arrangement, yeah? I'll keep you happy like Johnny did if you keep me happy, know wot I mean? You're still pretty tidy for a chick your age, I aint fussy, don't mind givin' you what you want if you get us a look in at GMC like yer did The Shank. . .'

I opened my vodka-numb mouth to explain that it wasn't like that for Johnny and me, it was - but suddenly I knew how totally pointless that would be. How would the likes of this fuckwit chancer ever understand that Johnny and I had genuinely loved each other, since it was unlikely he even knew what love was in the first place. Love to the likes of him was an on-off text conversation with an Indie bird whose haircut wore her and who let him do it up her arse for a backstage pass. The fool was only repeating gossip, regurgitating what the bands and my charming acquaintances in the industry had thought; that Johnny had bitten the bullet and fucked me in order to advance his career. That I was a deluded old bitch who had been taken in by a pretty con artist and couldn't admit I'd been had. Oh, of course in my darkest hours I'd thought that might be true, but Johnny had always proven me wrong, and I loathed this waster who in his blind vanity so patently thought he could do the same trick he assumed Johnny had pulled. Get him and his third-rate outfit an in at the company? I nearly laughed. What did they think I did at GMC? How much power did they think I had? Sure, I might be able to put a word in various ears if I really thought some artist had the right stuff, I had been able to give my boy good advice, who to talk to, who was who, that kind of thing - but make him into what he had become, if he'd had no talent, no charisma, no it-factor? Like some *Pop Idol* tele-Svengali manufacturing an ersatz star from shit? Jeez, they couldn't be that stupid - could they? Could they? I looked again at the idiot in front of me, his weak mouth, dead eyes and pallid, shapeless stoner's mug. Not so fucking pretty when you looked close, not at all - and I realised with a sick-ening shiver that yes indeed, they could be that stupid, and they were. He was. Around me, the party seemed to freeze and craze over like a stone-struck windscreen. I was suddenly dead sober.

'I don't think so, love,' I said, cold as a high mountain tarn. You can say 'love' where I come from in such a way it means the opposite. He might have been a Southerner but he felt the import of it alright. And he could see my eyes.

''Ere, no need for attitude, I didn't mean . . .'

But I was gone. Out of the pathetic Star Bar, out of the Astoria, out of the Life, out of London. It was over. I knew it.

It was over and I had two choices; go on stumbling through party after party, brainless shag after brainless shag - or make a totally new life. I poised for a second on the see-saw. Then I stopped dead in the piss-stinking, syringe-strewn alleyway next to the Astoria and looked round me at the grey, rat-nibbled unravelling mess of a

London dawn and took a deep, shuddering breath. There was only one way for me now. It was either go forward or - no, that was too crap even to contemplate; to be one of those worn-out surgery-screwed, guppy-lipped, Botoxed youth-craving old hags cruising the outer edges of party darkness? It made me nauseous just thinking of it. A silvery, savage voice whispered in my head like an angel speaking to crazy Joan of Arc: *what if Johnny came back and saw you like that? How could you bear it? Better he finds a nun than a whore*... But what could I do, what could I . . . The familiar seemed suddenly comforting, safe . . . No. I was made of sterner stuff than that, I had to be. So I put my old life away in a locked box in a deep, dark place in my heart and closed the iron doors of my will on it. It would never see the light of day again. Never. If I couldn't be with the love of my life, my beloved, my heart, I would never love again. It was a done deal and fuck anyone who thought that was wrong, or archaic or mad. Fuck them.

And another thing. I was going home.

Five

Say what you want, you can't beat IKEA for furnishing a place if you can't be arsed to shop. OK, you may have the sneaking feeling that there are fifty trillion houses globally tricked out with Bloggi sofas or Krigle bookcases with Bjorgi lamps shining coolly on the Fganno tufty abstract rug in shades of sludge and scarlet but what the heck, it's clean, new and vaguely tasteful in a homogenous kind of way. Inexpensive. Impersonal. Nothing heirloom, nothing with sentimental value - and that's what I wanted. Not a shred or whisper of the past, no backsliding and gazing drunkenly at Johnny's picture whilst listening to him singing about how much he loved his *'woman with sky-blue eyes'* as he put it on 'Kiss Me Or Kill Me'. Yes it's me, he wrote it about me. And yes, it does hurt even thinking about it, never mind listening to it; so in the bin it went. You don't buy an ex-junkie a wrap with a big tinsel bow on it for Christmas, do you? It would have been the same me keeping all those songs, just feeding the addiction. I needed to be clean.

Ho hum. Aw, fuck it. In fact, fuck it double. With knobs on, if we're going to be childish. So I got rid of everything, starting with the stupid clothes – except the infamously expensive black cashmere Brora wrap which was my comfort blanket – it all went to Oxfam; some haul, thousands of pounds worth of designer tat. I gave away the funky rock 'n' roll costume jewellery to my fellow secretaries at GMC (though I kept the good silver pieces like the Navajo squash-blossom necklace and the Keith Richards skull ring from The Great Frog). Johnny's little gifts went in the bin; they'd never been expensive, he'd never had any money, they were just funky, sparkly things his magpie eye had lit upon in some cheapjack stall at Camden or wherever. I'd treasured them, but now they were sodden with memories, too painful even to look at for long; the detritus of a storm-wreck. The furniture went with the flat which, naturally, sold for a colossal sum - the fancy car got snapped up in a second by one of GMC's new boy-execs. Nearly everything went. It was fantastically liberating, like jumping naked in a cold sea on a hot day.

I kept the cowboy boots though, all twenty pairs. And the big box of fancy perfumes - Narciso Rodriguez, Serge Lutyen, Keihl's Orginal Musk, Aveda Purefumes Number 6, the weird 400 year-old recipe E'spa stuff you couldn't get anymore, the pure organic patchouli and the boxed sets of Diptyque candles I'd bought by the dozen. Plus the moisturisers, cleansers, toners, exfoliators, brighteners, serums, eye-creams, body creams, butters, lotions, spritzers, scrubs, shampoos, conditioners, foot stuff and Aveda Hand Relief hand cream which gets the all-time prize for best hand cream with most inadvertently hilarious name. But not fake tan - I don't do fake tan, it smells like a burning dog-biscuit and turns me fluorescent orange. I could have dumped all that stuff I suppose, existed virtuously and cheaply on Boots own brand and Superdrug no-nonsense, no frills face-grease but there's a limit, after all. I can't part with my scent, lotions and boot collections, I really can't. That would be betraying my inner luxe-cowgirl, which would never do. Still, at least I suppose I always pong nice and walk like a winner.

Anyhow, It all made a tidy sum, let me tell you. More than enough for a mortgage on the two-bedroom flat in a converted wool traders' building at the bottom of

Leeds Road and the IKEA instant home. I got new kit, serviceable if not couture, mostly from Gap, which OK, was indeed black or denim and not that dissimilar to the old kit but much, much less teen-whore and much more suitably mature (in a tight, rock 'n' roll sort of way; old habits, y'know) and for me, positively matronly. I bought a Datsun fake Jeep in cherry red, too; it isn't the Ferrari but who cares? How long would an (albeit elderly) purple Ferrari Dino last round Leeds Road? About as long as it took the local twockers to jemmy the door lock, I should think. Ten seconds?

I went back to college. It wasn't hard to get a place re-training for social work. Yes, social work. Why not? It was what I'd meant to do before I got side-tracked into Showbiz. I was a tad elderly but they wanted mature students as the College got extra cash from the Government for re-educating the likes of me and anyway, they had massive quotas to fill and Social Services were so desperate they'd taken to advertising on local radio for workers. So I took my excellent but essentially useless First in English and my 'life-experience' along and they damn-near bit my hand off; in comparison to the former hairdressers and care-home workers they usually got I was a dream applicant. In fact the lanky fool who interviewed me got all over-excited about my tenuous Ultimate Angel connection and actually asked if I knew where Baz the bass-player lived in Bradford - as if he did, having moved to Surrey as fast as he possibly could years ago. But you see, Bradford lads, the Angel, oh aye. My arse. I smiled sweetly and said, naturally, I couldn't possibly divulge information that confidential, which I later learnt did me handsome as it proved I was good at keeping my mouth shut and presumably not yattering all my future clients grisly secrets all over

Town when pissed or stoned.

I can't say I engaged much with my fellow students. After classes, I went home and studied or watched TV, read or slept. I could have slept for Britain back then; I think all the coke-years caught up with me. Now, I'm back to white-eyed insomnia, but then I waded through heavy swells of formless dreams as if my body were administering morphine to itself. Sleep was all I wanted. Oblivion.

I made a couple of friends, of course I did. Sue and Renee were also Matures, and not the sort who went back to Uni to get laid which was what a number of the Mature women had all too obviously done. I'd rather have a wank anyday than be that desperate, to be honest - I mean, wasn't that what God invented vibrators for? It was painful watching them be creakily arch with anything in boxers. Had I looked like that post-Johnny? Jeez. I would look away and feel my face burn.

So Sue, Ren and I coffee'd and cribbed each other's notes, covered for Ren when her kids needed her, sympathised with Sue about her pig-husband and never talked about my past. I'd 'lived in London', had 'a corporate job'. That was all. I was a New Lifer, one of those ex-rat-racers. The Girls had read about it in *Marie-Claire* or *Red*, they knew the score. Stockbrokers turned Yoga gurus. Architects turned artisan florists. That kind of thing. I dropped hints about a long-term affair and let them think it had been with a married man who finally, after years of promises and lies, had gone back to the fold. They could understand that, it was mentally digestible for them. It wasn't that I didn't trust them, but I knew what rock'n'roll did to punters - and by that term I mean anyone not actually in the music industry - it turned them crazy; they stopped being pals and turned into fans, star-struck, even with the likes of me who never set foot on a stage in my life. Didn't matter, I was a Friend Of The Stars, as they say in the media. It was enough. If they'd known about Johnny, who was at that point, high in the charts and gracing the pop'n'rock pages of every tabloid with his fabulously out-of-it behaviour (did I see the fell hand of marketing there in the carefully staged paparazzi punch-ups, crazy parties, drug addiction rumours and perfect stoner-super-model arm-candy?) and intense live gigs that had 'em comparing him to Jim Morrison or a slew of other death-and-glory heroes, they'd have freaked out. When I saw the pictures, the cruel, biting worm of useless worry coiled in my gut; he looked so gaunt, so tired - not slim anymore but as bony as me, he looked - and I knew it when I saw it - wasted. But what could I do? That's the worst thing about still loving the ex, worrying is pointless. You can't go to the hospital, make the call, comfort them with cuddles - or go to the funeral; you're the past and the past is as they say, another country far, far away. So I said nothing, and distracted myself with course work, thereby getting excellent grades for the piss-easy essays and idiot projects.

Ren and Sue thought I was a right whiz-kid (no pun intended). Obviously, they thought, my previous high-velocity corporate life in London had left me with superb work habits which, they moaned, they just couldn't aspire to what with the kids, the lardy useless hubbie etc, etc. So I did a lot of their work for them. Why not? They were nice lasses under a lot of pressure. They were ordinary women, with ordinary lives. That's not in any way a judgement, I don't mean it nastily, but it was just a fact. They would have been unable to see me the same way again had I told them the truth. They wouldn't have been able to relax with me. They would have

43

been unable to resist creeping into that faded limelight, filching a little of that third-hand glory. *I know that Johnny Eliot's ex, honest - it's true, she's at college with me, yeah, she did my last essay for me! She's everso nice really, not at all stuck up - he broke her heart, he did, poor thing, yeah, she was quite a lot older than him, hmm, you know, an age-gap relationship, like that documentary on the telly last week . . . Started off as a bit of a toy-boy thing, I reckon prob'ly but it got all serious and . . . She's making a new life coz you know, she's from Bradford originally and . . .* They knew the way it went, how to word it - they were trained to it by all the celeb mags they scarfed up voraciously while pretending they never usually read them; well, only at the dentists. Punters don't see rock 'n' roll in the same way those of us who've toiled in its grubby bowels do; they saw glitter, glamour, freedom and a twenty-four seven party. We see it as a cross between the Carnie and a juggernaut, covered in flowers and crushing its devotees as they throw themselves in its path. Blood and magic, brutal and glorious. I couldn't have made light of it for them, I couldn't have been witty and cool. I was too burned by it, the scars still pulled and made me wince sometimes.

It wouldn't have worked so I kept schtum. Better that way. Better to have nice, easy-going pals. Get through the course, get a low-key job in Social Services, finish my life being vaguely useful to someone, somewhere, then fade away into the beckoning grey. Better to have no history, no past, because I had no future.

So I was born again as plain Annie. Nice enough, quiet, keeps herself to herself, had a bit of a sad life, bless her.

Oh yeah. I have seen the Glory, Lord. I have heard the trumpet-call. I was Born Again.

A fucking miracle, eh?

Book Two

Raphael

'Raise no more spirits than you can conjure down.'

Proverb

Six

'Look, Sam, you know what? I couldn't give a fuck, no, I really couldn't. It's not my life, right? It's yours, int it, yeah? You want to fuck it up, man, it's not for me ter stop yer. You want ter fuck up yer kids lives and their kids lives and on and fuckin' on, so be it. It's what yer mam did ter you, int it? Why break the chain, eh? Why fuckin' bother? Who cares? We'll all be dead shortly and that's that, so what the fuck.' I took a long drag on my black Sobranie and blowing the smoke out hard, eyed Sam Jagger with apparent despair.

Sam bridled and shifted Brittney on her lap like a fart-stinky badly trussed parcel. Disturbed, the baby burped a bit of unsavoury goo and Sam daintily wiped her rosebud mouth with the hem of her England shirt.

'Honest, you don't talk like a fuckin' social worker, you. Shouldn't you be tryin' ter, ter . . .'

'What? Get you ter send Liam ter school regular? Feed Jake somethin' other than fuckin' crisps an' pop? Stop smoking? Stop taking drugs - oh, please, spare me the bollocks, I know what you get up to, everyone does - stop shagging all and sundry? Practice fuckin' birth control? Well, I'd love ter, but frankly, darlin', would it do any good?'

Sam smirked. 'Well, no, but . . . Won't yer get inter trouble if yer don't, well, have a go at it and . . .'

I nodded, pursing my lips and looking sage. 'Oh yeah. I could get the fuckin' sack on account of you an' the way you go on. Don't look like that, I could, y'know, I've put meself on the line fer you and the kiddies. I could lose my nice little job an' be no end pissed off, no pension, no nothin' all on account of you. An' yer know what then, darlin'? You'd get a right fuckin' hard-arse bastard down here after yer, fillin' in forms, takin' the kids off yer like as not, fuckin' yer six ways and sideways, no mistake. A right little jobsworth Hitler, coz they won't want ter make a mistake like me again. So y'know, ball's in your court. Up ter you. What can I do? I'm only a cog in the fuckin' wotsit, the fuckin' machine. Brick in the wall, that kind of thing.' I shrugged, watching her carefully through the haze of fragrant smoke, studying the thoughts passing like scudding clouds across her peaked and pretty face. I'd taken a gamble, would it pay off?

'So, yer mean, like, if I do what yer say, 'bout the kiddies an' that, a bit like, you'll still be my case worker, you'll stop on, but if I don't . . .'

I waved my fag expansively. 'Up ter you, like. Sure, I've stuck me neck out coz I do think deep down, y'know, deep down you and the kids are basically sound, know what I mean? Yer just need a bit of a helpin' hand, like. But it's your call. I can't mek you do owt, wouldn't want ter, wouldn't try even. I'm just here ter, like, sort stuff out for yer. That kinder thing. You know.'

Sam looked thoughtful - self-interest, caginess, a genuine affection for her children, puzzlement then enlightenment passing across the surface of her face like wisps of cloud scurrying across the sun. No-one had ever suggested to her before that she might possibly be capable of competent mothering. Or indeed be competent at anything except Being Trouble, or Being Useless. It was a strange new concept to study, poke and mentally finger. Outside, the sound of dirt bikes revving echoed like distant thunder and a dog howled mournfully, then a chorus of mutts took up his refrain. *Call Of The* bleedin' *Wild*. I pulled myself back to the here and now and raised my eyebrows. Sam scratched her scalp with half-grown-off acrylic nails lacquered fuschia and striped with unsteady nail art flashes. I knew where she'd had them done. Down the road GiGi's Of Becksyke had a *Full Set For £20* offer on. There wasn't a woman in spitting distance who didn't sport a set of talons a mountain lion would be proud of. Kids throughout the village looked like they'd been savaged by eagles as their mums, sisters and aunties strove to control two centimetres of solid plastic when it came to feeding, changing and clothing their squirming offspring.

Sam looked at me and pursing her lips, nodded fiercely. 'Well, yeah, I mean, yeah - coz - yeah. OK, I'll 'ave a go, like. I'll, I'll stop wi't gear fer a bit, an' I'll cook a proper dinner, I can yer know, I'll do fish fingers an chips, an' beans, they'll like that the little 'uns, an' I'll stop in more of an evenin'. I mean, it's only proper, int it, only right. Gotta be responsible, int yer, I int a kid no more, after all. Yeah.'

Sam smiled, her face filling with the light and grace of her glorious revelation, causing her momentarily to transcend prettiness and achieve actual beauty; she must look like this, I thought, when some bloke she fancies at the boozer offers her a double vodka and Red Bull or a pill. It must worry him quite a lot until she subsides back into manageable ordinariness. Not for the first time, Sam made me think of St. Bernadette Of Lourdes, or at least, the highly-coloured saint card version I used to get at Sunday School. Un-saint Sam nodded vigorously, shaking her bleached pony-tail, jiggling Brittney who scrinched her snot-crusty little face up and made squeaking sounds. I looked away. Couldn't do babies.

Suddenly Sam looked anxious. 'Is that right? Is that what I'm supposed ter do, like?'

51

I smiled and stubbed my fag out in the overflowing *Souvenir Of Morecambe* ashtray. Sighing elaborately like I couldn't care less, I got up and shouldered my huge bag, trying to avoid dislodging the damp-smelling heaps of clothes and bobbly misshapen pure polyester bed linen that balanced precariously on the back of the armchair. I looked at the Modern Madonna And Child scene in front of me and wished, not for the first time, that I was a photographer, a film-maker or an artist instead of a social worker. I'd seen a photo once, a bit like the hazily illuminated tableau in front of me that had stuck in my mind - it'd been in a Sunday supplement, a portrait of an old half-caste junkie from round here, she'd obviously been beautiful once and the pic showed her as a glorious saint-like ruin glowing golden in the witch-fire of her decay and degradation; fabulous picture, unforgettable. Yeah, well - maybe Art could make sense of the idiocy of Sam's life. I knew I couldn't.

'Yeah, you're doin' the right thing, I reckon, darlin'. Best we just get on with stuff between us, don't want people interferin' do we? We can sort stuff, no problem. You just get Liam ter school fer a bit an' Brittney ter the clinic, an' make sure the lads have some nice scran an' we'll see how it goes, eh? Grand, I'll be off then.'

I resisted punching the air in triumph until I got in the jeep. Sam had three kids and was still under twenty. She had long-term 'substance abuse issues' which had started when she was about eleven and was why I was her own, personal case worker. The children had their own worker. The bloody dog probably had a worker too. It was that kind of family. Sam lived in a disgusting hovel of a rented two-up, two-down cottage on the outskirts of Becksyke village, that tattered trail of sagging houses and dusty little shops fading away along the straight road out of Bradford, and had been a major problem for every social worker she'd had during her short life. She was my personal little triumph; where others had feared to tread, I strode like a - well, like a broomstick wearing a yellow wig. Something from Fantasia's *Sorcerer's Apprentice*. The sheer enormity of getting her to consider - and I was by no means assured anything might actually come of it - cooking a greasy fry-up for the boys was a success of spectacular dimensions. Normally the whole family's diet comprised of cheap take-away burgers, curry, kebabs, pizzas or Pot Noodles supplemented by Jakobs Cream Cracker sandwiches done with an inch of cheap marge and industrial quantities of chocolate bars, biscuits and huge bags of radioactively luminous sweets washed down by non-diet pop or - if Sam was feeling particularly health-conscious - Sunny Delight. The kiddies liked the fluorescent-green one best. The fact that after eating all this crap Jake and Liam ran screaming round the house like demented banshees mainlining bathtub speed had nothing, in Sam's mind, to do with sugar or additives. They was a bit lively. A handful. Right little bastards. Stick one o' them knock-off DVDs on for 'em that'll shut 'em up. Summat kiddie, dinosaurs, they like dinosaurs especially ones that sing an' that. Oh, right. Tyrannosaurus Rex, then; Ride A White Swan, Jeepster, Marc's pouty head-shaking fuck-me glitter-eyed posing? No, Disney's cartoon saurians doing third-rate show songs in cartoonland. Shame.

I sighed, squashing my rising hysteria down firmly; I wanted to laugh not from amusement, but from the same reaction that causes people to giggle helplessly during granny's short, soulless shove off at the local cremmy. I'd been nearly two years on the job and by that time most people had ceased to bother doing anymore than the base minimum their job description demanded. I don't blame them for that, because no one tells you (certainly not the soft-focus, caring adverts for social workers in magazines and on the radio that reek of desperation in the face of insurmountable odds) what it's really going to be like. I would think being stripped naked in public and scrubbed raw with sandpaper dipped in white vinegar until you bleed, then having all and sundry tell you you're a useless wanker for crying would about cover it. Still, as Piff - my comrade-in-arms back at HQ, as we called the office - always said; *it's a war out there, baby girl, and we're just the bloody cannon-fodder. If you don't laugh you'll break your heart. Up and at 'em, Mighty Atom. Once more into the frigging breach, dear friends, once more.* I paused at the car and looked around at the gently rolling green hills folding away into the sweet rotting leaves and balsam-scented smoky blue of a glorious early autumn evening, the neat stitchery of jade and sage green shrubs overlaying the more distant gilded knots of trees that crested every rise and were just very faintly turning; oak, birch, and here and there, rowan swaying with garlands and clusters of ruby berries that glowed in the haze like a houri's earrings. If you could tune out the random blunt thud of obscenities, intermittent roaring of the dirt-bikers, the zippy whine of boy-racers gunning their GTIs, the chug of elderly artics labouring up the slight incline and the melancholic canine choir it was like a tiny little rural idyll. Bradford, you couldn't invent it. What a weird, secret puzzle-box of a place it was. Ten minutes drive out along Thornton Road, and after a final scrubby fringe of run-down houses flouncing tattily by the roadside, you were near as dammit in the country and the hills rolled away into infinity. Or Manchester, which was nearly the same thing.

I sighed, resisting the urge to light another fag. In London, all you smelt in autumn was the damp stink of exhaust fumes laced with the rancid exhalations of burger joints and kebaberies. At least here you could occasionally smell heather and wildness over the city sprawl. A mental Post-It Note sprang up in my head as I gazed gormlessly at the nearest rowan, heavy with fruit: Must remind Sam not to let Jake eat wild food; bad enough when he ate the dog's three day-old Chum.

Struggling with the faulty door of the now ageing jeep, I paused again to look at the view. A view, to paraphrase Dr. Hannibal Lecter, was all Sam had. The jeep coughed into life like a city pigeon on a cold morning and I chugged back towards town, listening to the ominous grinding sound of the bearings in the gear box, or possibly the drive shaft, dying. Not for the first time I wondered how much I'd get for a trade-in and what kind of vehicle I'd get next. Rather like dreaming of your next lover, I dwelt on sleek, expensive motors purring with power and then slid down the scale to reality and a second-hand Mitsubishi. This led neatly if illogically onto unsuitable thoughts about Johnny Depp and I was just reliving a choice fantasy about desert islands (*'welcome to the Caribbean, love'*) - when the beep of a horn pulled me round in time to wave at Gordon Bicker-syke the Dog Warden as he drove past me back the way I'd just come; after some rabid pitbull on the loose, or those cacophonous hounds. Or maybe one of the new feral hybrids, a Rottsatien or a Doberkita, demon-mongrels that resulted from their parents being kicked out when Master decided to replace them with more fashionable attack dogs.

I waved cheerily. Gordon was a nice fella, and bore the persistent ribbing about being 'Gordon The Warden' with good humour. Childishly, it always made me smile, since I have a weakness for those names that match their bearer's occupation; Mr. D'eath the undertaker, Ms. Reader the librarian etc. I mentally collect them, and while Gordon's didn't strictly fulfill the criteria, it was enough to make me notice him when we'd met at an office do somewhere. We'd got on well, chatting easily like old comrades. We liked the same kind of music, it turned out, and the same films. I'd fucked men with whom I'd had much less in common than that, trust me, but I didn't feel the urge to ravish Gor. We were more like pals and it's generally an error to shag your mates. I was pretty sure given a chance, he'd ask me for a date - he was divorced, with a kid his ex-wife had taken to Spain with her new partner. If he asked, I'd go out with him, but he'd have to make the first move, I wouldn't chase him, or anyone. But I did like his slightly bow-legged stocky figure, thick nut-brown hair scragged into a short pony-tail with a rubber band and calm, broad Northern face with a broken nose and eyes almost the exact same colour as mine, Viking blue. Calm was definitely Gordon, he radiated a sense of easy-going, rather serious serenity that gave gravitas to his homely face and probably accounted for his legendary skill with freaked-out mutts of all descriptions. It might well work on bad-tempered, baggage-laden women, too; you never, ever knew.

I'd had more than a few flings since coming home, but none of them lasting. Sure, I was often lonely but it was a price I'd willingly pay rather than saddle myself with an unsuitable bloke just because I wanted someone to come home to of a night. Maybe it was selfish, but I'd got my life running pretty clockwork and I preferred it that way. I'd had enough high jinks to last two lifetimes. Piff sometimes wondered out loud *what-will-happen-when-you-get-old* but, given her circumstances, wondering was as far as it went.

Thinking of Piff, I punched her number on the in-car.

Even through the metallic distortion of the phone speakers, her rich contralto flowed like honey off a spoon. 'Hey, baby, I was just thinkin' of you an' wondering what you doin' tonight.'

56

'Watching *CSI*. Washing my hair, shagging Johnny Depp. The usual. Why?'

There was a slight pause. 'Lina's - she's - oh, you know. She's fucked off again. I don't want to - how 'bout I bring pizza round an' we watch dead bodies bein' dismembered together, eh?'

'Course. I've got beer. And other stuff. And ice-cream, come to that. You wanna stop over? Sure, no problemo, you know that. Mi casa su wotsit an' all that. Look, sorry about . . .'

'Yeah. me too, But it me own fault, baby. I know what she's like, she's got a lot of stuff to work through, you know? She had a rotten childhood, it's gonna take her time to process it, she's just actin' out. She'll be back, eventually. See you around eight, OK? I've got a couple more visits and some paperwork, then I'll get my things and trot over to yours. The password is *Bertha Mason*. Bye.'

The phone clicked off. I laughed to myself. Bertha Mason, Rochester's mad wife whom he locked in the attic for years, and who eventually burnt the house down in her insanity, dying in the flames as she capered about on the blazing roof. *Jane Eyre*. Typical English M.A. Piff lit joke. Bertha Mason was a Creole, a bi-racial woman from a genteel, decayed plantation family. Young Rochester, be-witched by her wild, luminous beauty, married her, then paid the price for his impetuosity. That's how Piff saw Lina. Lina was always running off, spending Piff's money on drugs and other girls, then creeping back in a state of collapse vowing she'd never, ever do it again. And Piff always took her back, nursed her, adored her and covered up for her. Lina was an artist, after all, and artists had tem-perament, didn't they? They felt things more than other people. Lina was fragile, over-sensitive, she took things to heart.

Bollocks, of course. Lina was a third-rate painter and a first-rate user. Sure, she was pretty, though the years of partying were starting to take their toll, in my view. The golden skin was getting a tad crêpey, the slim figure a trifle angular, the famous bosom a teensy bit saggy. She certainly had a good line in wheedling, though, that was a fact. Piff fell for it every time, because Lina told her what she wanted to hear. That Piff was everything to her, that Piff, all sixteen stone and damn near six foot of monumental muscle, bone and fat, was a goddess, a nurturing angel, her protector in a cold, cruel world. It made Piff feel needed. It made me feel poorly, knowing what Lina was in reality and how she actually viewed her long-suffering meal-ticket.

But there you go. Love is indeed, blind as a friggin' bat. I had no room to talk and certainly no desire to judge and I got on with Lina as best I could for Piff's sake. Epiphany Grace Charlot, everyone's crass stereotype of the big, black mama; a strong, ball-breaking, no-nonsense Amazon, her red-streaked fancy braids tied up high with an 'African' do-rag and her signature jangling earrings flashing all the colours of the rainbow, was - behind her carefully culti-vated facade - a sweet, insecure, loving woman. Not the Dread Amazon of office legend, eyes blazing like catherine wheels, tongue like a whip and biceps of steel. She wrapped her pain in a web of cleverness, charm, secret kindness and razor-sharp efficiency; most people never got past the height, the weight and the hair. Most people, and I include co-workers, didn't realise she was gay, mostly because they were too scared to ask Piff personal questions, though they frequently brought her offerings of their troubles and quite often actually followed her cool, logical advice.

But Piff was gay, had always known herself to be a lesbian and had never had any desire to hold hands with, never mind marry, the nervous flat-top-'n'-fade besuited

Sunday-best boys with names like Trinity, Winston, Clarence and Curtis her mother brought back from church to tea with her huge, disinterested, unmanageable youngest daughter. How Mam had bridled with pleasure at the faces of those lost boys as they drooled over Piff's smooth, gleaming café au lait skin, perfect teeth, immaculate straightened hair still smelling of the hot irons and glossy with pomade, her long, long legs, big high bootie and admirably disdainful attitude. *'Big in leg, good in bed', 'more cushion for the pushin'*, as the old guys in pastel flat-caps playing dominoes cackled admiringly when Piff sauntered by in her shorts and skimpy tops (*'see me in me 'alterback, you say me give you 'eart attack'* sang reggae teen popstrelles Althea And Donna - so truly in Piff's case). Piff - fourteen with a bullet, just longing to kiss the girls and make them cry. Only generally, it was her did the crying since she never had the nerve to confess her desires to the pretty friends with whom she adoringly linked arms and tantalisingly had pyjama parties and hairdressing sessions. So near and yet so, so far.

But Piff's Mam's machinations were all for nothing. When Piff finally bit the bullet after her glorious University career and a torrid affair with a radically Sapphic black American visiting lecturer, which broke her heart slightly and did wonders for her confidence, and 'fessed up, you could have heard the screaming and wailing in the next county. Her mother fainted. Her sister wept and wrung her hands. Her father walked out of the house without a word and her brothers followed him, their jaws clenched so hard they looked like bags of walnuts. *Disowned* didn't cover it, it was excommunication, Piff was anathema. They got the pastor to come and try to exorcise her, which he had a go at, ranting and chuntering about demon possession, until Piff just walked out the door with her one suitcase and her rucksack full of books, tears glazing her round cheeks.

Recently, her mum and her sister had come round a bit. Her brothers and her dad were another matter. It always gets blokes the worst, lesbianism, I find - hits 'em where it hurts. Real lesbians, I mean, not dozy slappers playing at kissy-sucky girl-on-girl to turn some sad porno-mad bloke on. Now Piff looked for family in Lina and found a bottomless well of need and selfishness that provided a dark and painful substitute. Funny how the best of us act the dumbest, sometimes, isn't it? Like I had room to talk - not that I'd ever suggest I was a good person, far from it. Still, you know, self-knowledge is a tricky beast - you think you've got a bridle on who and what you are then boom-banga-bang, someone says a few words and you realise you're nothing like you thought you were. Piff thinks she's this tough, intellectually cool gal who's seen it all and doesn't buy into the bullshit, but all Lina has to do is put on those googly kitten-eyes and wobble that cute bottom lip and Piff's a goner. Whereas if Lina tried that with me - and she has - I'd laugh. Which I did. I don't think I'm top of old Lina's Christmas card list, but there you go. My heart pumps custard about that, frankly.

Oh dear. People eh? You be hard pressed to invent 'em.

I hoped Piff remembered to put double pepperoni on my pizza.

Seven

'My God, woman, your bathroom look like Harvey Nicks gone mad - how many products a skinny white girl with no man need? You been buying perfume again, haven't you? Some of them bottles still in boxes not even opened.' Piff alternated West Indian, Oxford and Bradford speech alarmingly; sometimes listening to her was the linguistic equivalent of a roller-coaster with the brakes gone. I sighed.

'I'll thank you to keep your remarks about my pitiful addictions to yourself, madam. Oh yes, and ha ha ha, this from a person who thinks Vaseline is a good thing - pass the olives, please.'

'Here you go. Vaseline is a modern marvel, lady, you can do all kinda thing with Vaseline, trust me. A jar of Vaseline and some Palmers Cocoa Butter - you don't need nothin' more than that. Excess is bad for the soul. You are on the slippery path to damnation with all that fancy goin' on. That stuff in the brown box that says Marrakech on it, what is it? Amber? That's nice. I had a go - do I not smell like a dazzlin' exotic temptress from the Arabian Nights, eh?'

Piff extended a shapely arm jangling with a multitude of thin bangles and draped in purple M&S cotton knitwear. I held my pizza slice away from myself and sniffed her wrist.

'Oh yeah. You reek of scandalous Sapphic goings-on in the decadent oriental hammams of Morocco, in my opinion. Slightly tinged with garlic. 'Ere, you didn't spray that around like billy-oh, did you? It costs a fortune, I had to send for that from Libertys in London.'

Piff's eyebrow raised elegantly in a manner that would have done Mr. Spock proud. 'Had to? Oh, I see. You *had* to. Some of us have to eat and pay our bills, you got to spend your money on scent. Oh dear, the devil got you in his snares alright. Want some coleslaw? It was free.' Her earrings - large mobiles constructed from brass coins and faceted mauve beads - tinkled like tiny wind chimes as she did the head wobble thing.

'Waste not, want not, give it here. Jeez, it tastes like floor cleaner. Is there any wine left or should I repair to my extensive cellar and unscrew another bottle of Morrison's finest Australian Red? Or crack that dubious flask of the Burgundy Unnaturelle I aquired from Tipsy Nights offie on the way home? Oh and bung the telly on, the clicker's by you - there - under that red cushion - I want to watch the news.'

Grumbling, Piff fumbled for the remote and flicked on *Channel 4*. 'I don't know why you bother, nothin' good ever happening. Fools blowing themselves up for no good reason and other fools shootin' anything that moves. Did you see that thing about the guy who sent those letters to the coppers claiming to be the Night Creeper, you know, and it totally fucked up the case for ages? He's in court now for pervertin' the course of justice or whatever. He says he did it to impress his friends - my God, they must have been imaginary friends 'cause I can't believe he had any real ones, me mind bogglin', I tell you, and . . .'

The screen glowed silvery blue in the dim light of the living room; slightly shabby now, the spanking sharp new furniture a tad battered, the matte cream walls a bit grubby here and there, the disorder of my life cluttering the surfaces and rumpling the rugs. I could hear Piff. I mean I could hear her voice but what she was saying drifted away like flotsam on a receding tide.

All I could hear, all I could see, was the television. The fucking television.

All I could see was Johnny's face, on the screen, then a cutaway to paramedics loading a gurney into an ambulance, an American ambulance - there was a bundle, wrapped, on the gurney and they loaded it into the - the newsreader's unctuous, gloating voice saying . . .

' . . . died today at his New York apartment from a suspected overdose of drugs. Troubled rocker Johnny Eliot, also known as Johnny X, of the pop group Velvet Shank who topped the charts world-wide last year with their single 'My Beautiful Blonde', had recently left the famous Cedars clinic in Los Angeles, California where he was treated for heroin addiction. With Mr. Eliot in New York was his girlfriend, the British supermodel Lainey Stone. Ms. Stone issued a statement today through her lawyers expressing her deep sense of loss and condemnation of drug abuse which - as a former addict herself, she stated - she abhorred. Ms. Stone, whose on-off relationship with the notoriously temperamental singer was the subject of considerable media interest, added she had tried unsuccessfully to help Mr. Eliot to overcome his problems, but to no avail. Mr. Eliot's body will be flown back to the UK for a private family interment when it is released by the American authorities. Mr. Eliot's mother was unavailable for comment but his sister Marie said her brother's untimely death was a crushing blow to a tight-knit family and a great loss to music. Robert Willerby, vice-chairman of GMC UK, Velvet Shank's record company, is in our New York studio: Mr. Willerby, a sad loss indeed and yet another musician dies in drug-related circumstances. Do you as a company feel enough is done to warn young musicians of the dangers of drugs in an industry that seems unable or unwilling to address the issue?'

Bob got to be vice-prez eh? La la. Look at him in his good black Boss suit, mourning. He's in mourning – for his cash cow, the fucker. Still, GMC won't go short, eh, Bob? There'll be the *Special Edition Memorial Album, The Memorial Concert Live Album*, and *The Best Of* and *The Re-mastered Tracks* and the *Previously Unreleased Tracks* and . . .

Johnny you can't be dead. You can't be dead, baby, my love, my angel - not while I'm alive, it's not right because darlin', if you're dead, see, if you're dead what's the point of me being alive, what's the point of breathing, of anything, what's . . .

The pizza slice fell from my hand in slow motion as I doubled up and fell forward off the couch onto my knees, knocking over the bowl of black olives and my glass of cheap red wine - it pooled on the laminate floor, coppery-smelling, rank. I saw my hand, outstretched, fingers splayed against the screen as if I were trying to reach through Bob Willerby's fat, pink, freshly shaved face to the truth, the truth - that Johnny wasn't dead, wasn't dead, wasn't . . .

But he was dead.

A great wind roared through my spirit; excoriating, icy, full of grit and ashes. It swept up and through my heart in an icy black vortex so agonising I retched and gasped for breath while Azrael closed his vast, night-black, crow-black, hell-black raggetty wings around me and turning his solemn, pallid face towards me, kissed my forehead with his livid poisoned lips. He paused, the Angel Of Death, while fetching my beloved from the world, he paused and I begged him to take me too but he wrapped himself and his burden in the tattered opacity of darkness leaving me alone forever in the maelstrom.

Alone, forever.

Eight

'Breathe, breathe slowly, come on baby, slowly - that's it, that's it - oh, Annie, what's the matter, sugar? Are you OK? Can you sit up? Can you . . . ?'

Everything seemed to have been bleached of colour. I felt as if I had been sucked dry of life and I was just an assemblage of bones wrapped in a tattered skin, no longer human, the fat hiss and sizzle of bloody living flesh desiccated into an ossuary and a death's head rictus. I was dead. I was dead.

Then I felt Piff gather me into her warm arms and felt her strong, steady heartbeat against my cheek. I smelt the warmth of her, powdery and sweet, the caramel scent of Palmers Cocoa Butter on her soft skin; human, alive. A hiccupping shudder dragged air into my deflated lungs.

'That's it, that's it, you're safe, you're OK, come on now, try to relax, eh, try to be calm. I'm goin' to call an ambulance, Annie, I think you had some kind of fit, darlin' - don't you worry now, I'll . . .'

'No, Piff, no, I'm - it's not . . .' My voice sounded like rotten silk tearing; the words spinning off into nothingness. I blinked dry eyes, my eyelids clicking in slow motion. 'It's not - I'm not ill, I . . . Piff, go - go over by the bookcase, see - see that box, the wooden box, the carved - yeah bring it here, please, sorry, I mean, yeah - open it, Piff, look at the pictures.'

My head fell back on the cushion Piff had put behind me as if the tendons and muscles couldn't support the weight of my aching skull and I heard, as if from very far away, her sifting through the contents of the box.

The antique cedarwood box that Johnny and I had bought as our Memories Box while we'd been on holiday in California. It held all the private photographs of Johnny and I, the letters and cards he'd given me and his e-mails, which I'd printed out.

Did I say I'd thrown everything away? What liars pride makes of us all.

And as Piff moved layers of paper with a sound like wind soughing in the branches of an old pine tree, just like the one outside our hotel window on that trip to Cornwall, where Johnny had tried to learn to surf and we got brown as . . . I smelt him, smelt Johnny; for a second I thought - what? That he was there, was with me, that he wasn't . . . But I realised it was his perfume, the one I'd had made specially for him by an artisan perfumier in New York, his own custom-made one-off blend. It had been hideously expensive but I hadn't cared as long as it had pleased him. It was all intense essential oils, layer upon layer of labdanum, patchouli, vanilla, vetiver, ambrette, frankincense, myrrh, amber, Bulgarian rose absolute, Oud wood – the list was endless and beautiful, like a scented prayer. The woman had said some of the ingredients would keep their fragrance for a hundred years, would never die. *Like me,* he'd said, *like us.* I'd put some drops of the heavy dark oil on a couple of cotton wool pads and put them in the box when we got it, now the fragrance - strange, narcotic, archaic - filled the room like his ghost, embracing me in memories.

The silence, broken only by Piff's breathing and the sifting shuffle of papers, seemed to go on forever. Like a computer screen displaying photographs on a slide show, images of my time with Johnny passed across my mind, I saw without looking what Piff was seeing:

Johnny and I laughing in a photo booth
Johnny smiling in a California sunset

66

Johnny and I snapped by an obliging tourist in Thailand
Johnny laid on our bed half-naked eating a bowl of ice-cream
Johnny in a studio living room playing acoustic
Johnny and I, cuddling, faces pressed side by side, photographed by Fred Dandridge
Johnny looking up at me, his face striped by the shadows of a hotel window blind
Johnny on stage looking like a tattooed fighting angel lit from within by hellfire
*Johnny holding up a bit of paper with the words **I love you, Annie** written on it*
Johnny
Johnny

'Oh, my God, my God - Annie - you told me there'd been someone, but I never. . . Is this who you. . .I'm so sorry, baby, so sorry, I never. . . I never would have thought . . .'

She put the pictures back in the box and despite the fact I'd asked her to look at them, despite the fact she was my friend and a dear one at that, I wanted to scream at her to take her hands off them, to stop touching all I had left of my boy. I turned my head away and tried to breathe slowly.

'Annie sugar, I'm - I'm goin' to put the kettle on, OK? OK? We'll have some tea, I - oh, darlin' I don't know what to say, you must feel - just try and relax, I'll bring you some nice sweet tea - oh, love . . .'

I rolled off the sofa like an invalid and crawled to the box. Shuffling through the dusty paper strata I found what I was looking for and crept back. It was a small monochrome art print, a photograph of Johnny's face in close-up, his eyes (those eyes, those eyes - razor wire dragged through my heart making my breath catch in my throat) seeming to gaze directly into the viewer's. It had been taken by Maurizio Paoluzzi for *Vogue UK* when they'd done a piece on up-coming unsigned rock stars. It had made all the other young hopefuls look pallid and amateurish by comparison and won a portrait award for Maurizio. I'd pulled a lot of recalcitrant strings to get Johnny on the shoot but it had paid off good style, boosting his profile a thousand percent and securing Velvet Shank a massive GMC contract. On the back of the print Johnny had written:

'For Annie my beautiful Blonde, my love, My Lady, my friend always and forever from your Johnny who loves you more than anything in the world you make my heart sing and don't forget it XXX'

I didn't have to look for it, I had it by heart. The print was still in the heavy silver Jorg Jensen frame I'd put it in and kept by my side of the bed all during our time together. I put it to my lips and whispered the silly phrases we'd used with each other, the things all lovers say, the precious, ridiculous incantations that we all hope will keep the night at bay.

I said goodbye.

Nine

'Annie? Annie? Oh, I'm sorry to wake you - are you feeling better? Only, well, there's - well, there's a bit of an emergency - and if you think you *could* manage, I mean, I know flu can be - but we really do need . . . If you could come in . . .'

As phone calls go it'd been pretty uninformative. To Bob Pritchard an emergency usually means something like the photocopier not working, or a computer on the blink. He alternated between hysteria over trifles (if men can have hysteria given it originally meant your womb was wandering round your body causing you to become unstable - but trust me, if men had wandering wombs, Bob's would be a Frequent Flyer) and lip-pursing, unreasoning dictatorship when he imagined his authority was being challenged. Which it never was because no-one except the newest recruit ever paid a blind bit of attention to whatever hobby horse he'd mounted that week.

Bob was a watery-eyed, chinless, lanky, beige eco-bloke who refused to use deodorant, with a pink-eyed, skinny, beige wife who favoured baggy sludge-coloured hand-knits from Peru, and two acne-studded, skinny, beige kids he obviously engendered on his missus by osmosis, because Bob was one of those people it's utterly impossible to imagine *at it*. Cruel, yes. True, definitely. He kept his job because no-one ever got fired in our line of work for being a dithery, incompetent, well-meaning pratt and he'd been promoted sideways so many times he'd have to start at the beginning again, and no-one wanted to have him back again second time around.

I'd had a week. A week to get myself under control. I'd even got a proper sick-note courtesy of Piff, who'd stayed for three days and then visited every day to Lina's barely-disguised disgust, empathy not being her strong point. Then Bob phoned, a quavering but unmistakable note of genuine panic in his reedy voice. So I went back in. Pausing to look in the mirror on the way out, I knew no-one would question my so-called diagnosis. I looked like - well, I looked like how I felt. Strung out to fuck. A thousand-yard stare and not a trace of anything human I could see.

Reflexively I sprayed myself with some perfume I'd bought because I'd thought how much he - Johnny - would have liked it; an amber scent reputedly laced with pheromones, the heavy glass bottle and solid metal pebble-shaped stopper the kind of thing he enjoyed. Would have enjoyed. I almost smiled. Even now, there I was, boots on, silver on, spraying myself with Ambre Passion like a good soldier strapping on her armour. Fight the good fight. Go get 'em girl, and all that crap. Yeah. The Black fucking Widow; unacknowledged Relict of a dead Star.

I suppose, looking back, I had that strange, high calm, that feeling of being in the eye of the storm, standing on a mountain top and watching the howling debris-filled tornado spiral round me whilst I was as detached as some kind of freaky ascetic; sanctified by the exhaustion of grief. I'd cried myself out, I was as tattered and faded as an old prayer flag whipping in the Himalayan breeze. Nothing lived in my head but emptiness, nothing moved in my heart but grief.

I smiled at the dead woman in the mirror. Whatever it was, Bobby-boy, bring it on. Oh yeah.

And he did. Sam Jagger's youngest boy, three-year-old Jake, the eater of dog-food and rowan berries, was missing. He'd been missing since approximately - no-one knew for sure - yesterday tea-time. Maybe. Possibly it was longer. Sam reportedly said she'd seen him for definite at breakfast but then what with her nail in-fill appointment and then an unplanned quick one at the pub with Baz who she'd met as she came out of the salon, she'd not got home as she'd intended. But it was OK, because she'd rung her mum who'd had the other children for the last couple of days to give Sam a break and left a message on her mobile to go and give Jake his dinner - meaning his lunch - not thinking for a minute that most mothers didn't leave their pre-schoolers alone in the house for two minutes, never mind two hours. Her mum was to stay at Sam's and give all the children their tea together, family-like, because Sam proper meant to be back to do their supper but she and Baz had met this old mate from school and . . .

It was a whining litany of excuses that ate up any sympathy Sam might have accrued for herself like acid eats steel. She'd gone on the lash leaving the children without even checking her notoriously flaky mother had ever received the garbled message Sam left on her dodgy knock-off pay-as-you-go mobile that was hardly ever in credit. Sam had no idea that everyone she spoke to, the police, the young case-worker subbing for me, and more sinister, a reporter from the local paper alerted by a police snout, despised her and thought she was cruel, stupid, ignorant and a danger to her children. She thought, her sweet flower face flushed and pink with tears and terror, that they'd understand her tortuous and self-justifying unreasonable reasoning. That they'd look after her. That they'd find her grubby, beautiful, tousle-headed boy for her and they'd have big hugs and it'd all be right as a trivet by beddy-bye-byes.

She genuinely believed this. After all, we were authority figures, we were there to care for her, she'd been told that

71

all her life. Naturally, you'd dis coppers in the pub and call them fucking pigs but if anything seriously went wrong - death, rape, brutality, suicide - they sorted it. Social workers were her surrogate family; the stern aunties that nagged you into being good. That had your best interests at heart. They might be a pain in the arse but they were educated and knew how to read and write, unlike Sam herself; therefore, they knew what to do in a crisis. All Sam had to do was weep until her cheapjack market-stall generic mascara tracked down her cheeks in inky rivulets and say how sorry she was with every gasping sodden breath and we would deal with this horror for her.

I need not tell you how wrong she was. Yes of course, it would be dealt with and search parties were already out and social workers already in place, but would it all be alright by bedtime? Hah. She'd so lost those kids, I could see it in Bob's tight mask of tension and resentment as he filled me in on the disaster, making sure I knew he thought my lax and bohemian (he actually used that word) approach to my clients had born this bitter fruit that he, head of department, was currently gagging on. He'd had to send Tamsyn to Sam's. Of course, she wasn't ideal but at least, having come straight from Uni, she was on-message in a departmental sense, whereas my message discipline (he'd been on an American-style New-Age-Goes-Terminator booster course recently and loved every gung-ho minute of it whilst publicly pretending to think it was ridiculous) was decidedly compromised.

However, he said, eyeing me as you might eye a pikey's mutt, Sam was not relating well to Tamsyn. She had done nothing but scream - quite literally scream - for me since this incident had erupted. She refused to talk to Tamsyn who was becoming very stressed by Sam's negative attitude and aggressive body-language and the fact Sam kept referring to her as that - ahem - effing stuck-up little - ah - well. The police had requested him to put me back on the case to save any further distress to the family (and themselves trouble, but he wouldn't say that). Reluctantly, he'd agreed to see if I was well enough and as I was . . .

He paused, taking off his glasses and cleaning them with a special little microfibre cloth he carried in the pocket of his cords for that purpose. His naked eyes were the exact colour of spat-out gooseberries. I thought about Tamsyn, with her fake-tanned unformed little mug and taffy-blonde *MTV* hair, her crap scrape-through post-80's degree and her incipient middle-class totty's navel-pierced beer belly, the ladette stigmata of her generation. I thought about Bob's huge crush on her that he thought was his Secret Passion. I thought about how he didn't know I knew he was sacrificing me to this mess - and possibly, if it got worse, the ravening wolves of the media - to save his pudgy, pimply arse.

I thought about Sam. And Jakey.

I got up, picking up my enormous bag and fumbling around, found my black fags. I stuck one in my mouth.

'Annie - you can't - this is a non-smo . . .'

'I know, Bob, I know. Phone Tamsyn and tell her I'm on my way.'

'Well, I mean of course you'll have full departmental backing, and I'm sure little Justin . . .'

'Jake.'

'What? Oh, of course, the stress, it's so - *Jake*, Jake, of course. Anyway, I'm sure little Jake will be found safe and sound as soon as . . .'

I eyed him narrowly. He believed every word. I walked out of the door as his sentence trailed away.

I drove like a pinball wizard to Sam's and parked the wheezing jeep beside the cop-cars, assorted scrappers belonging to Sam's vast array of exes and currents, and Tamsyn's new-style lime-green Beetle. With the usual fake pink gerbera in the dashboard vase. I paused to get myself together before walking into the unravelling chaos of a situation no-one expected would have a good outcome. Myself, I reckoned Sam's la-la mum, Joanna, or Jo-Jo as she preferred, would remember she'd farmed Jake out to one of her many unsavoury relatives or friends, or he'd wandered off and fallen asleep in a farmer's field and would shortly stumble home crying for beans on toast as he'd done before. I didn't think he'd been abducted by a sex-fiend or space-aliens because, contrary to popular belief, these were fairly rare occurrences. I was more worried he'd hurt himself and was unable to get home. I pictured him with his chubby little ankle sprained, fake white and gold baby-Nikes clogged with mud, sitting in a field close by in his filthy bootleg Man United shirt, crying those big blue eyes up, waiting for a 'nadult' to come and get him.

But though I knew it was going to be a long, arduous haul I was glad of the distraction, to be honest. I'd rung Piff on the way and she was trying to wangle things so she could come down, but her current case was still tying her up in court.

'You take care, you hear? Don't let that fool Bob pressure you. Tamsyn can deal with this, it's the job after all, she trained for this you know, like we all did. She gotta learn the real stuff sometime, he can't protect her forever and remember, you aren't well, sugar.'

'Yeah, I know. I'll be OK. What else can I do? Sit around in the flat forever? This'll be summat and nothin' mate, just you wait and see. And I can't do that Tamsyn, she'll just do everythin' by the book, you know she will, straight down the fuckin' line and she'll fuck it all up with Sam. Piff, I'm best off doing it myself, you know that.'

'Yeah, yeah. But I'll be round to yours later, baby, OK?'
'People will think we're in love.'
'With a skinny ting like you? Ha! Tink again, girl, you wish.'

I was alright. I was OK. If only I could get the bloody stupid song that kept jangling round and round in my brain out of my head, I'd be fine.

Wild thing, you make my heart sing,
you make everything

Bloody stupid song, our bloody stupid song, it rang in the empty, cold vault of my mind with the sinister, wheezing, hurdy-gurdy jauntiness of a mad clown singing in Bedlam.

Resolutely I took the fag from behind my ear, lit it, and squinting against the smoke, struggled out of the car with my stuff.

Ten

'Annnnnnniiiieeeeeeeee Anniiiiieeeee mybabby mybabby
mybabby he - they won't - mek em find im, mek em they
don't . . .'

Sam hurled herself at me from where she was crouching
by the sofa clinging onto Jo-Jo's huge knees. Her face was
blotched and swollen with weeping, glazed with snot,
and her hair stuck out like broken straws from her wonky
pony-tail. A dissolving crust of make-up left over from
yesterday's partying had given her huge panda eyes, and
rivulets of foundation and glittering bronzer tracked her
cheeks like cosmetic tie-and-dye. She stank of cheap body
spray, sweat, sex, unprocessed alcohol and that strange,
burning odour that pills mixed with booze produce. She
was wearing a torn blue sequinned paisley-print camisole
edged in black lace that barely contained her breasts and a
pair of dirty black knee-length shorts. 'City Shorts' I believe
they're called. Even on petite, hipless Sam they looked
crap. Her bare feet were bruised and filthy, her ruined
silver flats discarded like dead fish by the sofa. Several of
her fake nails were broken, dried blood beading the ends
of her torn fingers. The whole room turned to stare as she
flung herself headlong onto me, clinging like a sticky, rank
limpet.

More snot bubbled from her blocked nose as she
ratcheted gulps of air and chuntered like a toy robot
running out of batteries. 'My Jakey my Jakey my little
angel some fuckin' perve's got im mum's angel says so
I know it I do he's out there with some fuckin monster
oooh ohhh why don't they do somethin' Annie why

don't they go get im the bastards the fucking bastards the . . .'

Jo-Jo nodded sagely and re-arranged her colossal breasts and belly comfortably in her outsize turquoise T-shirt and layered brown print gypsy skirt. 'Oh aye. Poor little fella. In the clutches of a monster. Bein' molested as we speak by a filthy paedo. My Guardian Angel told me. Like on the telly, you mark my words. I've done the cards, see, it's all there. I'm prayin' to my angels all the time for him, poor little scrap.'

From out of her purple crotchet bag she produced a battered pack of Angel Fortune Cards and began shuffling them with the mindless dexterity born of long practice. Sam clung to me, gazing at her mother, her eyes wide with a mixture of fear, respect for her mother's well-known self-proclaimed occult powers, and loathing of the coppers whose faces were so devoid of expression you couldn't mistake what they thought.

I was about to reply to Jo-Jo's nonsense when Tamsyn came out of the kitchen bearing a tray crowded with mis-matched mugs. She put the tray on the floor in front of Jo-Jo who favoured her with a queenly nod, and turned to me, ignoring the sobbing girl slowly sliding down my body towards the floor. I semi-dragged Sam over to her mother and draped her in Jo-Jo's capacious lap.

Tamsyn smiled brightly. 'I made some tea.'

I bit back the remark I wanted to make - she wouldn't get a medal from me for lowering herself to stick a tea-bag in a cup - and thanked her. Irritating though she was, I couldn't let myself get angry. Anger was the knotty, brutal key that unlocked the gates I'd only just managed to force shut. I mustn't get angry no matter what. In my head that fluttering tag of music flapped and ragged; over and over, a honky-tonk repeat.

You make everything. . .

groovy

'Are you alright, Annie?' Tamsyn asked, a faint haze of concern fuzzing her smooth brow. Her expression suggested she very much thought I wasn't. Well, she was right, I wasn't, but what difference did that make? Life had to go on. I had to go on. I mean, I could not - you know, I could just die, we can all do that anytime, it's not, as they say, big or clever - but who'd know then about the love I'd had, my most precious possession, my devotion, my True Faith? Only Piff, and she could never fully understand it because no-one who wasn't me could ever fully understand the consuming immensity of it, how it devoured me alive and at the same time, set me free. . . No, I would go on because I always had, keep that votive flame burning. Its icy flicker had sustained me while he - Johnny - had been alive, in the world but lost to me. Now he was gone that ghostly flame could sustain me still. I'd never imagined he'd come back to me, you see, I'd never thought that, so now he never could it made no odds, in a way. I could go on and on and . . . Fuck. Fuck. Just had to keep hold of that cold calm, that cool detachment, it was my greatest friend. My shield.

So come on and hold me tight

I love you

'Yeah, just the flu, you know, takes it out of you a bit.' I shook my head, trying to dislodge the music that burbled in my brain.

'Have you got a headache? I've got some painkillers in my . . .'

'No, no - no really. Just got one of those stupid things where you get a song in your head you can't get rid of it. Silly. Annoying though – it's an old Troggs song . . .'

'Oh, I don't - but God - I know what you mean about songs, I like totally had that old Arctic Monkeys dancefloor thing in my head forever last week and I hate that kind of music usually but Charlie was playing it over and over. . .'

No, Tamsyn wouldn't have heard of The Troggs, never listened as Johnny and I did to the excruciatingly funny Troggs studio out-takes tapes every musician loves so much and that I got for him, wouldn't get the sly, sexy, country-boy silliness of the Troggs. 'Wild Thing' had been our song, guaranteed to make us smile, have us singing the chorus together, the source of a dozen private jokes meaningless to outsiders. The Troggs would hardly be Tamsyn's scene, even ironically, especially if she didn't care for the likes of the Arctic Monkeys and their many wannabe-street-poet soundalikes. Dreadfully common, lads like that, all a bit Artful Dodger; you could see the snobbery plain as day in her eyes and the faint pursing of her pearly-pink lips. It was nasty of me, but I bet she loved that whining chinless toff Hal Finch-Ellis with his hideously omnipresent hit 'Too Precious', or even poor old James Blunt.

Tamsyn smirked. She was big on smirking. If it had been an Olympic sport, she'd have got us gold. 'But yeah, James Blunt's my kind of thing, totally an oldie these days I suppose, but God, you know, I really love his voice and like, 'You're Beautiful' is like so totally my song, it's on my Myspace and people laugh but. . .'

I coughed loudly into my hand. She moved away, afraid of infection. The brief flare of our personal conversation was over.

At a quarantine distance she filled me in on what she knew, not much more than Bob had already told me, and left, not bothering to say goodbye to Sam, who was now invisible to her. But then, she was invisible to Sam, too. *Quid pro quo,* I thought, on the whole.

I spoke with the copper in charge. A decent enough, square-built woman, not stupid, with a flat Derbyshire accent and a no-nonsense attitude. She knew no more than anyone else, adding only that there were no known sex offenders in the area and that in her personal opinion, the kiddie had just wandered off. Didn't help the mum was so - er - *distressed* and that the local press had already got hold of the story. I refrained from mentioning it was probably a copper who grassed that one to the hacks. Anyway, photos had been taken by all and sundry before they could prevent it, on mobile phones, press Nikons, and cheap disposable cameras left over from holiday. The golden age of communication meant the excoriating glare of multi-media exposure before you could whistle Dixie. And what a photo-op: Sam had been outside running up and down, her breasts falling out of her flimsy top, screaming and weeping to all and sundry that angels had told her her son was being murdered by a paedophile. The substances Sam had ingested the night before had apparently not worn off. As to the photos, and the accompanying articles and internet crap - with the possibility of more and more looming on the horizon should the worst come to the worst - well, it wasn't good. The copper sucked her teeth discreetly and murmured that she couldn't imagine a useful outcome for Sam. We looked at each other, the knowledge of how completely disastrous it all actually was passing between us like a small but effective electric current. When it came to the Sams of this world, we'd been there, done that and bought the fucking T-shirt a hundred times before.

'Miss, Miss, 'ave you got a minute love, there's summat I need to tell yer.' Jo-Jo's catarrhal contralto - a Blues singer's dream voice - never ceased to amaze me with the husky, musical beauty of its tone, belying the true nature of its owner. That voice - warm, confiding and hypnotic - had wheedled wads of cash from credulous punters as her fat hands, glittering with CZ eternity rings, flipped the cards and she spun them long tales about how cruelly misunderstood they were, how despite what ignorant folk might think they were deeply sensitive and kind-hearted and how one day, after some sadness and a family row, they'd find love and happiness in the end. And someone special would give them a ring set with a blue stone - *mebbes an engagement ring, eh? One like dear Princess Di's, God bless her, England's Rose, eh?* It was all in the angels' hands and for an extra tenner, you could be gifted with a genuine lucky angel brooch, everso lovely and proper rolled gold.

Reluctantly I went over and sat beside her on the sofa. What fey bollocks was she about to serve up this time? Angels had flitted away with Jakey and taken him for tea with the Baby Jesus? I was still pissed off about her winding Sam up about paedophiles stealing her kid like some *News Of The World* sponsored oracle. But I pushed my irritation down hard; she was my client's parent, after all. No point alienating her unnecessarily. Later I'd try to have a word with her privately about being a bit more bloody tactful.

'I'll read for you, lovie, fer free like, see what the angels say,' she breathed at me, her chins quivering as turned her whole body slightly to speak to me. She was too big to move easily. Piff was a big woman but she was muscular, flexible and in proportion. Jo-Jo was simply stiffly and lumpily obese. A lifetime of boozing and eating vile, cheap grease-saturated food had given her this burden; her fat had the curdled, semi-liquid quality of melting wax, her upper arms draped with pendulous, flapping swags of flesh in a dreadful parody of wings, an earthbound, flesh-anchored angel of un-mercy, the opposite of her beloved spirits of light.

'Ah, no thanks, Jo-Jo, I'm not into . . .'

But it was too late. She was already shuffling the big, grimy cards.

Sam raised her head exhaling a sour whiff of body odour and the yellow stink of fear no-one believes in until they smell it. She'd found a filthy teddy of Jakey's, under the valance of the sofa where it had lain covered in that dust and crap that gathers under beds and the like - what my mother used to call *slut's wool* - and was clutching it to her bosom as if it were the child himself. Above the subdued but definite burble of activity in the room her cracked voice threaded like snarled and knotted embroidery silk.

'Please Miss Annie Miss, please. They might say summat to you, they won't say owt ter me. I'm bad me, I'm a bad mum I know I am . . .' Her voice rose, breaking on the high tones, raw with stress. 'I am, I am, I know I am, that's what you all think, you do, you think I'm a right cunt, I know you do, but you don't know owt about me, you don't - why don't you fuck off and do summat, do summat, find my baby, find . . .'

Jo-Jo flipped the cards unconcerned by this outburst as she had been unconcerned by anything Sam had done since her birth. People sometimes thought Jo-Jo didn't love Sam or her siblings but that wasn't true. Nothing human is so simple. As far as she was capable of loving anybody or anything that wasn't herself, Jo-Jo loved her children. Well, maybe 'love' was too strong, 'fond' was better; she was *fond* of them, but they didn't impact on her life in any particular way. They had brought themselves up, under the ponderous, disinterested gaze of their low-rent *magna mater* whilst wailing women crept up to the bungalow under cover of the night, paying hard cash to Jo-Jo for the tugging, agonising fish-hook of hope. No time for the kiddies when there was decent money to be made and spent on trinkets, baubles and holidays in the sort of hot places where you could get a decent English fry. Jo-Jo never took the children on holiday with her - wouldn't have been a proper break, then, eh?

I didn't know the other kids - they'd dispersed around the country and beyond, into the Bermuda Triangle of the Balearics - but Sam's life had been one, long howl for attention. Jo-Jo's lack of interest in her desperate little monkey-baby, all long skinny limbs and big pleading eyes, had screwed Sam's little brain into gibbering mush. She ate whatever drugs were offered her without asking what they were, drank like a piranha, cut her arms to ribbons on bad days, and her choices in regard to her objects of affection were notorious, not just in the area, but in at least three official departments. Jo-Jo had never hit Sam and her siblings, but the damage she did was real enough. There were people who came to Jo-Jo for readings who thought she was a living avatar of the Blessed Virgin, so caring, so understanding, what a wonderful person. And in her business life, she certainly gave that impression, because she wasn't really involved. In private, Sam begged for love and got her Uncle Barry's dick in her mouth from age six. Some substitute. Jo-Jo just looked away. *Barry allus were a wrong 'un*. No point causing a fuss, that's what happened to girls. No doubt it had happened to Jo-Jo in her time. Say la vee, an' all that. Barry'd lose interest anyway when Sam started bleeding, that's how he was. Jo-Jo's only interest, the thing she actually loved, that made her feel important, powerful, was her career as local fortune-teller, self-appointed wise woman, dispenser of curiously effective and intimately localised advice (*'get rid, lovie, his dad were just the same, them Tollers allus run ter type, look at their Robbie, no smoke wi'out fire there an' all'*) and general witch. It was much more satisfying to her than the concerns of her wild brood of changelings, none of whom, because of their pick 'n' mix selection of fathers, physically resembled each other or her, in the least. Was Jo-Jo a good, or a bad person? Depended who you asked. Depended on how the cards fell. Like all of us, really, if we're honest, which we seldom are.

The angel deck moved like water in her glittering, swollen hands.

I leant round the front of her, taking hold of Sam's trembling arm and shushing her gently. 'Come on love, stop it now, look, sit here and yer mam will do the cards for me. We'll see what them angels say together, OK?'

Sam nodded numbly and slid across the floor to me like a toddler scooting across lino on its bottom, and leant against my legs. I could feel the unnatural chemical fever burning in her, hot against my flesh. The back of her thin, dirty white neck as she bowed her head was pathetic. I sighed. The rest of the people in the room contrived not to look at this strange pieta. Outside the close fug of the tiny room, I could hear cars, coppers talking on radios and far away, the dogs barking and howling again, a disconcerting sound like a savage, demented choir. The rank smell of body odour, damp, gas fires and general filth was choking. I longed to just get up, walk outside and never come back. To get away from this stench of disaster, the clinging, greasy exhalation of inevitability.

You make my heart sing

How I wished that bloody song would fade from my head. Its knowing, faux-innocent, psychedelic atmosphere seemed to cast a strangely sinister light on the events un-ravelling around me; there was something weird in it, some-thing almost gloating. Like a smirking little devil perched on a high shelf playing a jaunty tune on the fiddle while awful cruelty, or rape, or murder, or the ruin of a life were enacted beneath his tapping, goat's foot. I shook my head again, but the song clung, like a miasma.

Wild thing I . . . think you move me . . .

'Here we go, you shuffle them now, dear.'

I shuffled the oversized cards, the pretend-renaissance images of God's legions faded and worn from constant handling. How many weeping girls, worried mothers, fu-rious jilted brides, agonised lovers had done as I was doing? Their faint voices, babbling like a distant beck, seemed to slide from the pack as I inexpertly cut and re-cut, distorted glimpses of their shadow-blighted faces overlaid the anodyne masks of the badly printed images falling through my bony fingers.

But I wanna know for sure . . .

'Tell yer what, we'll just do Past, Present and Future, shall we? Saves time don't it? I don't suppose you'd want Sacred Cross or owt, anyhow, I don't s'pose we've got the room fer a big spread, like.' Jo-Jo shifted her bones in the enveloping mass of herself and smiled professionally at me, the persona of her working self settling over her moon face like a chiffon veil.

'Now, you think of a question, you know, about the babby like, an' we'll see what we'll see, eh?'

Sam snuffled. Irritated, I tried to concentrate my mind on Jakey, picturing him, feeling him, smelling his unwashed kid self, seeing his spiky fair hair and pierced ear, the cheap Beckham-style gold and diamanté cross pendant glinting as he smiled up at me, his soft little mouth a pout of rose and smeared jam. . .

I couldn't. I couldn't. The pictures formed and dissolved into a tatter of darkness, as if he were dropping away down a bottomless well. I opened my mouth to speak, to say I really didn't want to do this, but Jo-Jo was speaking already, a frown on her smooth, pink forehead.

'Well now, let's see, shall we? Let's see what the angels say, eh? I used to use the Tah-rott, me, but these days, I find folk like the angels better. Not so scary, y'know, no funny pictures of skellingtons an' that. Just lovely angels wantin' to help us.' Jo-Jo paused, then her voice took on a slow, sing-song tone, like a mother telling a bedtime story. 'Look, here's Uriel, he's a proper Archangel, he's a Prince of Light, him, he makes us understand punishment an' dreams, he sends warnings an' that. He's very strong, very strong; what we sow, so shall we reap, that's what he says, which is right enough as we all know, eh? And here's the Seraphim of Eternal Love, he's ter comfort yer for lost love, he says no love is ever proper lost, like, that it's never dead, it's in our souls, our lost loved ones live in us forever an' ever, we only have ter open our eyes an' there they are, it's just that we won't see 'em normally but they're there right enough, they're . . . 'Ang on, I don't get it, this card, I don't - it int mine, did you put it there?'

Jo-Jo stared at me, a card in her hand, her face gelid in the dust-dancing light filtering through the drawn curtains. Shaking her greasy elf-locked hair she turned the card towards me. I looked at it, but I couldn't seem to see it properly, it was out of kilter, hazy . . . I strained to see, to understand what I thought I was looking at. A chill ran through me, someone walked on my grave. The hairs rose on my forearms like a dog's hackles and my stomach rolled. The room seemed to recede sickeningly, the noise muting, turning down to nothing. A thick, breathless stillness lay over us as she pushed the image closer towards me.

'I - no - I don't . . .'

The picture came into focus. The angel's face was hidden in his cowl by shadows that layered down to infinity. At his back, behind his huge, unfurling charcoal wings, were black storms coiling and building without cease and the maelstrom, thick with roiling shapes. His naked ivory hand was held out to me; a bundle of beckoning bones. Above his head, in a rip of smoky red fire was written 'Azrael'. As I read it, I tasted blood, coppery foul, on my breath and my pulse tripped a beat.

Come on, come on, wild thing . . .

It was unnatural past bearing; the real world had faded to a bleached rag and the here and now was this stew of insane impossibility. Panic rose in me like a flight of scared crows - I fought against the symphony of their furious tatterdemalion battering. My heart seemed to swell in my chest and the air started to shiver and craze over, a roaring filled my ears as if Something raw and terrified was hurtling down a dark tunnel towards me and I knew that it was trying to break through, whatever it was, that it was beating itself against the skin of the world, screaming, desperate, that it wanted to speak to me, tell me something horribly important, take me into itself. I couldn't swallow, my eyes were burning, I fought to catch my breath . . . I knew what it was, who it was, I knew and all I had to do was open my heart and he'd . . .

Then with a clamouring, sucking sound like waves dragging on a steep shingle beach, it was over, we were back in the room and Jo-Jo was looking at the card, nodding. Her deep-set eyes, of an unusual silvery grey colour, gazed at me with a fleeting shadow of wickedly sharp intelligence, before she looked down again and shuffled her bra straps comfortably. What did she know, this fat old woman? What had she seen? I wanted to shake her, scream at her to tell me but I couldn't, my brain seemed to be stuck, frozen, numb.

'I must be gettin' tired, all this worry. Fer a minute there I dint recognise it, must be gettin' mucky wi all the handling these old cards get. Eh, should get meself some new 'uns, but these are my lucky set, you know. Anyhow, right, it's the Guardian Angel of Children see? Holdin' a dear little babby in his arms. He's fer kiddies, see, ter protect an' care fer 'em, specially them as int loved as they should be, or who gets abused, like. Poor little 'uns. It'll be for your job like, lovie, cause that's what you do, int it? Lookin' after them as can't help themselves.' She nodded again, smiling calmly, those curious eyes buried deep in the shining red domes of her cheeks.

'See, see Miss Annie Miss, it's my babby, my babby wants me, he's telling yer, he wants me, he . . .'

Jo-Jo put the cards away and patted Sam absently. 'Yeah, he does, love, he does, we all know he wants his mammy, but see, the bad man's got him now like my angels said, an' . . .'

I was still disoriented and confused, but Jo-Jo's eye for the professional main chance - *Psychic Gran Solves Missing Jakey Mystery!* with any luck there'd be national headlines and she could maybe even add *As Seen On TV* to her cards and flyers - coupled with her apparent inability to comprehend the effect her repeated assurances that Jakey had been kidnapped had on Sam, who visibly crumpled further in on herself and set up a long, guttural whine of despair was enough to galvanise me. 'Jo - stop it. Please. Look at the state of her, it's not helping you sayin' stuff like that.'

Jo-Jo bridled. 'Well, Miss, I speak as I find, and I won't cross the heavenly voices, I am guided by a higher power, me.' She raised her eyes upwards whilst laying a hand on her chest decoratively. The very picture of a Victorian saint from a cheap Sunday School tract. She was such a sham, it was obvious - all that angel codswallop. Complete fucking nonsense. I wasn't one of her gullible, distraught victims. She couldn't con me with her fairground pikey routines. I shook myself mentally. Nothing had happened. Nothing. I was just over-tired, that was all and yeah, emotional. In mourning, as they used to say. It was close and airless in the tiny living room crammed with people, reeking of fag-smoke. I'd just felt a bit faint. Dizzy. Only natural. Nothing had happened. Nothing. Nada. Rien.

You make my heart sing

Nothing.

Wild thing

Best do something. I couldn't bear the thought of sitting in this wet tangle of women anymore. Do something definite, useful. Before Jo-Jo could trundle out anymore spiritual gems and the policewoman in charge decided to run her in for interfering in an investigation and being a total fucking arse. Fuck me, I'd give evidence against her for that, any day. I decided it was time to separate her and Sam. I looked at Sam as she sat, clutching the teddy in her bruise-mottled crossed arms, rocking, a silvery thread of snot spinning towards the floor, and decided to get her washed, brushed up and dressed in something

89

approaching decent. Something that wasn't cut low enough to show her belly-button. If she had anything like that in her limited wardrobe, of course. It might be superficial of me, but at least then there'd be no chance of anymore freak-show pics. It might help, a little bit at least.

I shrugged at Jo-Jo. 'Yeah, well, whatever. Look, I'm going to get Sam sorted out, get her tidied up a bit. Come on love, up we get, that's it, up, yeah, time to get a wash - yeah, but you'll feel better, you will, just - that's a girl, come on now, yeah. We want Jakey to come home to a nice, clean mum, don't we? Yeah, course we do. Look, Jo-Jo, please, leave it alone with the paedo stuff for a bit eh? Eh? Let's just hope the angels have got crossed wires or summat, eh? It's all gonna be alright, it is, we've just gotta keep steady, yeah?'

I saw the copper nod at me and I heaved Sam up off the floor, the sock, toy, ashtray, fag-end and crumb-strewn floor. She hung limply from my arm, boneless and unresisting, the low whine still jerking from her interspersed by gulps as her breath caught with sobs.

At least I could get her presentable. In case anything happened.

In case Jo-Jo was right.

Eleven

'No, this morning, early, some old bloke walking his dog - dog went mad, barking its head off, pulled him over to the bushes an' there - yeah, yeah - up by that old farm on the road out - yeah, Wuthering Heights, Jeez, shouldn't joke about it, it's well lonely up there - oh, Piff, it's fuckin' awful. That poor little sod. There's reporters all over the shop, the coppers are in a right state an' Sam - the doctor had to give her an injection, proper knocked her out. For the best, really, God knows what she'll be like when she comes round.'

'You had any sleep, sugar?'

'No. No, not really. Well, I kind of sparked out for ten minutes on Sam's sofa but no, not really. Tamsyn's covering for me so I can get a kip then go back for when Sam wakes up. The other kids are staying with their auntie. Oh, Piff, I could fuckin' kill Jo-Jo, I really could, the old cunt. Sorry, language, but there you go, that's what she is. All that rabbit about her bloody spirit voices telling her about paedophiles and now she's got the reporters in a fuckin' bidding war to get her story. Yeah, no, honestly, she has, sitting there like a lardy fat Queen fuckin' Bee on her mobile like there's no tomorrow. I note she's got credit quick enough now - pity she weren't so fuckin' keen to shell out a tenner when Sam rung her to look after the boy. She loves it, Piff, loves the attention. I'm not being awful, you should see her, it's disgustin'. Never mind that the child's - Jesus.'

Piff drew her breath in and even over the phone I knew she was doing that head shake and cheek sucking thing she did when she was despairing. 'Is it true he was - that - oh, poor, poor little thing. Poor little boy.'

I drew a long breath. I didn't want to think about what I'd heard, how Jakey had been found, it was horrific; the bloke who found him was in hospital with a suspected cardiac and grown coppers had puked like kids. 'Yeah. They reckon he was, well, he was - he was got at by animals, big animals, dogs probably - after - least I fuckin' hope to God it was after, I hope he was dead before - you know. Aw, Piff, I don't want to think Jo-Jo was right and it was some fucking paedo but it's lookin' that way, even the coppers are making noises about it being probable. Some bastard took Jakey, killed him, then just dumped him and the dogs . . . Jeez, you know, Gordon's always banging on about feral dogs, packs, no-one pays any attention, well they will now for fuck's sake. God in heaven, Piff, I can't imagine what the press'll make of it. Fuck what a mess. I can't . . . It's just fuckin' awful, mate, awful. No other word for it.'

I was only half listening as Piff told me to get some rest and she'd see me tomorrow, Lina had an opening tonight, she didn't want to go, but Lina was in bits, her nerves, she was so high-strung at the best of times, the other artists she was exhibiting with were all so difficult, so obstructive, Lina was totally stressed out. I said the right things, of course, but Lina's fits of artistic temperament didn't really cut it in view of the day's events. All I could see was Sam's little oval face fall apart like white ash in a fire when the news came in. I thanked whatever deities I could think of she'd fainted before she found out what state he'd been found in. Eventually though she would find out; it didn't bear thinking about.

It was a beautiful evening. The sky was a deep, tender blue scattered with diamond-chip stars, faint wisps of cloud veiling a crescent moon as fragile as a twist of silver wire. The lights of Town looked as pretty as a sentimental postcard, I could hear the hum of traffic and a girl's laughter floating up from the street below. The candle burning in front of Johnny's photo in its lovely silver frame set on the table by the sofa, was scented with amber and lavender. I looked at him and a pain like glass cut went through my heart. When I saw that angel card, that stupid - Johnny, my love, my darling, my wild thing, had it been you? So frightened, so desperate? What if I'd let you in, my beloved, would you have stayed? Would I have had you with me again? Would I ever have another chance to save you? The papers were full of stories about your crazy life - was there nothing you didn't try, didn't take, didn't fuck? That rib-rack bone-puppet Lainey Stone, her beautiful, vacant face like an empty vessel waiting to be filled with whatever the viewer chose to pour into it, had already sold her story about your roller-coaster life together to some celeb mag complete with your stoner love notes that canted round and round your apologies for not loving her as much as you loved someone else, someone lost. Was it me, Johnny? Was it? Or was I being vain beyond belief? Deluded? Ridiculous?

Oh, Johnny, I would have taken care of you, protected you, and guarded your spirit like I was meant to - if only I hadn't been born so many years too early. What did you used to say? I'd been impatient, I should have waited for you in Heaven, we could have come down to Earth together. Now you raged and screamed on the Other Side, and there was nothing I could do for you except remain faithful. As I always had done, despite who I'd given my body to. But never again, never again. Faithful unto death now; it was as pure and savage as nature, as irrational and archaic as a dream; the mystic union, soul marriage. Who'd understand it but you, another bloody Catholic? I picked up the picture and kissed it; cold glass returned my kiss. Cold, cold, cold.

I sighed. Nothing bad could happen on a night like this, it was too beautiful, too gentle. *L'heure bleu*, the French called this time, there was an old perfume by Guerlain called that - sweet, vanilla, musky. I'd had a bottle once. No, on a night like this, nothing bad could happen. Nothing wicked.

Just a child murdered by a living devil, then so ripped up, so torn apart and mutilated he was only recognisable by his remaining Nike trainer and a cheap gold and sparkle crucifix earring; all his little face gone, his soft rounded belly a bloody ruin, all his flesh . . . The dogs had left nothing untouched, nothing.

When I finished being sick, my body purging in shuddering spasms, the acidic vomit burning my throat, I crept into my unmade bed and shivered my way into a fitful sleep. I dreamed of a dark, steep-sided stony valley, moonlit to a mercuric silver, a river flowing through it strong and fierce. As I got close to it I saw it wasn't water at all, but a wild racing torrent of black wolves, pouring along the valley bottom, snarling and yelping. Now and again one of the beasts put its great shaggy head back and howled, and they'd all take it up, a brute carillon, their eyes glowing phosphorescent, their long teeth gleaming. Terrified they'd see me, I shrank behind a grove of wind-blasted trees. As I stepped back into the shadows I stumbled and looking down, saw the body of a child, and ripping at his soft throat was one of the wolves. Blood, dark and glittering in the moonlight, dappled its jaws as it swung its head round to look at me. In an agony of fear I tried to turn away, but the wolf gazed at me, still and tense as a drawn bow.

It had human eyes.

I woke screaming, sweat drenching me and the sheet sticking to my back clammy and sour.

Twelve

Bob looked at me accusingly, then pulling down his spectacles, pinched the bridge of his beaky nose, rubbing the sore places where the nose-pieces sank into his flesh. He closed his eyes as if to block out the very sight of me. I was tempted to stick my tongue out at him while he couldn't see me but restrained myself. Barely.

Bob was a man who had striven all his life to avoid real responsibility whilst craving the ego-rush being a boss gave him. He liked filling in forms, attending conferences, stuff like that, it comforted him, assuaged his conscience, made him feel he was doing good. Or as he said it, Doing Good. His wife crawled on her belly whining about her sterile life to a deaf Protestant God at some happy-clappy New Age Church - Bob gave his soul up to the incantatory triplicate hymn of bureaucracy and bound himself in supplication hand and foot with the unbreakable cords of red tape.

The Little Jakey Tragedy, or *The Little Angel Killing*, as the media now called it, was an unstoppable virus eating his own, personal hard-drive. And it was all my fault. Questions had been asked. My methods, procedures and work practices had been criticised. Remarks were passed about my appearance - all that black, was it Satanic? And the negative body language I'd never been aware of apparently suggested I was arrogant and conflictual. Aggressive, even. My head of department - Bob - had been called into meetings, and not in a good way.

He could not, he felt, in all honesty, support some of my decisions, decisions made without consulting him, to those Higher Up. He really couldn't. He'd said as much to the committee convened to look into the structural and communicatory interfaces being set in place to control this dreadful situation. He'd been forced to admit - against his will because as I knew, loyalty to his team was paramount to him - I was a rogue in his department, and that he had been poised to send me for re-training at the least, when Little Jakey had gone missing and then - um, died. Whilst he was under my care. My care. Mine. Not his. Not directly his, that is.

It was official. I was the scapegoat. Bob would throw me from the sleigh as a blood-sacrifice to distract the ravening media as he thrashed the team onwards into the coming dark. He opened his pink-tinged goosegog eyes, and gazed at me with carefully constructed sorrow.

'So you see, Annie, my hands are tied. You simply cannot, I repeat, cannot, be allowed to continue with this client. It would be completely inappropriate, cause even more distress to a client already in a dreadful situation. I've given Fatima the case notes and she will be the client's core contact from now on.'

'Sam's a racist, Bob.'

'What?'

'Sam's a racist. She thinks the BNP are lovely blokes who're all out for England, English ways and good old meat and two veg. Fatima is a devout Muslim who wears the hijab.'

Bob bridled. You don't see men do that often, but it's interesting when you do. He looked like a strand of cold spaghetti waving in a stiff breeze. 'I don't think remarks like that are exactly helpful, Annie. The client has to be helped to realise such attitudes don't. . .'

'*Sam*, Bob, she's called *Sam*. I daresay given time, she'd get used to Fatima, hijab an' all. Sam isn't exactly that bright, and the BNP promised to get her roof fixed just like they promised old Fred next door he'd get a new bathroom, all courtesy of the council if they got in. The usual lying bollocks. But none the less, Sam believes all Asians are dirty Pakis and terrorists to boot. Or she thinks she does. She doesn't include Harun at the shop who's a right fuckin' smasher, the spit of that bloke in *East Enders*, or Dr. Aziz at the kiddie clinic who's ever such a nice lady, proper posh, and very understanding, apparently. Sam's a fuck-up, Bob, like all of them - she isn't rational, educated or analytic. Come on, you know stuff like this, we all have to deal with it non-stop. If none of this had happened, and you were just sacking me off the case willy-nilly, after a couple of months, and if Fatima could stick her nonsense, Sam'd think Fatima was everso understanding and lovely too. Given time, if everything was normal, you could probably train her out of her racism to some extent, and trust me, I've been trying. But this isn't normal. Her child has been murdered. If she can she'll rip anyone near her into tiny little pieces just to let her grief and fury out for ten seconds, just to give herself some relief from the pressure of her guilt. And it's only going to get worse. She's incredibly self-destructive at the best of times, she's . . . Look, d'you want the press to get pictures of Fatima, crying her eyes up, with her scarf torn off and all her papers chucked out the door into the street? Because Sam will do that, if not worse. She's slap-happy; she thinks braying the shit out of someone is perfectly normal, a normal reaction to anyone who upsets her. Everyone she knows thinks the same. D'you want a pic of Fatima with a bloody nose in *The Guardian*? Sam won't understand that lashing out is - what? - inappropriate, or care how it'll look, that the papers'll present it as another brick in the wall, another reason to condemn her. OK, OK - send Andy, if you have to send anyone else. He's older, got experience and he's steady.'

I paused, tripped up by my own tirade. Bob looked outraged. I had that numb feeling you get from banging your head against a brick wall. My ears were ringing. I felt slightly sick. Concussion, probably.

'I really don't think it's your place to tell me . . .'

I took a deep, supposedly calming breath and looked up at the dismal poly-tiled ceiling. A stain shaped like a small but determined mountain range was creeping from the outside wall. The pin board covered in brightly-coloured and infinitely unattractive information leaflets had shed a pamphlet on Hepatitis like a deciduous tree losing the first leaf in autumn. It lay on the floor dejectedly, the idiotically simplistic cartoon figures meant to engage young people in the war against Hep gesturing with desperation etched in every line of their rubbery, non-specific figures. The whole place smelt of instant coffee, dust, dirty industrial carpeting and computers. And Bob, of course.

I could hear him talking, with one part of my brain. *It wasn't my decision, etcetera etcetera. He would do what he thought was best for the client under the circumstances.* I repressed a smile at that, it was Bob-code; he'd send Andy. At least poor Fats would get off the hook. Inshallah. I knew she'd have put a brave face on it and done her utmost, but it would have done no good and her courage would have gone for nowt.

I looked at my hands; knobbly, red-knuckled, long spatulate fingers. One thick, irregular silver band on the third finger of my left hand. An antique from Ethiopia. Johnny had one too, we'd bought them together as friendship rings from a shop in Islington. I looked at my ragged cuticles. My skin getting crêpey, a liver spot or two forming - tiny harbingers of decrepitude. Johnny used to say I had beautiful hands, and not a night went by I didn't cream them with some expensive unguent, not a month went by without a proper manicure from that mobile manicure girl that did all the offices and got done by Tony from Publicity.

Johnny would never see me get properly old, now. I'd never have to see him flinch imperceptibly at my kiss or hear him make excuses to get out of fucking me. I was safe from that, at least. I must get a copy of that album, with 'My Beautiful Blonde' on it. I wanted to re-read the lyrics. I had them by heart but reading them - somehow it would bring him closer again. He always tried so hard with his lyrics, fancied himself quite the poet; how adorable he looked as he scribbled on scraps of paper, brow furrowed, sexy fat lower lip pushed out in concentration. I used to get him fancy notebooks, but he always lost them, all except that big Moleskine one with the pocket in the back where the scraps got stored, he did his journal in that one, he . . .

'Annie, are you listening to me? I realise you must be tired, but I do think . . .'

Outside, I could hear the muffled thud of the latest Asian rap track approaching and receding in a crushing wave as some lad gunned his motor down the street, bass system on full. I could see dust motes floating lazily in cracks of light filtering through the knackered vertical blinds, I could feel Bob's drone bouncing off my skin, the frequencies sailing towards me through the viscous air then rebounding off into the room and dissipating in the stultifying, grinding normality of it. I was off Sam's case - literally. Maybe once upon a time I'd have fought him, tooth and nail. But I knew better these days. As Piff said so rightly, what was the use of trying to stop the juggernaut? What was the use of standing there, waving your arms, shouting your head off, yelling that you knew best, that you'd spent long hours building up a fucking relationship with Sam, that'd you'd (how unprofessional) grown to be fond of her and her tumbling brood, that you were really getting somewhere with her but look, OK, it was an inch at a time, that . . .

That you'd loved Jakey. Loved his funny little ears with their silly Beckham earrings, his dirty baby paws, his sticky-up golden hair, his round face that promised beauty to come. That you'd hoped you could do better for him than his mother ever dreamed of.

And now he was a lolling, bloody ruin on the pathologist's steel table, with no-one to kiss that hand goodbye, those cornflower eyes goodnight; no one to rock him to sleep singing silly old pop songs as lullabies . . .

You make my heart sing

That you had been unable to save him from terror and pain so appalling the mind flinched at the mere thought of it, as it crept round your consciousness like a poisonous, mottled snake.

That you had been unable to save - Johnny. You'd failed both of them and now they dwindled, side by side, into the dark forgetting of the dead.

So come on, and hold me tight

Who'd hold them tight? Who'd hold them as they screamed against the great dark? Who'd . . .

'Annie - *Annie* . . .'

'What? Oh yeah, sorry Bob, sorry. Yeah, very tired I'm afraid, not much sleep. You know. A bit stuffy in here, don't you think?' I briefly wondered if he knew how he smelt to others or whether he thought about it at all. Maybe he was proud of being an all-natural, as-God-intended, three-day-old-sweat-whiffy bloke; nah, look at him, it never crossed his scurrying, maze-rat mind.

I sighed. I didn't like myself for being mean about Bob. I had worked hard to try and feel sympathy for him, I really had. I knew, I'd always known, by his lights he meant well. But the Road To Hell was indeed paved with Good fucking Intentions. Like most men, he was single minded; put him on a straight path with a definite goal and he was happy. He didn't handle emotions very well and thought they were messy, obstructive and a bit scary. Well, he was right enough about that.

And apart from anything else he was my boss. He had the power.

Which is why, the following Friday, I found myself as duty worker, bouncing the jeep up the rutted track to the isolated farm we all called Wuthering Heights, on an emergency call out.

Thirteen

The paramedics grunted slightly as they heaved the stretcher into the maw of the ambulance. They must be extra tired, I thought, because the woman wrapped in blankets and strapped in the plastic cradle was tiny; bird bones and a wispy halo of faded hair fringing the translucent, yellowed skin of her forehead, wrinkles netting her eyes, and her mouth grey-lipped. She looked ancient, but she wasn't. According to Jim, the ambulance guy I knew slightly from another case, she was only late forties; she looked twice that. A terrible, gut-wrenching sweet-sour ammoniac odour crept out of the open front door of the house. On the washing line to the side, worn, discoloured sheets, pinned up anyhow, some trailing in the mud, flapped weakly in the faint breeze. I had a brief word with the coppers called out along with the ambulance; call from a neighbour, woman found collapsed, no known relatives, no-one else on the property, no farm beasts or pets, nothing. The copper got into his car folding his notebook away and talking into his radio. He gestured for his partner to drive off and they jounced off down the track.

'Hey Jim - what's up, d'you think?'

'Well, number of things I should think. Reckon she's been in that condition for years - the fistula. Bad home birth I should think, never saw a doctor. That and the diabetes, she's in a right state now, poor thing. Very weak. Wouldn't like to predict an outcome, like. I 'spect she was ashamed - you know how it is. Women's troubles. Mind, we don't see it much over here anymore but int Third World - they 'ave travellin' fistula clinics an' that but if they don't get mended,

102

their people just kick 'em out ter fend fer themselves like, ostracise 'em, say they're not women anymore, treat 'em like lepers. It's a stigma thing. I mean, some of 'em aren't even in their teens and their lives are over. We had a talk about it a few years back. Terrible.'

'A whatula?'

'A fistula. An obstetric fistula, to be proper about it. You know.'

'Jim, would I ask, mate, if I did?'

He scratched his bald patch thoughtfully. 'Yeah, sorry. OK, it's when you have a kid, right, an' during the birth, you get damaged, like. Maybe it was a long labour or some-thing, no docs there, and the wall between - well in this case, poor lass - between her vagina and her bladder got damaged, made a hole, like. Leaks urine through inter the vagina an' then, well . . . Or it can be the other way. Either way it's repairable, you know, but she never got seen to. Incontinent, loads of infections I should think, lot of pain, lot of distress. Smell. Nasty. Like I said, you don't see it like this much over here.'

'Fuckin' hell - yuk. Ouch.'

'Yeah. Ouch is about it. Must 'ave been bloody awful for her. Talking of which, the neighbour - if you could call her that, there's no one round here for at least a mile any direc-tion - says they were dead religious. Her an' the sister. She passed away about a year ago. Sarah here'd been on her own ever since. Obviously just couldn't manage anymore. Neighbour noticed all the groceries piled up at the bottom gate by the mailbox an' called the coppers. Easy with that, young Darren, that's a person, not a sack of flour. Can't get the staff these days, you really can't. 'Ere, terrible about that kiddie, eh? Stuff that goes on these days, wicked.'

'Yeah, yeah. Bloody awful, really.' I winced at the cliché, but how else could you say the unsayable?

Jim made as if to get in the ambulance. I followed after him, not wanting to delay him but needing to know more. 'Why was stuff left at the gate, d'you know? Why didn't they bring it to the door?'

He stopped at the tailgate. 'Neighbour says they were told not to, no-one was welcome, they wouldn't see anyone. Meter men only, an' them on sufferance. An' anyhow, delivery lads, postie, were all frightened of the dogs. Haven't seen any meself, but - look, she's over there, best ask her yourself - Darren, off we go lad, righto Sarah love, don't worry, try to relax now, we'll get you right soon enough.'

A long, serpentine braid twisted in shades of corn, silver and white flopped off the gurney like a living thing parasitically attached to the skull-thin head that rolled from side to side in distress as the bundle on the gurney twisted feebly. My plait was long, down to my waist nearly, but this braid must have reached down past the woman's knees; it was so long as to seem almost unnatural, in this day and age of obsessive grooming. She seemed to be saying something. Disjointed scraps of words, muffled, breathless, jerked from her bloodless mouth. I leant forward as Jim tidied the braid away and started to shut the doors.

'The boy, the boy - they don't - the boy - oh don't - oh, please I can't go - the boy . . .' Her voice was reedy and breathless with distress and her faded grey eyes were unfocussed and wandering. 'Gentle Jesus, meek an' mild . . . Becca, Becca, don't . . . I'm sorry, I'm . . .'

The doors shut and the ambulance set off down the track. I stared after it. What boy? And dogs? That put the willies up me, dogs. I dialled Gordon - better not take a chance in a run-down, isolated place like this; too full of broken-down old outbuildings, barns, and dark little nooks and crannies. Bang up close to the moor, too. Plenty of places to hide for a dog pack - a thought flashed across my mind: Could these be the dogs that had savaged poor Jakey's remains? It was nothing of a distance from here to where he was found if you went across the rough. My God - it could be. Scenarios from TV programmes about crack forensic departments in Las Vegas staffed by skeletal supermodels and beardy deaf blokes flashed through my mind. I could see it all, the lost toddler, the evil bastard who killed him, then the scavenging dogs. It all fit perfectly. I felt a surge of excitement, we'd get the monster who killed Jakey all right, it was a done deal. I walked across towards the neighbour woman, holding the phone to my ear.

'Gordon Bickersyke here, can I help you?' He sounded very far away and crackly.

'Gordon - it's me, Annie, Annie Wynter . . .'

'Oh, hiya, how are you? What can I do for yer?' The line burbled slightly and I wondered how good reception was, best make it quick. I gestured, smiling brightly, at the neighbour woman miming to her to hang on, I wouldn't be long. She shook her head whilst exhaling, as if in despair of how annoying people were. I was. Whatever.

'Look Gordon, I'm up Becksyke, at Fellstone Farm off the - yeah, Wuthering Heights - ha ha - they've taken the remaining tenant to B.R.I. yeah - well, there's rumour of a dog pack living in the - well in the barns I suppose, I don't know, anyhow, I thought, it might be same one that - you know, that did that thing to Jakey Jagger and . . .'

'Whatever you do, do not - are you listening now - do *not* approach any dog you see there, even if it looks harmless. I mean it love, don't. I'm on my way, should be there in about twenty minutes, and I'll get the vet over with the tranquilliser gun - I'd rather you didn't, like, go looking for dogs or owt? Don't be brave, it's not safe. I know what you're saying about the kiddie, it could fit and

105

I've had reports about feral dogs round by that farm before, it were on my To Do list ter check out. Just wait 'til I get there, yeah?'

'Oh, yeah, totally - no problem, big dogs scare me stiff, mate.'

'It's the little nippy 'uns chewing yer ankles you have ter worry about, in my experience - no, really, don't go rootin' around until I get there, OK?'

'Sure, see yer.'

I pressed the red phone icon with relief. Gordon was so reliable, he'd sort it out - if there actually were feral dogs round the farm and it wasn't just a yappy King Charles and two Chihuahuas grown into *Hounds of The Baskervilles* through a potent brew of speculation, gossip and laziness on behalf of the anaemic teen delivery boys from the local Co-Op.

'Sorry about that, Mrs - er . . .'

'Elcar, Betty Elcar.' She bridled, doing a far better job of it than Bob had. 'I'm the one as rang the ambulance, for that poor soul. Dreadful, how she lived, dreadful. We did try to help, like, but it were no use, her sister wouldn't 'ave none of it, sent us off with a flea in our ears.'

The sun was heavy in the sky laying a thick yellow light over everything, like golden syrup idly twirling off a spoon, glazing the dilapidated buildings and the boggy, weed-sprigged front yard. It looked almost idyllic in a run-down rustic way, and I could imagine some cheesy adman setting a homely bread advert here; apple-cheeked farm-wife kneading a wholesome loaf for her ruddy-faced, cheery family. You could do that in pictures, because on telly you wouldn't smell the stink still wafting from the house. That'd put the mockers on any romance straight away. My thought must have shown on my face.

'You can smell it, then? Awful, int it. I daresay that were why no-one were welcome. It were Sarah, summat wrong wi' her we reckoned - and we were right enough it seems, poor lass.'

I realised how still it was now the ambulance and cop car had gone. A dead quiet hung over everything, giving a dreamlike quality to the place. My mind scratched around a bit at a thought I couldn't place, then it clicked. No bird-song. No territorial blackbirds chittering, no wrens, no magpies, no nothing. Just silence.

'Ah - you knew she was sick then?'

'Oh aye. Summat anyway. Mental problems we thought. You know.' She circled her finger against her temple in the age-old sign for insanity. 'Any road up, we did 'ave a go at . . .'

'Excuse me, who's *we*?'

Mrs Elcar looked irritated, I was obviously annoying her with my pathetic inability to read her mind and be up to speed with thirty years of local gossip. 'The other Sisters an' meself, like. We . . .'

'I'm sorry? Sisters? Are you a nun?'

She looked outraged. 'I beg your pardon, Miss, we 'ave no truck with the Church Of Rome and its goings on, or them as seek to imitate it, indeed not. We're The Reformed Unity Brethren. Sarah an' Rebecca were too, An' their parents, old Brother an' Sister Bell. An Elder was Old Bell, for many year. We're a small congregation, to be sure, but our strength is the strength of the Righteous. Do you know Our Lord Jesus, Miss?'

I resisted saying anything smart, it never worked with religious fanatics and fanaticism was the light shuttering behind this woman's face. 'Ah - so, Sarah - and her late sister, did they, I mean, were they a regular - did they attend services, that is . . .'

Organised religion still made me uncomfortable, even idiotic little Protestant sects, of which there were still a good number in the area, each with their fierce tribal codes, their hierarchies, and their firm and unshakeable belief that they were the only Right ones in an increasingly Wrong universe.

Mrs. Elcar - Sister Elcar - pushed a wisp of fine, greasy mouse-coloured hair back behind her ear with a smug expression. Nothing was to escape the severely middle-parted do that terminated in a tight knob of a bun. 'They lapsed after their parents were Called ter Glory an' Received by Our Lord. Stopped Attending. The Elders went to remonstrate with 'em but it were no good. Rebecca said as how she knew best for her an' her twin. They was twins, see, not identical, but still. Twins. Rebecca allus was the stronger though. A big, hard-faced piece, like a man. We don't believe in women putting on a man's clothin' see, as it says in the Bible. Not natural' - here she glanced at my black bootcuts with a moué of distaste - 'but Rebecca, allus in men's attire, like, an' she cut her hair, which we Sisters never do. That's int Good Book too, should you wish ter look it up. We never cutteth off our hair. Sarah dint, but Rebecca - well.'

I flipped my plait casually. I hadn't cut my hair for years. Maybe that would help me into Heaven. Summat for God to grab hold of. 'Oh, so Rebecca looked after everything here then, until she, that is . . .'

The plait flipping obviously cut no ice with Sister Elcar, since her expression of disapproval only deepened. 'Aye, she did everythin' until she was Received inter the Gatherin' Of Saints nigh on a year since. If she dint go t'other place, that is. It were a heart attack, very sudden, no warnin'. Well, leastways none she told anyone about but that were her all ovver. Close, like. Sarah were on her own then but she still wouldn't see anyone, said Rebecca forbid it. I spoke to her a couple o' times through the letterbox but that were it. I come up for another go, thinkin' ter take her back ter the Brethren, an' I saw the groceries piled up, then Sarah, fallen int mud, after trying ter pin her washin' up. She was allus washin' an' all by hand since Rebecca would have no truck with machines. The Lord alone knows how long she'd lain there, cryin'. No one ter hear round here, like. So I went int house - terrible state it is - an' rang the police an' ambulance.'

'Oh, I see.' I began fumbling in my bag for a smoke. The thought of that poor woman lying in the yard on her own - it put cogs on me. Would that be my fate one day? An old woman, dying alone, no-one knowing or caring?

Sister Elcar looked up at me, her face a tight, red mask, weathered and archaic. 'Beggin' your pardon, Miss, you don't see. You think folk like me who're committed to Our Lord are a bit simple, like, don't yer? A bit wrong int head? Outter touch wi the real world. Well, before I found the Brethren an' Mr. Elcar, I were a prostitute on the Lane. Aye, that shocks yer don't it, you'd not thought o' that, that I might have had a life before. I'm not proud of it but it's the truth an' I won't deny it nor cease ter bear Witness ter my sins. I'm no whited sepulchre. I sold my body fer silver coins, me, drank strong liquor, were full o' demons. I were the worst o' sinners. But thanks to Our Lord an' Mr. Elcar, I were saved. You think I'm an' old woman, don't yer, just a silly old biddy. But I seen stuff that'd mek you bring up yer dinner, that I have. Now, Rebecca Bell were a domineerin', man-hatin' bitch, pardon my language, a right piece o' work. She wanted control of everythin', her twin included. She were a devil, right enough, cold an' cruel as winter. Sarah were a soft little thing, simple almost, it were like Rebecca got all the strength and left none fer her twin. There were rumours . . .'

I blinked. She had me there, right enough. Curiosity - my besetting sin, or at least, one of them - overcame my pride. 'What rumours?'

Sister Elcar looked away, thrusting her jaw out. 'I don't care ter speak ill o' the dead. But it were said Rebecca Bell were unnatural. Wi Sarah. It were true they allus shared same bed, allus, until about a dozen year ago or so when Sarah got ill. Then I 'spect the stink drove Rebecca out. I don't say it were true, but if it were, well, it's buried with her an' I don't see Sarah lastin'. Let's hope Gentle Jesus thinks fit ter take her to his lovin' bosom - more sinned against than sinnin' that 'un.'

There was a kind of inverted satisfaction in her voice as she said this. I wondered if Jesus ever despaired of the humans who worshipped him, ever thought about packing it in and leaving them to their own devices. Maybe that's what gods did in the end, just got sick of it and buggered off to some place else, away from humanity and its endless cruelty and whining. Perhaps the Christian god had done that centuries ago and his devotees just hung on, dialling and re-dialling, like discarded lovers trying to get through to their erstwhile squeeze whose phone was firmly and permanently off. Like I'd done, when Johnny left, when my little godling had left me. Still, what would I know, lapsed Catholic that I was. Beyond redemption, me. No pearly-white wings and matching halo set for me, no meeting up with my lost loved ones in the great Beyond. . .

Wild thing
you make my heart sing

No, not that - not that. Not now. I couldn't think about

him now. I couldn't succumb to that, to think I might see him again. I wouldn't. I wouldn't. I'd never see him again. I had to believe that, to know it or the rest of my life would be pointless because I might as well go to him now. I could live a life of faith and devotion, still do something useful in the world, but not if I was dawn into thoughts like that. It was too alluring, too sweet a prospect. I pulled myself back to the present, out of the vast temptation of the past. Sister Elcar was already gathering herself to go, good deed done, but there was one last thing I had to know.

'Um, it's possible Miss, er, Bell's illness was caused by childbirth difficulties. Did she have a child? She was talking about a boy before she was taken away. Do you think there could be anyone else on the property?'

At last Sister Elcar looked surprised. Bullseye, I thought. That pinged yer.

'A kiddie? Sarah? No, not that I know of - Sarah? No. I doubt she ever spoke two words to a man that weren't her dad or - oh, I see what yer gettin' at.'

That pinged *me*. I hadn't thought of father-daughter incest - my God, had they all been at it? A regular *Deliverance*-style paedo ring, just the kind of thing to light Jo-Jo's fire. 'Oh, I - yeah, well . . .'

The woman's body sagged a little. She sighed heavily. 'Owt's possible I s'pose. But I can't see it meself, not that y'know what goes on in folk's houses, not properly. But it weren't Old Bell got her pregnant, if she were. He were dead before she got ill, by a long while. Sarah took bad about the time Rebecca sold all the farm beasts an' the machinery, turned off the hands, not that it were more'n two at best o' times. Locked herself an' Sarah in from then on. We thought it were grief finally overcomin' em, like. Mebbe it weren't, mebbe it were summat else. Happen we'll

111

never know now. But there int anyone else here, tek my word on it.'

She turned to leave. 'Oh, I wouldn't stay here on yer own, Miss, there's dogs somewhere about, that I do know. Big uns. You can hear 'em howlin' of an evening. Rebecca allus kept at least a couple o' them big rough Alsatians herself, huge things, said it were in case o' burglars, but I reckon she just liked ter look the part, if yer get my drift. I shouldn't wonder they aren't runnin' wild somewhere, nasty beasts. The house keys are ont kitchen table, by the way, I looked. I'd lock up an' get off if I were you.'

She smiled; it lit her whole face up like a beacon. You could see then the pretty girl she might once have been, before cruelty and then God got hold of her. 'Yer not a bad un fer a heathen. Yer try ter do good, which is more'n most. God loves yer, even if yer don't know it. Yer troubles will be over in the Glory ter come.'

I smiled back. She wasn't bad for a Christian, despite the God bollocks.

Fourteen

I watched Sister Elcar trundle off and went back to the car. I leant back against the bonnet, putting my face up to the setting sun, trying to catch a few last rays, topping up the Vitamin D before the long pull of winter brought months wrapped in layer upon layer of ill-assorted fleeces, acrylic scarves in shades of mud and manky bobble hats. Unless you were a nineteen-year-old girl on a night out, of course, in which case you popped on some wispy sequinned lingerie, strapped yourself into a pair of vertiginous heels, wreathed yourself in J-Lo or Britney's latest pong, slipped on a shimmer of diamanté and pasted on enough make-up to act as a barrier against frost-bite, then trotted out come ice or snow with twenty quid and a teeny-tiny mini-mobile stuffed into your deep-plunge Wonderbra. Some poor sod groping your tit could end up dialling America. The other day I read a columnist in a posh Sunday Supplement saying that sort of dress code classified you immediately as a 'Northern slut'. Well, whatever - but I bet he wouldn't last ten seconds dressed like that in the kind of wind-chill we get round the Town Hall taxi rank come December, the wet twat. Pardon my language, as Sister Elcar would say.

I shivered. This place gave me the creeps good style. Clouds were passing overhead in that weird fast-forward unravelling tatter that was so characteristic of Bradford and gave us the curious light effects in town that had toddlers running after reflections which chased across the ground as if there was a sun-sized disco ball twirling in the sky. In the city centre it was pretty; here, it made the house and sagging outbuildings seem to shift and leer as the shadows swelled and shrank. I listened for dogs. Nothing. The dog pack thing was probably an urban myth anyway. Even Gordon admitted he'd never actually seen one in full cry, or whatever it was they did, he'd just got eyewitness accounts and like the coppers always said, nothing was so unreliable as an eyewitness. Anyway, Gor and the vet would be here soon for their dog hunt, and good luck to them. They wouldn't need to go in the house, so I'd best lock up, then wait in the car. Just to be on the safe side. You know.

Sighing heavily for no good reason other than the bone-deep fatigue that, increasingly, dragged at my heels and made me feel like someone had opened a spigot in my heel and drained all my strength away - like Talos the iron giant in that old *Jason And The Argonauts* film - I went into the house. Taking a breath of fresh air, first, mind you.

What can I say? It was grim as fuck. Just what you'd expect. Rubbish piled up everywhere in tottering heaps, pathetic bits of spoiled food littered the kitchen. A brown film lay over everything like a layer of indelible shit. The walls were done in ancient beige-painted anaglypta with a dreary swirl pattern or peeling dun cabbage-rose wallpaper, unshaded bulbs dangled from muck-encrusted wires, the ceilings were tan with dirt and the floors uncarpeted, just bare boards. It must have been as cold as a penguin's bum in winter. The whole place looked like it was stuck in a time-warp. Nothing had been touched since 1950 and modern conveniences, like, oh, Fairy Liquid, 100-watt light bulbs, Dettox, white paint or soft toilet paper, hadn't been invented. And shouldn't have been, in the opinion of the occupants of the house.

As I stood in the awful filthy hallway, trapped in the vile stink of ancient piss, infection and despair, a spasm of intense anger flashed through me, catching me unawares. It neatly ripped through the mental bubble wrap of knee-

114

jerk clever cow witty remarks and carefully cultivated cynicism that I'd wrapped myself in from the start of my career in social work – no, be honest, that I'd used as a defence from year dot. Forever. Funny Annie, daring Annie, Annie honest you are a one, the things you say, you should be on the telly you make me laugh that much.

Annie, you're so quick, my Funny Lady, my love

Wild Thing I think I love you

Johnny – oh, oh, my beautiful Johnny, I . . .

I shouldn't be here doing fucking scut-work so a spineless shit like Bob could save his lazy arse and shift the fucking, *fucking* blame onto me, ruining my chances of doing anything except get the bloody sack most like, having to find another job at my age, like, doing what? What could a forty-something ex-rock 'n' roller, ex-social worker with a bad rep actually *do*? Work in B&Q stacking shelves? Or in the garden department? What the fuck did I know about lawn care? Oh, I know. I should have been married, shouldn't I? Grown-up kids at university, growing old with a grumpy husband with rampant nasal hair whose eye wanders guiltily over the perky nubile charms of our daughter's summer holiday bikini-clad buddies. I should be ensconced in a comfy circle of matronly friends who go to readers' groups, do yoga, try to keep cheerful and pretend they don't mind being side-lined, sex-and-love-starved and ignored by a society that regards older women as so much tedious, hormonally-challenged rubbish, fit only to be dosed with Prozac and jeered at by fly young male comedians on the goggle-box. Well, fuck that for a game of soldiers, mate. No way on earth. Not after *my* life, after *my* love; if I was going to live, then by God, it wouldn't be that kind of trickling down to nothing sad and sorry half-life.

My mind ran ahead, leaping obstacles, worrying at solutions. Never give up, never surrender. Yeah - if I sold up again I could go abroad, maybe work at a recording studio somewhere, one of the big European residential places in Spain or France running the bookings - they always needed people like me, people with real industry experience not a faked-up wannabe CV, people who wanted to stay put, not marry the rock stars and bugger off leaving them in the lurch. Yeah, I could . . .

I wanted to ring Piff, have a good moan, maybe arrange to go out somewhere, the pictures or something. Her acerbic attitude would be a tonic, snap me back to steadiness. But she wouldn't be back off holiday for another couple of days and I wasn't going to ring her and chunter on about how crap I was when this was the first proper break she'd had in two years; she and Lina were in Goa, so Lina could be artistic and soak up the exotic atmosphere, paint some lovely pictures. She'd screwed a grant for just that - I wondered if the arts people realised it would all go on parties and drugs. Or indeed, if they'd care. They must have been soft in the head giving her the money in the first place - but still, it got Piff a holiday. Pity it wasn't anywhere she would have chosen. Piff hated beaches and all that, I wondered how she was getting on. I wondered . . .

Fuck it, oh fuck it - never mind anything else, I should be with Sam. I should be looking after her. She'd be freaking out now, proper hysterical. Poor, poor little bitch, poor little fucked up scrapper. How could they be so stupid, how could they take me off that case after I'd worked so long and so fucking hard getting her to understand the basics of living, never mind caring for - oh, Jakey, Jakey; how unspeakably bloody awful, how brutally savage you had to be crushed out of existence by some evil fuck. What God could bring a beautiful, healthy child like Jake into the world then wipe him out of it with the casual fly-swatting cruelty of an insane despot? If Sam couldn't have him, why couldn't I? For that matter, why couldn't I have kept my own, precious lost baby? Or had my Johnny's child? Why couldn't I have had his child to love after he'd gone? It was so fucking unfair, so completely bastard unfair.

Furiously I looked into every sordid, smelly, mean room, checking the semi-rotten sash windows were closed - and most of them were nailed shut with handfuls of six-inch nails as if someone was ensuring there was no hope of escape - and turned off the gas and water. Then I locked the front door and stood shaking with fury in the yard wishing I could strip off then and there and wash myself with neat Dettol. How could anyone live like that? Or if Sister Elcar was right, force their own flesh and blood to live in pain, fear and terrible distress for some twisted reason that died with them when their congested heart burst with the strain. I cleaned my hands as best I could with the remains of a bottle of Evian and made a mental note to stock up on antibacterial hand-wipes for the future. I couldn't seem to get the foul creeping stench of the house off my flesh - it gave me the heebie-jeebies. Then I fumbled a fag out and lit up, inhaling deeply and shaking the tremors out of my legs like dancers do after a long practice.

I checked my phone, not that I wouldn't have heard its polyphonic android twitter if it had gone off, but it was a reflex we all had these days: check the phone, someone might be getting in touch, we must all stay in touch. I sighed and took a long drag. *Come on Gor.* I needed to get off, I couldn't bear it here. Still full of adrenalin and residual irritation, I stared off moodily towards the furthest out-building which was parallel to the back end of the house. It was a good-sized, crumbling, sag-roofed structure that might once have been stables. The cavernous double barn doors had rotted off their hinges and were propped in a friable heap against the sidewall. The clouds flooded across the sun again, light shoaling like frightened fish across the gaping jaws of the ruined building.

I took another deep drag, squinting against the smoke. The chasing rays lit up something lying on the floor of the stable, just inside, close to the edge of the splintered doorframe. It caught my attention, with the lure of the half-seen. Something small and white. Out of place in the dinginess of the farmyard. Small and white - solid, not a scrap of paper or cloth. It jagged at my mind, a fishhook thought, a half-memory.

Without thinking, I walked towards the stable. Throwing the half-smoked cigarette into the mud I tried to focus on the white thing, but the sun went in again and I could only see a faint luminosity. Really must get my eyes tested. What was it? It looked like - was it - where had I seen something like . . .

I stepped over the ruined threshold and stooped to look at the white object. It was a child's trainer. A white Nike with a gold swoop. A baby Nike. A white - my God, my God, it was Jakey's trainer, Jakey's missing trainer. There was blood on it, dark and clotted, it was Jakey's . . . I felt a thrill of excitement; just like on the telly, I'd helped to solve a murder case, found an important piece of forensic evidence. When Sarah had said *the boy*, she'd obviously meant Jakey, her sister's dogs and - I'd been right, I had to ring the coppers, get them back here, get . . .

Out of the thick darkness to the side of me, deep in the shadows of the broken-down stalls, came a low, throbbing growl; it multiplied, a terrible harmonic of warning and threat. It was as if the dark itself simmered, glutinous with the most primitive of all terrors, the ancestral memory of predator attack. Instinctively I turned towards the noise

118

while, at the same time, my mind screamed at me in a berserk gabble to back out of the building slowly then run to the car, lock myself in, and drive off. To get away, to run. Because of all the many stupid, thoughtless things I'd done in my life this was the most devastatingly dangerous. My body started to obey the instinct to bolt, but half-blinded by coming into darkness from sunlight, as I turned I caught my foot on a tangle of rope and old harness and stumbled, banging into the doorframe, turning back unwillingly to face that terrible sound. The growling increased, deep and savage, thrumming against ribcages, catching breaths and champing against ivory teeth.

How slow it was. No time to run anymore as the shadows resolved into more than a dozen hell-hounds, ragged, dusty, gas-yellow eyes flaring, wet red tongues lolling as they stepped forward with a grisly precision, placing blunt-clawed paws almost daintily, hackles raised in ragged ruffs, great broad heads lowered. All breeds and none, they were a feral melting-pot of the discarded and dumped, a wild pack, the living avatars of our criminal lack of responsibility and blind belief that we humans were the lords of creation, able to make monsters for our pleasure then throw them away when we were bored, or wanted a new toy.

It felt like someone had pulled all the tendons out of my body. A hot weakness drenched through me, my heart pounding like a jackhammer, my muscles slack with horror. I could feel my bowels and bladder loosening and my mind start to yammer and shriek with panic.

The dogs inched forward. Frantically I tried to remember anything I'd ever read or heard about dog attacks, but all I could recall was the awful devastation those grinding jaws could wreak on flesh and bone: noses bitten off, faces eaten, lumps torn out of calf and thigh, a photo of a man's forearm turned into a shredded, bloody tangle by a pit-bull.

119

I was panting, my systems shutting down as I fought for breath and tried to struggle back out into the yard and find my phone to call for help. The lead dog, a massive, brindled old German Shepherd crossbreed as tall as my waist, its thick fur a raggled mess of burrs and knotty tangles, white scars bisecting its greying muzzle, its ears notched and torn, detached itself from the pack and stopped within six inches of me as I frantically pressed back against the stable wall, trying to edge across and out of the doorway.

This was it. No escape. If I moved wrong the brute would tear out my throat with the fluid ease of a butcher slicing steak. Don't look it in the eyes - don't do anything sudden - don't . . . Scraps of information fluttered through my head raggedly. Somewhere I'd read if you sang quietly and calmly the rhythmic sounds distracted the dog from his attack mode, but all I could think of was that foolish old song. I started mumbling reflexively, the silly words becoming a desperate prayer to the God I'd so rubbished earlier.

Wild Thing you make my heart sing oh blessed Virgin Mary help me you make everything dear God save me oh please Wild Thing I think I oh Jesus Jesus not this not this oh

Then out of the massy dark, from the seething heat of the lair, rose a creature so unnatural it ripped at the very heart of the world, tearing apart the order of things, making a shuddering nonsense of everything I'd ever taken for granted or believed, a thing beyond my experience or understanding.

My lungs laboured to catch a breath and an acidic wave of adrenalin shivered through me. Half-fainting I slid down the wall.

It moved towards me, sniffing the air.

Wild Thing.

Fifteen

The big Alsatian fell back, growling, with the rest of the pack as the creature moved through them with a stooped, loping gait towards me. It stopped, poised, just short of my feet as I huddled against the wall, just in the cold shadow of the door, fractionally outside the red-gold gleam of the setting sun that poured its beauty into the ruined stables. My hand fumbled automatically in the pocket of my zip top for my phone but the flimsy jersey fabric twisted and caught at the aerial stub. I could hear myself still singing in a droning mumble but my mind was outside of all that, outside of everything, looking down from far away at the monster sniffing at my boots.

The dogs yipped and growled as the creature crouched down by my feet and the big dog started forward causing my stomach to flip with terror. Again I had the weird sensation of watching from the outside as the creature turned its shaggy head and snarled in a reverberating brute threat that the dog, its eyes fixed on me, ignored. In an instant, without any hesitation, the creature launched itself with incredible, springing speed at the dog and seizing it by the neck threw it to the barn floor where they fought in a savage wrestling match, dirt and fur flying up into the light from the door as the whole pack barked and howled; some of the other dogs inching forwards and back as the fight rolled into the stalls where I could see mangy, half-grown pups and females with pendulous, milk-heavy teats back away snapping and yipping.

It was my chance. Before the horror of what was happening could start to paralyse me again, I tore the phone from my pocket and flipping it pressed re-dial, knowing the last number I'd dialled was Gordon's. The little machine trundled through its procedures as I began crawling towards the door, trying to get up, not looking at the melée that screamed and tore behind me. I heard ringing, then Gordon's voice, small and far away as I scrambled up, tearing my jeans, ripping my free hand on the jagged broken wood of the door frame.

'Hi Annie, yeah, I know, but I'm on my way, love - had to get some stuff for the vet, bit of a detour but . . .'

'Help me help me Gor the dogs in the stable I went in the stable oh the dogs I can't get out there's so many of them they're they're massive it's Jesus Gor help, help they've got me there's a thing in here a monster Gor help help me . . .'

The phone spun out of my hand, tumbling out into the yard where it lay, far out of my reach. A red rip of fear swirled through me as jaws closed on my ankle, crushing through the thick leather of my cowboy boot, dragging me back down.

I fell back, sitting on the floor, against the wall again. A kind of horrid calm filled me, white and shiveringly cold, and my will to fight evaporated like icy, iridescent vapour rising from black water. With a curious detachment born of shock, I gazed at the dogs and the lowering Alsatian, crouched on the floor in a tail-down, ears-back posture of submission, half its ear ripped apart and a bite oozing across its muzzle. It looked cowed, but not beaten, and its amber eyes were fixed with obsessive, enraged intensity on the thing that held my ankle, not with powerful jaws, but with an incredibly strong, filthy, human hand.

I stared at the thing, unable to process what I was seeing. The information filtered through my terror in disjointed particles, sliding slow as treacle into some semblance of order. It wasn't a beast, it was a human. A human. I could barely see a face, so dreadlocked, matted and crawling with fleas and lice was the shock of black hair that hung down in ratty tangles nearly to the floor as the creature squatted on its haunches gripping me with a hand whose curved, broken nails were as thick and heavy as claws. As it shifted slightly, a musky, feral smell rose off it. The choking stink spoke of this thing never having washed in its life, however old it was, and threading through it was a hot funk of aggression and maleness that I instinctively knew, but could not have properly described if I'd smelt it anywhere else, at any other time. It was the reek of testosterone and dominance that had allowed the creature to beat the great Alsatian into crawling submission and kept the rest of the grumbling pack off me. It - he - let me go, sniffed my boot, and with a strange, hopping motion kept smelling me, up the length of my body, his nostrils dilated and damp, until his head was close to mine.

He was naked, and hair felted his arms, chest and belly, growing down his back, coarse and ragged - not from his head, not long hair, but down along his neck, from the dark, dirty flesh itself, like a lion's mane. His spine, knobbly and curved, seemed weirdly elongated and his shoulders and arms were over-developed and packed with densely hard, lean muscle as far away from a gym-trained body as you could get, giving him a hunched, simian look. His forearms were rippled with an interweaving muscularity and wholly out of proportion to his upper body. He crouched, his breathing rapid and shallow, as I hummed, tears and snot tracking my face, and tried with all my remaining will power not to faint. I had no doubt whatsoever, none, that this creature could literally tear me apart into bloody collops if he wanted to. His legs were bowed and powerful, the knee joints swollen, scarred and knotty, like his callused elbows and thickened wrists. His genitals were contracted, testes pulled back into his body like a warrior's. He was like a hideous bio-machine; a destroyer of worlds, impervious, unconnected to his human origins, or a beast-man from some far distant primeval era.

I knew, viscerally, in the strange frozen no-time stasis that kept me sitting there, kept the dogs back, kept this monstrous thing crouched by my side, that this was the boy Sarah had spoken of. Not Jakey, but this warped and ruined thing. I'd been wrong, dazzled by arrogance, so pleased with myself for solving the mystery, helping Sam, the coppers - proving I was better than Bob, than everyone. If curiosity was one of my sins then, pride, deadliest of all, was my nemesis. Pride had led me to this horror and now my life hung in the hands of a creature out of time and reason. I felt more hot tears leak from the outer corners of my eyes, but for what? My own stupidity? The thing was sniffing again, this time at my wrists and the soft crook of my elbows. I'd worn that heavy, amber perfume that morning, the one supposedly laced with human pheromones. Could this thing, with his razor-keen sense of smell, catch it? What would such an alien odour mean to him, who'd only ever known the animal smells of the dogs and the earth scents of the wild heathlands? Would such a strong man-made perfume annoy him, distress him? Would he be puzzled? Spooked? Would he attack? I only knew I'd best keep still, keep very still and breathe slowly, do nothing to startle him or make him angry.

Suddenly the Alsatian gave a low growl and the thing swung his head round and snarled back, a terrible sound coming from a human throat, and a wave of revulsion swept through me. It was completely reflexive; the thing was neither truly human, nor animal, he was an abomination, and suddenly everything in me revolted against him. The atavistic, cellular desire to kill him, destroy the unnatural hybrid, obliterate him from the world, rose in me as the desire to dominate had driven the creature. It made me catch my breath, and the slight sound brought that strange, terrible face back round to me.

He was never fully still, never passive and accepting as you and I - civilised and tamed - are. Shivers ran through him in little shocks, his skin twitching like a fly-bitten horse. Dark eyes flickered incessantly, scanning all the time, assessing, and the light caught them, showing an eerie underglow, phosphorescent disks flaring briefly like a cat caught in headlights. His jaw was thick and bunched with muscle and he seemed to have had his short, snub nose broken at some time because he breathed harshly through a mouth that showed long, yellow incisors and front teeth chipped in the middle forming a triangular notch. His breath was foully rank and old blood crusted the corners of his cracked lips. A horrible thought passed through my stuttering brain. Jakey's blood. My God, it could be Jakey's blood. Oh, no, no, it was too awful to think of. I felt my mind starting to shut down with the burden of it and again, I fought to stay conscious.

I must have shifted slightly because quicker than I would have thought a person could move, he pushed his face into mine. I shuddered, and recoiled without thinking. Again, that tilting of the head and his breathing, shallow and quick. Then he made a sound. It was a mewling, almost plaintive noise. The effort seemed to cause him distress, as his throat worked convulsively and his ribcage heaved like bellows, dragging and sucking air as the sound choked out, clotted, like vomit. Saliva roped in thick cuds from his mouth as he tried to make the sound again. The creature, his terrible, strange head on one side, pushed at me with the swollen, reddened knuckles of one hand and made the noise again. This time I recognised it. The oldest sound in

125

the world; the sound that birthed all other sounds, the most universal, most holy and savage sound humanity ever makes.

'Ma . .'

He crouched beside my thigh and laid his filthy head in my lap, the vermin running so thick on the bits of scalp I could see, that his knotty hair moved. The stink of him was appalling; it made my gorge rise.

'M – ma . . .'

A tuneless, monotonous hum vibrated in his chest. He nudged into my belly.

Hysteria rose in my throat, choking me. I knew who this thing - this boy - was. It was Sarah's son. The child that had ruined her physically and brought her twin's wrath down on her. What had Rebecca done, in her rage and cruel tyranny? Thrown the infant into the barn to kennel with the dogs? You heard about such things, wild beasts suckling abandoned human infants, caring for them along-side their own young - wolf girls in India, dog children from the disintegrating anarchy of the former Soviet states, gazelle boys from Africa, all raised by animals, growing up no longer human, weirdly changed by their wild lives, outcast forever, never becoming like us. Discarded by humanity, they knew love only from their brute families, proving yet again that animals are kinder to us than we ever are to them. Which of those dog-mothers, watching us so intently, their real children huddled behind them, had suck-led this unwanted baby?

This boy was a feral child, like so many others I'd read about over the years in sensational books and newspaper accounts, or had seen on television documentaries no better than freakshows. But a true feral child, here, in Bradford? Not six miles from the city centre? But then, Bradford wasn't like most cities: six miles and you were out on windswept, deserted moorlands sweeping in folding fells through hidden valleys and erupting in weather-carved crags. This area itself was a by-word for isolation and semi-rural poverty; neither country nor town. The farm itself so set back and hidden by the lee of the hills you couldn't see it from the road proper, and there was nothing human built between it and a long run over the tops as far as Manchester; moor joining moor, some beautiful, some cursed with an evil history like Saddleworth. You could hide an army here, never mind one boy.

But how did he escape the notice of the authorities? I remembered all the cases of neglect and cruelty I'd dealt with; children, with no names and no paperwork, running with cig-burn sores and impetigo, tied in piss-sodden cots for days on end. Kids aged five left alone with a box of pot-noodles and a kettle while mother went on holiday to Ibiza; beaten half to death and stuffed under the sink in lieu of a baby-sitter for weeks on end like one youth I'd had to deal with, who'd grown crippled and simple because of it. They called him 'Monkey', poor bastard, where was he now? No-one had given a flying fuck about him - this boy had at least survived, but at what price? Of course this feral child was possible, the farm being as it was, the neighbours and everyone else warned off and Rebecca's guard-dogs a very real threat. If it could happen in the middle of a bustling city like Moscow, which it had, there was no problem in it happening here. I felt disgust start to turn to the ache of pity. Poor kid, Jeez - poor tortured, abandoned child.

He turned his face up towards me again, those flickering eyes slightly stilled, quieter, and I saw the fine modelling of what would have been a beautiful face before it was distorted by his short, savage life. He had high, round cheek-bones, a square, strongly modelled cleft chin, and a thick sweep of curved eyelashes fringing deep-set, almond-shaped eyes - dark blue, not brown as I'd thought. Dark blue, like lapis lazuli, and like that precious stone, a few gold flecks coruscated in the iris. His eyebrows were a perfect calligraphic arc. Fine curls spiralled on his hairline, escaping from the matted verminous knots of his hair. Under the ingrained dirt of years, his torn and scarred skin was ivory, tea-rose and gold. He was mixed-race, I thought - my God, that would have been the final straw for a woman like Rebecca. Who was his father? Who . . .

He butted me again, insistent, humming. He seemed tranced-out, almost drugged, like cats when they knead and paw at you convulsively. I started to hum too, it was obviously what he wanted; what memories had I stirred in him? Did Sarah sneak out of the house at night and try to care for him? Did she rock him on her lap, pressed against her pain and fear, terrified of the dogs who crouched in the shadows? Did she sing foolish lullabies and give him her breast until Rebecca found out, trapped her inside that awful house, locked the heavy doors and nailed those windows shut, leaving the child she loathed to the moors, the animals and the grace of God?

Time ceased to matter. I felt myself detaching from the world because, surely, I was going to be killed when this insane little amnesty was over. The thought seemed distant, as if I were thinking of someone else's fate. A story in the newspaper, a piece on *News At Ten*. I pushed thought of the inevitable end of my stupid, stupid behaviour away. There was only this; another woman's lost son holding me, the silly phrases of my dead love's song bobbing raggedly in my head. Soon there would be terror, pain and blood. Now there was only this curious peace.

Wild thing
you make my heart . . .

128

I hummed the simple melody and the creature crept closer, turning so he was curled round me, and I put my arms around him because foul with dirt and strangeness as he was, there was nothing else I could do. Under the ruin and neglect he was a child destroyed by terrible cruelty, the fury of one insane woman and the helpless weakness of another. What he was, we had made him; he was innocent, whatever he'd done, because you couldn't blame a beast for its nature. He was hungry. His family was hungry. They hunted, found food and ate. Deadly simple. Poor, poor little Jakey or a stray lamb. It made no odds to the beasts.

sing, you make everything

I was fairly certain what it was this creature, rocking and juddering, crooning mindless sounds, had done. I was also certain the world would scream in absolute horror and if it could, if it were able, it would cut his throat or put a bullet in his head or string him up, secure in its righteous fury and revulsion. To preserve civilisation. To avenge a child they would have previously considered the corrupted offspring of a deranged whore. Now Jakey would be a martyr and this creature truly what I'd told Gor, a monster.

So far away. I was so far away. I could see a face, sweet and familiar beyond bearing in my mind, a smile, dark eyes, a fall of thick bronze hair. . . Johnny, Johnny, oh my love, my angel, my . . .

Wild thing

Then I heard a voice, and the screaming and shooting began.

129

Book Three

Gabriel and the Gabble Ratchet

'Yet ah! Why should they know their fate,
Since sorrow never comes too late,
And happiness too swiftly flies?
Thought would destroy their Paradise.
No more, where ignorance is bliss,
'Tis folly to be wise.'

Thomas Gray

Sixteen

'Annie love, can you hear me?' Gordon's voice, barely audible over the rasp of the creature's formless humming, was little more than a breath but hearing it sent a shock of adrenalin through me that jerked me back to the reality I'd drifted so far from. He must have been directly behind me, right next to the stables doorframe. The creature felt the change in me and heard Gordon's voice all at the same time and stiffened, a low growl reverberating in his chest as he raised his head from my belly. I felt a wet, clammy roil of fear slither through my guts. It was now, whatever was going to happen, it was now.

The dogs caught the strange scent, heard Gordon's voice, and ears pricked, amber and yellow eyes flared. The big old grey-muzzle started to get up, teeth bared in a guttering snarl and the females snuffled their pups anxiously.

'*Wild Thing, you make my* - yeah, yeah, I can hear you Gor they know they know you're oh God Jesus Gor - *you make everything . . .*'

'Annie, just do as I say straight off - on my count of three throw yourself out the door, OK - one, two, *three . . .*'

With my last remaining strength and in the certain knowledge this was my only chance, I hurled myself side-wards. As I scrabbled messily for the open door, I banged the side of my face on the splintered door frame and felt rather than saw Gordon grab me hard by the arm and yank me bodily out into the failing light, into the yard, then drag me full tilt towards the house.

The creature was an inch behind us, running in his un-natural, crouching way, howling like a banshee, a sustained scream that rippled with frequencies way out of human use. Within the formless inchoate rip of it I could hear the dreadful refrain - *Maaaa - Maaaaaaa*

I could hear Gordon swearing as we flung gasping into his van, slamming the doors shut and reflexively locking them. It was then I noticed the police vehicles, the vet's van - and the marksmen. At the same time, I saw three big policemen who must have been beside Gordon at the stable, wrestling the creature to the floor, throwing a blanket across him, pinning him down with their weight. They had a hard job of it, and at first, I thought the guy who ran across from the vet was intending to help them, but instead, he held out his mobile, then ran back. At the time, I didn't process that, because I was too busy shaking and watching the marksmen shoot the dogs, one after another, as grey-muzzle - his ruff of thick fur raised, his head lowered - stepped into the barn doorway to defend the pack's lair, his younger lieutenants flanking him.

It didn't take long. They all went down in jerking, bloody slow-motion, as it seemed to me, though in reality it was all very quick, a matter of seconds, really. Then the bitches tried to bolt but were shot one after the other along with the half-grown cubs loping beside them, all the bravado scared out of them. Last of all was the old female, her heavy belly low to the ground, as she tried to run to the creature. The first shot, the only mis-shot, caught her in the hindquarters, and she crawled on, dragging her shattered leg. I couldn't watch, but I heard the howling, the creature's howling, as the second shot took her in the head, not six foot from where her foster-son lay on the ground on his belly, his hands bound behind him with cable-ties, two coppers holding him down with the blanket while the other, white-faced with pain, held out a bloody wrist, bitten to the bone.

After the marksmen checked the barn, the vet and her assistant brought the tiny cubs out in wire carriers. I could see them cowering, panting in fear and I could see the vet and everyone else staring at the creature as he writhed and screamed on the dirt, trying to twist round and bite his wrists free, trying to bite anyone who came within reach of him.

The faces of the marksmen were professionally cold as they put their rifles away in long bags, flexed their hands, rolled their necks and shifted in their clothes like athletes stretching after a long run. Whatever they might feel, they had been trained to hide it. The others, the vet, her assistant, the coppers - including the bitten one, despite the pain he must have been in - looked at the creature with a queasy mixture of fear, revulsion and disgust, as if he were the devil himself. You could see it in them, in the clenched fists of their faces, the reflexive loathing of the not-human, the not-animal, the unnatural hybrid, the beast-man, the were-wolf. Just as I had when I'd first seen him, before I'd fully realised how he'd come to be like that, the way he'd suffered. If I could make them understand that, make them see the child beneath the snarling mask, they'd feel like I did about him, that he deserved our pity not our hatred. But now, without that knowledge, every primitive reaction struggled with their understanding of how the world was, how things were done, how we behave. If they could have, they'd have shot him too and called it an accident. I don't know, even knowing all I did, maybe they should have. At least it would all have been over quick.

I was so cold. I could smell the sour stink of fear on me and the roiling in my guts told me I'd best get to a toilet as soon as I could. I was shaking but I had the mad desire to laugh. It was all so insane. It had only taken moments, everything jumbled up together, but I felt as if years had passed, ages come and gone, mountains worn down to nubs of stone and the sky bleached to the dead silver of a dying universe. I was freezing, and was just about to say so but I found my mouth wouldn't work, my voice wouldn't come. Gordon, his own face ashen under the permanent sun-stain of the outdoors man, put his big old fleece jacket round me. It smelt of washing powder and, faintly, of dogs.

'Are you - you OK, love? There's an ambulance due, you'll be in shock, did it - did it hurt you? Are you bit? Christ, it's - Jesus, look at it, what - I've never seen - I'd never have thought - it must have been livin' with the pack for years, fucking hell - sorry for swearin' but . . .' He shook his head, wisps of hair pulled out of his pony-tail stuck to his cheeks with cold sweat. Without thinking, he pulled the elastic band out and raked his hand though his hair and re-did it. I watched him. It was like watching an alien do something you've never seen before, though it was Gordon's habitual gesture I'd seen dozens of times. Only now, everything seemed different, distanced, unknown.

Outside the dusty van window, I watched the coppers manhandle the writhing, snapping creature into the back of a van. They slammed the doors - just as they did, the ambulance drew up, the vet drove off and one of the marksmen spoke briefly to one of the coppers, both of them nodding and sucking their teeth. *Bad business, this. Aye, not good, not good at all.* I could almost hear them. The copper jerked a thumb at the van and the shooter nodded again and turning, got into his vehicle with the others and drove off. The bitten officer went to the ambulance.

It was over.

'I think you should see a medic, love. Come on, can you manage?' Gordon put his arm round me and with enormous, unspeakable gratitude not only for him saving me, but for his humanity, I leant into him. He hugged me

136

briefly, then getting all practical and blokey, pulled the fleece round me tighter and patted my back.

'Ey, now then, come on, you did brilliant, you did great. It's all done now, lass, all over. Come on, let's get you seen to.' He was steady now, the adrenalin gone out of him, the still, calm Gordon returned.

The world shivered and jumped back into place, like a film re-winding. It was real, it had all happened. I opened the van door and vomited into the dirt, over and over again.

Seventeen

'Miss Bell? Sarah? Can you hear me? Just nod if - OK. Sarah, my name is Annie, I'm a social worker. I - I found the boy, Sarah, I found . . .'

On the bed, cocooned in glassy sheets and white cellular blankets, trapped by a web of drips and machines, the grey light filtering through dirty hospital windows leaching the last colour from her papery face, Sarah Bell moaned without opening her eyes and rolled her head on the slippery pillow. The motion caused her plait to fall as it had when she was taken into the ambulance; no-one had unbraided it, it seemed. I picked its length up from the floor with a faint shudder at the oily texture and musky odour of it, and placed it by her arm. How many weeks, months or even years had it been since she'd washed her hair? It was unthinkable in the modern West, not to wash your hair, shower, use a deodorant, yet Sarah Bell knew nothing about the things society had whole conversations about, had never even listened to the radio if the house was anything to go by. She was an anachronism, a survivor from another age. Eyes still shut, she felt for her braid with a rough, reddened hand and coiled it round her wrist, as if its smooth weight gave her comfort.

She was dying. The operation to repair her fistula had gone well, if she lived she'd be relatively normal again, but she wasn't going to live; she didn't want to. The ward sister had said as much, concern mingling with professional frustration on her face as she explained how Sarah was sinking, receding further and further away with every dawn, no matter what they tried. I explained my reason for visiting -

a very edited version - and it was agreed I could talk to her as long as she wasn't distressed; but she was very weak.

'Sarah? Please – can you tell me who he is? Is he . . .'

'My baby. My little baby.' The voice was as faint and thready as the chime of heather bells on the high tops. She opened her eyes and gazed at me, like a child. Her eyes focused on my plait which had flopped forward. Her face relaxed; did she think I was like her, did my long hair - did my bruised and scratched cheek - make her feel reassured?

'What's his name, Sarah? Does he have a name?'

She moved her chapped, colourless lips, swallowing hard as though something were stuck in her throat. She closed, then opened her eyes, staring into the catastrophic past. I could see me, the room, the hospital, the world fade away for her and only her dream life remain; the capsule of her strange, simple mind enclosing and protecting her from the brutality of her life. The fugue state that the mis-treated hide in, chanting disjointed *la-la-la's* to block out the actuality of pain and terror. Her voice had the same curious sing-song tone Jo-Jo's had when she told the cards; it was the whispering unworldly voice of the seer, the shaman, the prophet, the spirit world. An incantation. A hymn.

'He is Adam, the first of God's children, he come from me in blood an' muck but it touched him not an' he was as beautiful as the sun, and I loved him more than my own life, more than the land, more than . . . But she called him devil, she said he must be cast out, my baby, she said he was filth, animal filth, an' he could not be with the Chosen. So cruel, so cruel, she were the devil, not him, she . . .'

'Did Rebecca say that, Sarah, did she . . .'

Her hand tightened convulsively on the braid, twisting it tighter round her wrist.

'Is he dead? My son? Is he dead?'

'No - no, he's not, he's alive, Sarah, he's - he's OK, love.'

I lied. It was true he was alive, but OK? I couldn't explain to her, I couldn't. 'Sarah, who is Adam's father? Where is he? We need to find out if there's any family, if . . .'

She twisted fretfully under the bandage of starch-glazed sheets and her faded eyes bloomed with memory.

'He spoke to me, no-one else dared, she'd thrash anyone as spoke to me, but she weren't there, she'd gone to buy stuff for the beasts. He said I was pretty. Said my hair were like silk, like flowers. I had washed it with proper stuff that she brought home once, not with soap like usual, it smelt lovely, like Christ-mass marzipan. I were drying it in the sun, he took hold of it, said it were so long, an' the prettiest stuff he'd ever touched. He smiled at me. I went to him, in the barn, where he slept with the beasts. He were so good wi' the horses an' such, good hands. An' he were so handsome, despite him being dark, coloured, like. He were strong and gentle. He come from somewhere foreign, his voice were like singing. He said he'd take me there, it were warm and nice, not like here. I went to him, I did, that night when she slept, an' the next, for weeks. I loved him an' he loved me. He were saving his wages for us ter go off together - an' then she found out, found out I were - she sent him off, sent him away, said he were a nigger bastard but he weren't. He were kind, kind. But she said she'd have the police to him, say he forced me, hurt me, that they'd lock him up, beat him - but he never hurt me, only she hurt me. He run off then. Never come back. My only chance, my only - but he were a hired man, a foreigner, she said he dint have no proper papers, shouldn't have been here, she were the boss, who'd believe him over her? She sold the beasts, the machinery, everything. It were bad, bad, she hurt me, tried to kill the baby inside me, kickin' me, takin' her cane or Dad's belt ter me like I was a kiddie. But she couldn't get rid of my boy, not even her. Gentle Jesus wouldn't let her, He protected me an' my baby. She were that angry, I thought she'd kill me, screamin' an' screamin', hours on end, fer days, kickin', hittin' . . .'

Her voice faltered and she coughed weakly. I helped her take a sip of tepid water from a plastic beaker.

'Sarah, you don't have to, I mean I can come back another time, it's alright.'

She turned her head and gazed directly at me. There was an incomprehensible enormity of pain in her face; not physical, but the terrible agony of a brutalised mind.

'She thought I were simple, Becca did. They all did. Simple. But I weren't. I just wanted somethin' ter love.'

'Adam.'

A softness stole over her face as it had when she'd spoken of Adam's father, illuminating her like candle glow. 'Aye. My baby. He'll be well grown on now, is he tall like his daddy? Have you seen him, Miss? Have you? I wanted to see him, I did, I wanted to be a proper mam to him but she wouldn't - she - then when she - went ter Glory, I couldn't - I dint seem ter, I only went ter the yard, to the gate fer the food no further. I dint wander about, she allus said I were never ter wander about, said I'd get meself in trouble an' if anyone caught me, I'd get took away. Locked up somewhere, in a bad place. I allus thought somehow she might come back, catch me noseying about, I were that frit. I dint want ter see no-one, not even the Brethren. *She* allus said I were a leper, like in the Book, cursed wi' filth after I had my boy as a punishment from the Lord fer goin' outside the family, goin' against her who was part of me like I was part of her, that we were all we needed an' I'd destroyed it, let the Serpent in, ate of the apple. That's why I were blighted, for my sin, not fit ter see folk or owt like that, that they'd shun me, be disgusted. The doctor says that's not true, that it were just an accident but I - I - it don't matter now. I am grateful, like, ter those that helped me, I am, but this place, oh Miss, it's like what Becca said, I'm locked up in a bad place, fer bein' bad. Miss, I - don't you think it's - it scares me, so big, them devices, the noise, the way the folk talk. . . So tired . . . My boy, my son, is he . . . What's become of him, please, Miss?'

The brief spurt of energy left her, and she seemed to shrink even further into the stiff bed linen, her breath gasping and heaving in her bony chest, pitifully thin under the hospital issue gown. I patted her arm and looked away. The sight of her reminded me of another mother, another lost son, another woman asking me what had become of her boy. Sam, I hadn't forgotten you, what a state you must be in now with the press at you, Jo-Jo selling you to any journalist who offered her a fiver - her version of your life national tittle-tattle. I couldn't get near you, I was forbidden even to ring you, *not in the client's best interests*, poor Sam. How much they had in common, these two women, and how little anyone would ever know it.

'Have you seen my boy, Miss?'

Had I seen him - seen Adam? Did I know what had become of him? Gentle Jesus, meek and mild, suffer the little children - oh yes, I knew what had become of him, but how in the name of that pallid Messiah could I tell Adam's mother he was in Hell?

I looked at the gaunt form lying on the bed and it crossed my mind that just as Sam and Sarah were alike, so were Sarah and Adam, this ruined woman and her strange son; both kept from the world so-called normal people took so completely for granted, the world of giant supermarkets, the pointless chunter of mobile phones, out-of-town shopping malls. The dead eye of the television, cars that ate the land like metal locusts, drugs that everyone took but no-one admitted to, spoilt Western children with blank adult faces blinkered by the caul of market forces that turned them into drunks, junkies and whores for profit while their parents whined and moaned and scrabbled to stay young forever. A world so complex and skewed that the Minotaur's labyrinth was a short stroll on a sunny day by comparison. Sarah and Adam were links in an old binding chain, worn and patinated, turning in and around each other in a kind of blissful ignorance that rose above the morality of the day like a hawk soaring above the fells, riding thermals we couldn't even see, never mind imagine - their humanity only a frail mask, the primitive simplicity of their natures neither good nor evil, merely driven by the need for food, a mate, to reproduce, to be pack leader or the mother of a son.

'Is he - is he beautiful, my boy?' I barely heard her over the burble of the machines.

'What? I'm sorry, Sarah, I was miles. . .'

'My Adam, is he beautiful, like his daddy were?'

I saw again the stinking, verminous creature warped by his feral life, the broken teeth, hair a matted ball of filth, the weird chatoyant eyes, a gold-flecked blue as dark and velvety as a gentian, the curved sweep of eyelashes and his full, scarred mouth a re-curved bow.

'Yes, Sarah. Yes, he's beautiful, he is.'

She smiled. Her fine, wrinkled skin pale, aged before her time by illness, hard labour and abuse; the faint reddened patches on her cheeks giving her the look of an old china doll crazed with hair-fine cracks. The white light of the hospital, filtered by coarse blinds and punctuated by the gem-like studs of red or green LEDs blinking on humming machines, wrapped the room in a palely opalescent haze that despite its determined clinical modernity had an ethereal, frosted glass-like quality, like an angel's wings in an old illustrated bible.

143

In my bag were the Special Guardianship forms I needed Sarah to sign, that would make me the creature - Adam's - guardian. One of the nurses could witness them. If Sarah signed them, if I could make her understand, then I could stand between Adam and the storm. I'd tried to protect Johnny, and failed. I'd tried to protect Jakey, and failed. I would *not* fail this child, come what may, and despite what any of the blind, ignorant fools out there thought. Yes, he'd done a dreadful thing - or his pack mates had. Yes, he'd broken a great taboo - but he knew no better, he was not to blame.

In the Middle Ages they gave public trials, just like the ones they gave to human criminals, to animals who'd offended against humans; they hanged dogs that turned on their masters, cut the throats of bulls who'd trampled some-one's child. This was the modern world. They'd shot the dogs that had undoubtedly hunted and killed poor Jakey. They couldn't put animals on trial now - but they could sacrifice Adam and they would. The media was already slavering for him to be punished - *The Mail* had started a 'bring back hanging' campaign because some psychologist had said he would be incapable of remorse - and he would, because he would never know he'd done wrong in the first place. Adam did what he had to do to live, like all of us - he found food. That's all it meant to him.

To us, he was a cannibal who helped kill, then eat, a child. I'd known and cared for that child, and the thought of his death was terrible - but destroying Adam wouldn't help him, wouldn't bring him back. It wouldn't. Adam wasn't a child-killer, he wasn't a violent paedophile; he was an abused and ruined child himself. Someone had to speak for him, they did. *I* did.

I thought about the forms in my bag. If Sarah signed, my life would change forever. I'd taken them from the office before coming to the hospital. I'd hoped desperately Piff would be there but she was on call-out. No-one else had said anything, in fact, no-one had spoken to me at all. It was as if I were invisible, or contagious. No-one wanted to be infected with whatever madness had driven me to put everything on the line for - not that they'd use those words in public, but by God, that's what they said in private - a fucked-up pill-head whore and her dead child. What would they be like if they knew I was going to stand guardian for a feral cannibal killer?

I'd had to be quick, before Bob caught me and sent me packing, or de-frocked me or whatever happened when you were in disgrace - I used the office phone and my shaky authority to find out where Adam had been taken, it wasn't hard. There was only one place he could go, really, at least until a facility more suitable could be found, or built for him. He'd been taken straight to Bankcrest House. They took all the savage child-flotsam of society jettisoned by family and community; after they reached sixteen, they got parcelled out elsewhere. Officially it was a maximum security young offenders facility. In reality it was the antechamber of Hell: the only prison I'd ever visited where the staff were visibly afraid of the inmates. See, in an adult prison you could form relationships of one sort or another with the lags, mostly. Unless they were terminally bored, it wasn't worth their while to kick up a fuss, cause trouble; the price was too high, so uneasy alliances were formed. At Bankcrest you were dealing with pre-teen rapists, arsonists and murderers. The very word 'relationship' was completely and utterly meaningless to them. And there were their families, too - or at least, the ones that bothered turning up. The ones that didn't actually come to see little Darren (aged eleven, down for sodomising and strangling his five year old cousin at the Christmas party) but came

145

to find their own shaky redemption, to lay the blame else-where, to be assured they were good parents really and little Darren allus had bin a proper fuckin' bastard, choose how. *Not our fault.* Nothin' to do with them drinking them-selves witless of an evenin', brayin' seven bells out of the little cunt when they fancied it, makin' the kid suck his dad off and laughing when he took a hit of weed aged six or a chased the dragon with Uncle Bob while upstairs his stick-thin, bug-eyed Auntie Carole took it from behind from a fat punter with a picture of his kids in his wallet for twenty quid an' no rubber, scratchin' her calves bloody all the while. Bankcrest took all the fry-brained little Darrens and glued, splinted, bandaged and stitched those shark-eyed remnants of children into semi-functioning human beings that didn't wet themselves in public or stick knives into anything that moved. If they couldn't fix the kid, they contained them, like nuclear waste.

I phoned and asked to visit. They said under the circum-stances I could have a meeting with the head of unit. I agreed. Something was better than nothing.

I knew, at a cellular, instinctive, unreasoning level, that if I didn't do something for Adam, no-one else ever would and he would suffer the torments of the dammed, in the most appalling terror and agony, until he went screaming insane, died, or was broken into a mute and cruel submis-sion. I didn't blame Bankcrest, they'd do their best. But it was no good. The world had smelt him, had seen images of him, he couldn't be safely hidden, he was the greatest freakshow on earth for his appalling fifteen minutes of infamy.

I'd seen how the real world looked at Adam. How they handled him. What they'd done.

Eighteen

'Sarah, can you manage to talk to me for a couple more minutes? I know you're tired, but if . . .'

She shifted fretfully in the unravelling sheets. As she moved a smell of antiseptics and, faintly, blood, rose from the bed like a sanitary incense. The coal-tar odour of sickness; cut flesh and phenol. Sarah looked exhausted and I felt guilty for pressing her but if I didn't, and the forms didn't get signed, her son would vanish into the maw of bureaucracy forever, no-one's responsibility, everyone's burden, shifted from one facility to another as everyone tried to get rid of this insoluble problem. Like Genie, the American girl kept in total isolation most of her life, Adam would be studied by scientists and doctors both of the body and mind, well-meaning, well-intentioned individuals who'd despair when the money for their particular Adam Project ran out and yet again, this bit of living detritus would be foisted off on some other facility where he'd bang his head bloody on the walls of his cell pining for the moors and a breath of unconditioned air. No-one would love him - how could they? He wasn't a cute Disney *Mowgli* singing a jaunty tune to a lovable bear. He was strange beyond most people's imaginings. Even if they could bring themselves to care for him he would be torn away from them when the cash vanished, and their hearts would be broken.

I looked at the woman who'd sheltered him in her body as the stick broke across her back and her insane twin kicked her black and blue for daring to love someone else. The least I could do - I mean the very fucking *least* I could do was care for her child.

'I'm alright, Miss. I'm just - sometimes I feel better then I don't. Miss, I can't rest till I know who'll look after my boy, I can't. You're the only one who's spoke of him, oh, please, I know I - I dint do what I should've but who'll tek care of him?'

Ignobly, I felt a rush of excitement; Sarah herself had given me the opening I needed. I saw the ward sister looking at me warningly from the door holding up five fingers - I had to be quick.

Trying not to gabble, I calmed myself and spoke quietly. 'Sarah, I'll look after Adam, but you have to sign this form so that the authorities will let me care for him until you're better, then if you can get a lawyer and write in a Will too that I'm to look after Adam always, that would be even better - but you know, wait until you're stronger and . . .'

She looked at me. She'd caught the patronising note in my voice, the *now-then-my-dear* tone. I winced inwardly. She blinked slowly, her eyes locked on my face.

'I'll not get better. I'm Called an' I must go. Becca, she beat me an' she beat Adam the same, with that fancy walkin' stick of hers - when she could catch him, but Sheba turned against her, protected my boy. It drove Becca mad, her own dog turnin' on her like that. Even Sheba were a better mam to my lad than I ever wor, Jesus knows it an' so do I. I'll sign yer form, if you promise, promise me on the Book, that you'll do right by him, that you'll tek care of him, please - no-one else knows, no-one - promise me. Promise me, Miss.'

Time bound us in a tight cocoon, the monster's mother and I. We looked at each other with the most perfect understanding, a communion that didn't need words. She gave her child over to me and, in my heart, a chamber long-sealed opened to receive him. I thought of all the prayers I'd seen in my life - the Mass, my father drunk and begging the Holy Mother to forgive him his trespasses as my mother and I touched our bruises and winced in silence, each blaming the other. I thought of Sister Elcar's sturdy invocations and the gentle lucidity of Julian of Norwich's prayer that all should be well. Sarah Bell and I prayed together, silent as deep water, the limpid and fathomless prayers of women for their children, the agony of leaving, the joy of shouldering the beloved burden.

I took her hand in mine. 'I promise.'

'Thank you, oh, thank you. Where shall I write, Miss? I'm not afraid no more now. Not afraid.'

I fished the crumpled forms out of my bag and putting them under her hand, helped her scrawl her name. A child's writing, italic, unpractised.

She grasped my arm. 'Tell him - tell him I loved him, I did love him. Tell him - ah, tell him I'm sorry, I'm sorry.'

'Now then, I'm afraid I'm going to have to ask you to say your goodbyes. Sarah needs her rest, don't you, Sarah love? You'll not get better otherwise, eh?' The nurse briskly tucked in the loose sheet and fixed Sarah to the bed. A winding sheet, I thought, and no bridal gown for Sarah to be buried in. She looked at me, her eyelids bruise-blue and fluttering with fatigue.

'God bless, Miss.'

There was nothing else I could say but the thing she needed to hear. 'God bless you, Sarah.'

'Aye. We'll meet again, Miss, safe in His keepin' - an' my Adam, too.'

The nurse looked blank. She'd heard it all before, no doubt. Daylight atheists, submarine Catholics, the penitent and the last minute convert, everyone suddenly finding that the thing they jeered at most in the safety of their material life was the only rope they had to cling to when the dark fell.

I picked up my stuff and walked out to the nurse's station. The cheery pastels were faded white at the edges and dirt seamed the corners. The walls were untidily dotted with posters warning of MRSA and exhorting everyone to wash their hands. No amount of drooping pot plants or blandly modern abstract prints could alleviate the sense of a battle lost before it began. No postcards from Miami and Malaga blu-tacked to the wall alongside the telephone, or get well soon cards could make it a good place to be in, a calm, healing place; the people who designed these warrens must never have been sick, I thought, or they'd have done a whole lot better job of it.

'Um, Sister, could I bother you to witness this guardianship form for Miss Bell?' I saw her glance curiously at my scraped and bruised face, then look away - none of her business, after all. Domestic, probably. Oh dear.

'It's her son,' I continued in a soothing, professional tone. 'He'll need care when she - if she - doesn't pull through. Probably even if she does.'

At last the nurse looked surprised, her over-plucked comma eyebrows raising and her head wobbling infinitesimally. 'Her son? I thought - we didn't realise he was still living. We assumed . . .'

I put on a look of confidential piety and leant closer. 'Special needs. Very special. He wasn't with the family, you understand.'

A gloss of sentiment spread over her face. 'Oh, shame. Awful, isn't it? Poor Sarah, and that poor mite. Yes, I'll witness it - just let me find my pen, where is it? I'm sure I . . .'

As she bustled, I saw a copy of *The Sun* in the waste bin. It was half-unrolled where it had been thrown. The front page was visible. It was from the day after they caught Adam. I'd seen it before, of course, and all the others, but it banged in my chest like a dull blow all the same. The banner headline read simply **CANNIBAL.** The photograph was the one taken by the vet's assistant on his mobile. Everything that was distorted in Adam's scarred face was thrown into sharp relief because he was straining up against the pinioning blanket; his too-muscular jaw was distended, his mouth wide showing the broken and over-developed canine teeth. His nostrils were flared with the effort of breathing and his eyes strained in terror, the whites showing all round the iris. You couldn't see the blanket or the coppers. Just that terrifying face, grainy, pixillated, a creature from myth and legend, a chimera, a predator. The few seconds of video footage of his capture the man had also taken on his phone from the safety of the vet's van was the most hit film on Youtube and the internet. It had been shown on just about every news channel in the world. The vet's assistant had sold his treasure for a small fortune and done his own eye-witness accounts which cast him in the light of a brave soldier, as had the vet, the coppers and the Co-Op delivery lad, who hadn't been there but alongside the postman was the only outside contact with the farm and was totally thrilled by the whole thing. He kept mentioning his little band every time he got interviewed; he'd probably get signed on account of it - as dear old dickheaded Vinny used to say; *'you couldn't buy publicity like that, poppet, we'll shift a shitload of product with that sorta exposure, ber-ring it on, baby-cakes. . .'*

Gordon, The Brethren, and myself had refused to comment. None of us, it seemed, thought it was a duty or a privilege to be on TV or in *The Clarion* spilling our guts. The press were at me like flies round cowshit, non-stop phoning, hassling, wheedling. They loitered outside the flats practically twenty-four hours, asking the other tenants questions about my private life, if I had men up, was I gay,

151

oh, keeps herself to herself, eh? A recluse, like? Ah – a bit strange, maybe? It was driving the whole block mad with curiosity. People I'd never said a blind word to said hello very brightly to me in the lift and one woman I'd never even seen before introduced herself as 'Flat Six' and asked me to dinner. Oddly, I said no. She looked livid, and my bet was she'd sold her dinner party on the strength of my being there before she'd even asked me.

I didn't take calls but let them go to answer phone before checking who they were from and I'd made sure the media-dogs hadn't followed me here to the hospital, like they followed me everywhere else. At Morrisons they'd watched intently, photographing me as I bought loo-roll and yoghurt. Still, coming from the dear old world of rock 'n' roll I at least had some foreknowledge of how they'd go on, but I doubted Gordon did. It must be driving him completely mad. I must ring him. And Piff, too, I must ring Piff, I must get her to understand, to help me.

Pen in hand, the nurse caught me looking at the paper. 'Dreadful, isn't it? That - well, I don't know what to call it. I suppose we should all feel sorry for it, the creature, what-ever it is, but I can't bring myself to, personally. I shouldn't say it, but really, they want to put it down, you know, save the tax-payer the money. We could do with the cash they'll spend keeping that thing locked up. Ugh, horrible, isn't it? That poor little Jakey. Like I said to our Sarah, I only hope it was quick for him, over fast, you know.'

Startled, I studied her face. Did she know? No, there was nothing but conventional revulsion in that round face. Jesus, had Sarah seen that picture, did she know . . .

I cleared my throat, trying to look sympathetic. 'Did Sarah see that then? Does she watch TV? I know they didn't have one at the - in her home.'

'Did they not? Oh, that's brave. I couldn't do without

my soaps - I like to relax after being in here - I couldn't do without the telly. But yeah - come to think of it she doesn't like the TV being on, never puts it on herself. Says it frightens her - fancy that! Still, no accounting for tastes, I always say. I didn't show her the papers to be honest, if the telly scares her I should think that horror would. It proper gave us all the creeps, really. No, it's rest and quiet she needs, proper care, then she'll be right as a trivet in no time.'

'Has she got a Bible?'

'A what? Oh, sorry, yes, I see, religious. Well, no, d'you think she'd like one? I could get the Chaplain to lend her one - she'd probably just give her one, truth be told, I'm sure they've got lots of spare copies. It might comfort her, mightn't it? That's a nice thought, I'll ring down and get the Chaplain along before she goes home.'

'Thank you - and thanks for being a witness. I'd better go and get everything sorted out - you know.'

'Oh, it's my pleasure - are you actually Sarah's actual worker, then? Because another lady came this morning, an Asian lady, in a scarf, you know . . . Sarah wouldn't speak to her, just pretended to be asleep, you know what these older folk are like, they can be a bit prejudiced and . . . '

Shit. I should have known Bob would want this stitched up like a kipper for the department. 'Ah, well, I'm Miss Bell's son's worker, properly speaking. Always a bit of cross-over, with this kind of case.'

I smiled as she nodded understandingly, one mere cog in the gigantic infernal machine of bureaucracy to another, and picking up my bag, I pushed out of the swing-doors, narrowly avoiding being decked by a bloke who'd pushed in at the same time.

'Sorry mate,' I said, doing that typically english thing of apologising when it wasn't my fault. He stared at me for a second, then without speaking, shouldered past me and walked briskly towards the nurses' station. I sighed. Rude bastard. Some people don't even know the meaning of courtesy.

I was halfway down the corridor when I heard the commotion. The ward sister, her plump face red and angry, was ordering the bloke out of the doors, threatening to get the security, saying she was going to contact the hospital administration immediately. She didn't notice me, fortunately. Now she knew the truth about Sarah Bell, she'd know I'd been more than a little economical with the facts. I looked round for a hiding place as the bloke, covertly giving the finger to the nurse's back as he adjusted his jacket, started down the corridor. I quickly nipped into the Ladies. He'd nearly recognised me in the ward, it wouldn't do for him to spot me now.

I hadn't shaken off the press, after all.

Nineteen

I remember sitting behind my modernistic Scandinavian pine desk at GMC shortly after I'd scored the gig as Vinny's personal assistant, simultaneously buffing my nails and talking to the girl at Fabrice's Flowers about getting twelve dozen long-stemmed red roses delivered to the Ultimate Angel photo shoot the following day, the phone tucked into the crook of my neck like they always tell you is *so bad for you* in magazines, when the frosted glass door burst open and Soozi from Lula Dolls flung herself tearfully into the big red leather armchair.

I terminated the nice flower girl and dropped my buffer into my desk drawer while Soozi gazed at me, her tiny face a mask of tragedy. Like many female pop singers and fashion - as opposed to glamour - models, Soozi was the size and shape of a stunted, anorexic twelve year old, with a head slightly too big for her body. Lollipop girls, I call them, they look weird in real life but they always photograph well and Soozi was no exception. Her industry-standard silicone tits and collagen Paris Pout helped too, otherwise she'd have had nothing to burst out of her designer stage skimpies or support the tons of hi-pearl lipgloss stuck on her gob. She maintained her sylph-like figure by the copious use of cocaine and eating Kleenex to kill what appetite remained. Little girls all over Britain strove to emulate her. She did GMC proud.

Lula Dolls had taken Best Newcomer at the televised and much hyped *Music UK Awards* (or as we called them fondly, the YUK Awards) the night before. Soozi had no idea, like most artistes, that it had cost GMC an arm and a leg plus copious amounts of complimentary Moet, whores, and bugle to get her that dubious distinction. She chose, like most of 'em did, to believe it was sheer talent that won the day. Given her recently elevated status, I was surprised to see her so distressed. Not bothered, you may note, just mildly surprised. Soozi was a stupid, rude, egomaniacal, talentless mini-diva, with the personal charisma of a trout and the ambition and drive of a pit-bull with a jalapeno stuck up its arse. Not an unusual combination in the music industry, but her shiny, dainty prettiness and undoubted ability to look good on camera had more than compensated for her complete inability to actually sing. Soozi relied on the Melodyne, a wonderful machine which automatically put even the most unmelodic voice in perfect tune. And then there's playback; the art of mime, I find, never palls.

So as Soozi snuffled dramatically I inwardly heaved a sigh and put on a look of intense sympathy. After all, that's what I was paid for.

'I want to see Vinny.' It was not a request. Armies have marched and died for generals less driven than Soozi.

'Ah, well, er . . .' I stalled. Vinny was asleep on the sofa in his office. He'd partied hard at the YUK after-show and the enlivening effect of industrial quantities of the devil's dandruff had finally worn off. Waking him would be a problem.

Soozi pouted crossly, creasing her thick layer of Dior lip-gloss and toyed with the white-gold and diamond key pendant the fancy jewellers Bijoux-Bijoux had given her for name-dropping them in interviews. "Ave you seen the fuckin' papers? 'Ave you? Fuckin' unbelievable, the fuckin' twats. I won that fuckin' award fair an' fuckin' square, an' the bastards are sayin' it shoulda gone to The Big Zeros - The fuckin' Zeros! That bunch of fuckin' scruffy indie cunts! Fancy themselves the new fuckin' Oasis - pathetic. Un-fuckin' -believable.'

156

'Woah, yeah, right . . .' I began, wondering what the hordes of screaming fans and their mums and dads would make of Soozi's gutter-mouth if they knew about it. Naturally, she was all sweetness and light in public, but we weren't the public, we were her personal punch-bags like everyone who worked for her. I knew where the story had come from - without doubt it had been *arranged*, shall we say, by The Big Zero's company, our rivals, Palatine. Oh well. Nothing sold better than a band war. With any luck, the bands could be goaded into public slanging matches and hopefully, a punch-up at a festival or happening club. Everyone benefitted. Except the musicians, of course, who made complete dicks of themselves in the full glare of the media - but this was the music industry, who cared about *them*?

'I hate the fuckin' press. Get me Vinny right *now*. I wanta sue 'em. The *Zeros* - fuck me, I hate *them* too, the wankers.'

She fumbled in her bag and lit a Marlboro. Sticking her chin out like a pissed-off pug, she stared at me furiously.

'I'll get some coffee for you, Soozi, and wake - er, tell Vinny you're here. You just try to relax - and con-gratulations on the award, you looked fabulous on the telly, really, that Hernando dress was gorgeous.'

She snickered. 'Yeah, he aint gettin' that back wotever he might think, the tosser. He should be fuckin' grateful I wore his shitty dress, not bang on about it bein' a loaner. Arsehole.'

I sighed and mentally added the price of the dress to the Lula Dolls bill. As I poured espresso into a moaning Vinny I thought about how people in the industry both loathed and needed the press. Soozi would have been the first to scream blue murder if the interviews, features and photos weren't there for her. It was part of a professional recording artist's work to do as much press as possible, whether they loathed rabbiting on about themselves endlessly as some genuinely did, or it was their sole reason for living, like Soozi. It was part of the gig. It got your work - or your face, in Soozi's case - in front of the public.

But no-one actually liked the journalists, the all-out professional ones anyway. Of course they weren't all bastards and bitches, sometimes there was an honest one, a decent one - creative, interesting, one who'd stuck to their ideals and tried to do their best, maybe working for a left-field paper or on a late-night radio show, but very often, they didn't stay the course for long and dropped out, did something else. And it was so tiring and stressful working with the media. The turnover in the press office was huge - it seemed a glamorous job until you tried it, then the constant bargaining, grovelling, begging, and inventing stuff that might tempt the media's jaded appetite just wore you out. The only thing the hacks jumped for was scandal, and not every artiste was willing to expose their personal lives to public scrutiny in order to get the column inches, despite the press office's desperate pleas.

Personally, I had a sad fascination with those artistes who constantly railed against press intrusion, but flounced in shrieking if they weren't in *The Sun* every day. The lengths they were prepared to go to be famous were mind-boggling. We took bets in the office about what stunts they'd pull next; would indie-pop hero Jamie confess to being a crystal meth addict, accidentally release pictures of himself taking drugs backstage at a famous festival, attempt suicide and go into rehab (celeb mag exclusive)? Would former girl-group sensation and now failing solo singer Manda frantically drop two stone (tabloids speculate deliciously on possible anorexia and berate her for being bad role model for young girls)? Would aging chart-tart Teena admit to the illegitimate baby she had aged fifteen

(*Channel Five* mockumentary about their reunion)? Would internationally successful ex-boy-band chick-magnet Marky come out of the closet at last and - no, that would never happen, trust me. It still hasn't. Anyway, the likes of them and the media were an unholy marriage, a co-dependant partnership built on mutual need; one to flog copies and the other to feed their appalling addiction to fame, which is every bit as hard to kick as a lifetime's heroin habit, believe you me.

So on the whole, everyone agreed - however personable and amiable journalists might seem, you couldn't ever trust them. If you were an artiste, you had to think carefully about every tiny thing you said and did in front of them - dealing with that was a strain some artistes understood and coped with better than others. Just as some coped better with the hurtfulness of being made to look a complete wanker in print by someone they thought they'd had quite a pleasant chat with in the pub. After all, most musicians hadn't signed up to be diplomats, they just wanted to play their music and have a good time doing it. No-one taught them the rules of engagement, no-one told them the truth. They didn't understand that journalists had to write stories that *sold* their papers, not do five hundred words on what sort of pick-ups went best on a vintage Les Paul.

Entertainment and music journalists could be bad enough, but as for the mainstream media - man, they were plain old scary. They were a rabid dog biting itself to death, programmed to endlessly generate conflict and yet more conflict because that's what sold best of all. Nothing personal, you understand, they were just doing their job and in order to successfully do that job, they had to be without conscience or empathy of any kind. Of course they would protest loudly and long how unkind, unfair and wrong that was, because no-one's going to admit they're a complete cunt, are they? Course not. Everyone likes to think well of themselves, likes to think they're doing a worthwhile job, and journalists love to think they're hard-bitten heroes, proper writers dealing with the raw nitty-gritty of the human condition, not hounding some poor bastard to screw the last acid drops of scandal from their personal fuck-uppery. But at the end of the day, they're wage-whores, and trust me, you need a very long spoon to sup with that kind of devil.

And often, even if you didn't invite them in like GMC did, needing the exposure for our cash-cows, they came over the threshold anyway, because once they focus on you, you're no longer a living, human person, you're copy. You're the story. You're their mortgage payments, their kid's school fees, their holiday in the sun. You're a walking pot of gold no matter what awful thing might have happened to you or your family. They'll do anything, say anything, and promise anything to get what they need from you - anything. It's horrible and cruel, you say? True, true. But it's how it is. Raging against it changes nothing, except how they slant the piece. I knew all this, I'd worked in an industry where dealing with the press was my daily dose of poison, it made me immune to some extent. What it must be like to be an ordinary person suddenly put on their hit-list, when you had no experience of them before, I couldn't imagine.

They'd eat you up and spit out the bones before they swarmed off to consume the next big story.

Cannibals.

Twenty

I might have avoided the journalist at the hospital, but getting into my flat was like running the gauntlet. When I finally got in, after nearly losing it big style with a short, skinny cow who went at me like a ferret at a rabbit, I found a letter from the Residents' Committee saying they 'deeply regretted' the 'ongoing nuisance and disruption' caused by there being journalists virtually camped outside the building and cluttering up the street. Or whatever. I was too exhausted to care. I don't know what they thought I could do about it anyway and I recognised none of the names of the committee members - and come to that, I had never been asked to attend a meeting or be a part of their smug little junta. Fuck 'em.

Too tired to eat properly I wolfed a pot of yoghurt and an elderly banana washed down with tea. Necking a couple of extra-strong ibuprofen, the sort with added muscle-relaxants, I crawled under the crumpled duvet, taking Johnny's photo from the living room to put under my pillow. Yeah, pathetic, but it comforted me. As I lay waiting for my muscles to unlock and my head to stop throbbing, I felt almost unbearably lonely. I wished Piff would get home - only another day. Taking Johnny's photo out I looked at it and remembered how beautiful he was, how it felt to lie next to him in bed, the tenderness of his kisses, the sight of his sleeping face, smooth and golden, the way his thick heavy hair gleamed bronze in the shaded light of the old bedside lamp.

At some point while I wept, sleep took me into the dark. The phone woke me.

I didn't pick it up in time and scrambling around grog-gily I flipped it and looked at the time: 2.30 a.m. Bollocks, maybe it had been Piff. Probably a bloody journalist, more like, trying to catch me in an unguarded moment so I'd break down and whimper about how terrorised I'd been, and how distraught I was, like some ghastly celeb-tart banging on about losing her *Big Brother* contestant boyfriend to some other telly-whore. Must change my number, or just get a new bloody phone altogether, whichever was easier. Tomorrow. I'd definitely do it tomorrow.

Grumbling, I crawled back under the covers.

It rang again. Angry now, with the formless, childish anger of someone raggled out of a deep kip, I picked it up about to give out some serious abuse.

All I could hear was the brutal muffled *thud-thud* of hard house and a woman crying, terrible, wrenching sobs choked with snot and breathless with hysteria.

'Who is this? Calm down, tell me who you are. Wh . . .'

'Whydja - why - why dja dump me? Why don't you come an' see me no more? My baby's dead an' you fucked me off you did, like I were rubbish, whydja - it's not fair - I 'ate you, I 'ate you - my baby - you never give a shit didja, didja, you lyin' lyin' fuckin'- that fuckin' thing that fuckin' thing had my baby - fuck fuck fuck - why?'

A terrible clarity dropped through me, white, sharp and cold as winter dawn. 'Sam? Sam - listen Sam, it wasn't me, my bosses said I couldn't. . .'

'Bitch - you fuckin' - you bitch you cunt - they told me, that fuckin' stuck up twat told me, said you fucked it up, said you weren't comin' no more - you promised me, you promised me - you said it'd be all right you said it would be . . . Help me, you help me, they're all bastards, all on 'em, bastards, they say fuckin' - they say crap about me but you said it'd be all right - oh get *offa* me you fuckin' bastard get offa me - don't give a *shit* if it's your phone, you fuckin' - *I want my baby I want Jakey I . . .'*

The phone went dead.

Calls received listed a private number.

How many ways could I fail? How many people I'd promised to care for could I fail to protect?

Twenty-one

Piff sat in the easy chair by the window, the one I liked to chill out in and watch the high, ever-changing skies and the clouds that swept over the city in ragged diaphanous veils stitched with coins and seeds of light. Piff wasn't looking at the view, though. She should be, I thought, it was pretty dramatic today. Thunderheads boiled up in the west, dense black and gravid with rain that wouldn't birth because of the wind gusting through the canyons of tall Victorian buildings that made up this quarter of the city. I could hear the faint Aeolian howl of it through the double glazing.

I hadn't put the lights on, just lit a couple of big candles. The dim, grey light from the window showed the ashy tone of sunburn on Piff's usually glowing complexion. She looked drawn round the eyes and mouth, rather than relaxed and rejuvenated as I had expected her to be after her exotic holiday. She toyed with a jingling cascade of thin jewelled bracelets enamelled in varying shades of deep red that toned with her big garnet pashmina. She looked worried. However worried she was, she wasn't anything like as worried as me. I could have got a gold for England at the Stress Olympics, easy. But I tried to look calm. No point two of us being in a state.

I put her tea down on the table and sat back, sipping mine. 'I like those,' I said nodding at the bracelets. 'Very pretty - and the pash, very chi-chi. Souvenirs?'

She blinked and let the bracelets clink together as if she were ashamed of being caught fiddling with them. 'Oh - yes. Lina gave them to me - she was workin' with an artisan jeweller on a - on a painting, you know. Got a good price, not that you need to, everythin' so cheap out there, it's a scandal. Made me feel guilty, you know, payin' so little for stuff an' them havin' so little themselves. I got about six of these wraps. I got you one, a black one, I knew you wouldn't have colours, I - oh, never mind all that. Christ, girl, what happened? Are you alright? I saw - the papers, when we got back, that - creature, that boy - and poor little Jakey, it's just horrible. The press, it's like a circus, a freak-show - I can't believe it, they're even outside here, it's . . . But you, baby, it's you I'm worried about.'

So was I. I looked at Piff's dear, sweet round face and managed what I hoped was a re-assuring smile. I was so glad to see her - of all the people I knew, had ever known, really, Piff was the person I knew would understand what I'd had to do. She wasn't some straight, blinkered, ignorant sort, the type who'd shy away like a nervous pony at the thought of it all, who'd say, like so many did about anything they found in the least little bit disturbing, *'I just don't want to know, it's horrible, disgusting'*. We called them Ostriches, that sort of person. Piff, though, I could trust. Implicitly. One hundred and ten percent. She'd know how best to help Adam - and me. I wasn't pretending I didn't need help with all this, far from it. I might be doing something crazy and quixotic but I wasn't deluding myself. Quickly, I sketched in for her exactly what had really happened at the farm - as opposed to the highly-coloured media version - while she rested her face on her hand, elbow on the chair arm, knuckle on her mouth, nodding occasionally but never interrupting; so Piff, so serious.

'But I'm cool, Piff, I'm OK - no, I am, really. Yeah, I mean obviously it was pretty fuckin' scary but it was all so quick, honestly, I hardly had time to take it all in. Gordon was amazing, really, deserves a bloody medal, bless him.'

165

Today, I went to see my new son. Waiting in the reception at Bankcrest, looking at the cheery paintings done by the children, the cups and awards they'd won in prison competitions, the bunch of faded artificial flowers in the hand-thrown pot on the windowsill, the heavy locked doors leading into the facility itself. Outside, at the end of the long drive, hidden from me now by the curve of the road and some trees, a pack of journalists snuffled and scuffed around the high wire electric double gates, their faces relaxed into neutral, their bodies studded with cameras and recording gear, chain-smoking out of boredom, probably, and grinding the fag-ends out on the floor, the brief rush of watching me drive in and the resultant clamour over. They'd found Adam quicker than I'd hoped but I wasn't surprised; money talks.

'I'm going to take Gor out for a slap-up meal when this calms down a bit, just to say thank you. I - I keep ringing him, but I can't get through, his phone's always turned off, I expect he's even more hassled by those fuckin' journalists than I am, I mean, he's a proper *hero* – they love all that, don't they? He wouldn't though, would he? You know - blokes like Gor, God, last thing they want.'

Drinking tea in the Director's office, tea with milk which I hate, watching him control his anger at the journalists, watching him take all emotion other than a practiced good humour out of himself, watching him being professional, good at his job, me trying to be the same, failing, acting a part, the cup shaking slightly in my hand as he talked about the facility, the inmates, the programmes for rehabilitation, then sighing and steepling his hands as he finally got to Adam. They'd got him pretty heavily sedated. The Director didn't like it and neither did the staff dealing with Adam but they had no choice. He'd had to be cleaned up - it had been a major task, his head shaved because they couldn't untangle his verminous locks, nails clipped, his teeth looked at by the dentist, the doctor for his check up and vitamin injections. The Director picked up his notes. You're his guardian, Ms. Wynter, you must have your reasons for

166

taking on something like this on but I must warn you, he'll never be rehabilitated in any meaningful way, it's too late. He has no speech, no - understanding - no socialisation whatever. The major building blocks of normal child development just aren't there and they can't be put back. He's strong, and apart from some intestinal parasites etcetera, very healthy considering his experience. He could live for many, many years but he'll never be out of an institution. I have to tell you - we have already had a request to transfer him as soon as possible to Whitecliffe Medical Research Facility in Buckinghamshire - you've heard of it? No? Oh, it's -it's very big, very well funded. Very well supported by various government agencies, you know. They want to study the - er, Adam. They think he may prove to be invaluable in our understanding of human development and behaviour, growth patterns, the psychology of aggression, how we can become stronger, faster, more adaptable, that kind of thing. There are many and varied applications for that kind of knowledge, they say. Adam is the most extreme case we've ever seen in this country, you see. A true feral child. So rare. The Director looked out of the window. His voice was very steady. I can't refuse them. I've had instructions from higher up. Much higher up. Anyway, whatever happened, I couldn't keep Adam here, we don't really have the right environment for him. He needs to - well. We just don't. I'm putting him in the Little House Annexe when he's recovered a bit. It has a - well, a run, really. A yard. It was built for another boy, extremely autistic, very violent; he was calmer outside than in. It backs onto the woodland, at least Adam will see trees, for a while. Whitecliffe is a fully enclosed facility, top security. The other boy? Oh, moved on. Another place like this but more isolated. In Scotland.

'Annie, Annie - I'm sure Gordon was great, but you - you don't look OK to me, girl, you look terrible. Have you been eatin' ?'

I laughed. Not humorously. 'I can't - Piff, I've - you don't look all that yourself, darlin'. Didn't you have a good time?

167

I got your postcard, it looked fantastic, you said you were having a ball.'

Piff averted her face. 'I don't like hot places. Not, you know, very hot. Beaches, that kinda thing. I'm not built for it. The food didn't agree with me, I got sick for a few days. I mean, it is lovely - of course it is. Lina did great work, beautiful tings but - it's party central, least where we were. I couldn't - I couldn't look after her. She was out all hours - I mean, she's an artist, I know, they have temperament, they have to experience things but . . .'

I felt the old irritation with feckless, graceless Lina resurface. Selfish cow. 'You mean she left you alone all the time, didn't she? Oh, Piff . . .'

Her face said it all. Hours by herself in the hotel. Lonely walks in the evening on the beach. Striking up conversations with other guests as she ate alone. Making excuses while Lina fucked anything that moved and necked whatever drugs and booze came her way. Same old same old. What fools love makes of us, even decent, intelligent people like Piff.

She shrugged, unhappily. 'Oh, you know how it is, we had a huge row. Typical holiday row, you know, you can't wait to get away together, then you start relaxin' an' *bang*, out it all comes. But she said - some bad stuff. Very bad - I should forget it, but I can't, so I don't know . . . But come on Annie, stop tryin' to avoid the issue. Have you booked in for counselling? Jackie Harvey's very good, really . . .'

Going down to the holding room. The Director explaining what I needed to know as we walked. Staff looking at me as we passed, me wondering if they knew I was the Monster's foster-mother now. Wondering what they thought. Wondering if they hated me for caring about Adam. The child-killer. The cannibal. Looking in at the observation window. Adam - oh, Wild Thing - how fucking dreadful, how horribly, agonisingly pitiable you looked, rocking in

168

a corner, shit and food strewn round you, the bright, white light and your shorn head throwing the heavy brow-ridge and cheekbones of your strange, compelling, terrified face into sharp relief, the prominent incisors visible as you drooled in your uncomprehending agony of fear, the drugs fogging your senses, confusing you, the sound of you on the intercom - Maaaa - ma Ma-ma . . . The Director saying forensics had been, taken samples while you slept, drugged and docile, they'd show what you had done, consumed. Maaa - ma Ma-ma . . . The look on the Director's face, the terrible, terrible helpless pity of it all, my heart tearing apart hot and fibrous in my chest, my heart . . . Wild Thing, Johnny, Jakey, my baby, my baby . . . Why was the world so fucking cruel? Why were we so fucking - so fucking bastard cruel? What a savage species we were. Adam, Adam. Watch us torture this strange, fragile, savage child with experiments and drugs just so we can make better bloody soldiers or whatever, hurting and terrorising him until the weird matrix of his mind shatters into a million pieces just so some fucking professor can write a paper on how long it took to destroy him - rather than that we should put him out of this misery, out of his misery, we should do that or . . .

Set him free.

The memories and the real world overlaid each other in a jittering splatter of images for a second and I felt myself jerked into the present like a fish on a hook. I looked at Piff. Her kind, tired eyes. The words tumbled out of me, almost against my will. 'I'm his Guardian, I did the Special Guardianship thing, Piff. His mother - I got Adam's mother to sign the papers. She's dying, she couldn't protect him anyway, she's not - not strong. But I can, I can protect him. I had to do it, I had to, d'you understand?'

'Adam? What - who - what d'you mean? Oh, my God, my God Annie, that - thing - that boy, you mean you've . . .'

'His name's Adam, Piff. Adam. I know, I know he's done something awful, unforgivable, but he didn't realise, he

169

didn't - he's more animal than human, Piff, he's only a child, he's been screwed up, abused, hurt all his life, he's - he doesn't understand, he's not like us, not all fucked up, civilised, he's natural, of nature, he did what he had to do to survive, that's all - I mean, I know Jakey - Piff, I loved that kid, I did, you know I did, but he's gone, he's gone and Adam - he - *someone* has to stand up for him. They have to, I have to - oh, Piff, Piff, they're going to experiment on him, the government, I heard it all today at Bankcrest, I went there to see my - to see Adam - the director all but said it was the bloody military who were going to fund the research, I mean, he said, you know, *government interests*, but everyone knows what that means, it's the military for God's sake, no-one else has the money for that kind of - huh - *research* and . . .'

Piff pulled her shawl closer at her throat, her bangles jingling. Outside, the great clouds wrapped themselves over the city like a cloak of storms. Piff stared at me for a moment, then blinked and carefully put her hands in her lap, the pale ivory palms catching the light like turning fish in a dark sea, her falling bracelets accompanying her movement with their chinking, arrhythmic tune. I started to speak again but she cut in. Her voice was very calm, very steady. Professional.

'Annie, you gotta think about this, girl. Just think, think about it. Look, baby, you've had a big shock, a couple of big shocks - Johnny, then Jakey - you're upset, confused, not yourself - it's natural under the circumstances, of course it is, but you shouldn't be takin' any big decisions right now. Let me call Jackie, set up a session, we can sort. . .'

Sudden anger flashed through me, my face felt stiff and hot with it, my jaw muscles bunched hard, biting down on the words that teemed irrationally behind my set lips. Piff - you too? For *fuck's* sake. No. No. Not you. Not you. No -

170

I'd depended on you - believed in you - don't go straight on me now, don't be a fuckin' Ostrich when I needed you so much.

'Don't. *Don't* Piff. Just don't.' I almost stuttered with tension. 'Don't - don't do that voice on me, I'm not a client. I'm not a fuckin' *client*, Piff.'

The candles guttered in a draught as, outside, the wind whipped a skirl of dust up into the clouds. The room darkened slightly, dusk falling properly, true dusk, not just the tenebrous stormlight. I took a deep breath, staring at the candle for a moment before looking back at Piff. The ghost-glimmer of the little flame danced in my eyes for a second, dazzling me. I shook my head to clear my vision.

'I'm - I'm sorry, Piff, I'm sorry, sorry love. I just - it's just, I have to do it, make the stand, d'you see? Someone has to and who else cares? Look, when I was in the barn, right, and I first saw Adam, I admit, I was fuckin' horrified - disgusted even. You know, a big part of me just wanted him the fuck away, I wouldn't have cared if he died, whatever, because I was so - everything was so fucked up. But Piff, I can't explain, I - I just knew, right? I just knew he was mine, and he recognised me, he called me Ma, he . . .'

Piff rubbed her forehead where the sun had caught her and the skin was dry and dull. 'Annie, wait - wait a minute, you're goin' too fast. Try and be calm. Now, you say the boy called you *mum*, but now surely, he meant his real mother, didn't he? Not you, sugar, his real mum. And, darlin' how could he possibly recognise you? Be logical, he couldn't have, could he? Now, I'm not sayin' . . .'

'But you are - you are saying it's all bollocks, not in those words but that's what you mean. You weren't there, you didn't - he smelt me, he knew me, I held him in my arms and . . .'

'And you admit you were terrified, you were just waitin'

171

for him to attack you. Oh, Annie, listen to yourself - this boy - who even you say is far from normal, violent, and may well be retarded, recognised you never havin' *seen* you before, thought you were his mother, and now what is it? The government are goin' to spirit him away and the military want to experiment on him? Annie, it sounds like a film, Hollywood, not real life. Listen to yourself, baby, please, you're not makin' sense. You're worn out, you're depressed - you need help. It's nothin' to be ashamed of. I know you're strong, stronger than most, but sugar, everyone needs lookin' after sometimes, we all do, we just do. Look, people in extreme situations can suffer from syndromes, things like Stockholm Syndrome, Post-Traumatic Stress Syndrome, you know this, you do - baby, you're totally stressed out, you must feel it yourself. Sugar, I'll do anything to help. . .'

I stood up. I had to make her understand. Piff looked at me, alarmed. 'Annie, sit down, come on, we can sort this out, we . . .'

'He called me *Ma*. Not mum, not anything stupid like that. He knew I wasn't his blood mother, he knew that, so he called me *Ma*. It's the oldest word ever, it's the most universal - he came to me, he didn't hurt me, he gave himself to me, *me*, like he knew I was his mother now, like he knew I'd lost - lost my Johnny, my baby, lost Jakey and he knew - I knew - and he - I saw Johnny's face, I did, so strong, so fuckin' real in my mind - Piff, it was like a message, a sign, I don't believe in all that crap, I don't, you know I don't, but I know what I saw and . . .'

My fists were clenched and the hair stood up on the back of my neck. I couldn't believe, I just could not believe Piff didn't see the whole mass of connections; she of all people knew life wasn't neat, tidy, compartmentalised. Weird shit happened everyday and who knew it better than us, who dealt with its wreckage every day of our working lives. Couldn't she see that crazy though all this was, and I'd be the first to admit it, it had actually happened - it had happened to me, whether I liked it or not. Like Johnny had happened. Like him dying. Like me losing my baby. Like Jakey dying. It had all fucking well happened, woven its strange pattern, and there was no undoing it. OK, OK, yes, it did all *sound* mad, I could understand that, I wasn't nuts, but really, if you looked at it properly, it *wasn't*. You just had to put aside your prejudices; your straight ways of thinking about stuff and it all fell into place. It was like - oh, there's no modern way of saying it - but it was like my Fate was on me and I had no choice but to comply with it. Just like in the old stories I'd studied at University; my *geas* - like Beowulf, like Diarmud and Grainne, like Perseus, like Jason, like the *Mabinogeon's* tricksy chants. Stories like that aren't amusing tales for the kiddies, they're vastly and archaically deep and reek of old magic, Mystery and the symbolism we've wilfully put aside in order to be good, secular consumers. They tell unchangeable truths, they show us the mutability and unreason that's the seething core of what we foolishly think is our ordered existence. Christ, I did my bloody thesis on it, for fuck's sake. I remember every word and I'm not so stupid as to imagine it was all a lot of boring academic bullshit designed to annoy students and cruelly keep them from their partying for a few hours. I knew the truth when I read it. I knew it now.

But Piff - Piff was looking at me with the shutters firmly down behind her eyes. I felt the damp warmth of frustrated tears flush my face and I struggled to hold them back. Blubbing wouldn't help. I wasn't some hysterical cow weeping like a fountain because things weren't going her way. If they weren't, I had to turn things around, be clever, make Piff see. I had to be calm. As it was, this was all wrong, not how I'd planned it, not how I'd thought it would be, at all.

A sudden realisation of my complete isolation washed back through me. Other people had families, a circle of friends, people they could call on for help. A partner. All I had was a brother who despised me, and a mother dedicated to a false idol who spent her declining years trying to expiate her great sin - me - by being a pillar of the church. A boyfriend, a husband? Who amongst the men I'd occasionally bedded - and let's not pretend it was anything else on either side - since I came home could measure up to my Johnny? There'd never been even a whiff of a contender. Perhaps Gordon, at a stretch, not that he was exactly a pin-up, but he was kind, steady, maybe if I'd made an effort we could have hit it off - but now? I couldn't even get him on the bloody phone, who knew what he was thinking - and what he'd think if he knew about Adam.

Friends? Oh, I hadn't needed them. Oh no. I had my memories, my pride, after all, hadn't I? Stupid, stupid, stupid. How I'd yawned through the clumsy student bashes, then the dull dinner-parties with their soggy, ill-cooked food served up by colleagues wrongly convinced that if that oaf Jamie Oliver could do it, so could they. The in-turned conversations, the sour wine, the kids playing up, the houses that smelt of dogs and bickering - what did that mean to me who'd partied with the stars, eaten at the best restaurants, drunk the finest champagnes, done the best drugs? I couldn't tell them about my past, it would have sounded like rank boasting, they probably wouldn't have believed me anyway and if they did, well, we'd have had even less in common after their initial fascination with the showbiz dazzle-dust faded, and curiosity turned to jealousy as inexorably as their bad coffee turned to bitter dregs.

To be honest? I'd thought myself above them. What a nasty little counter-culture snob I was. There they were, doing their fucking best, trying to have a life, trying to bring up their children decently, struggling to make the payments on the little house, wondering where their youth had gone, where love had gone, what was to become of them and all I could do was be a snotty, judgmental cow. But it was no good. I couldn't be like them. I'd seen too much, done too much that was outside of anything they knew. I wasn't better than them, but I was different. We had no point of contact other than work. Even then, they disapproved of my attitude, my ways of dealing with the clients. Many's the time I'd ground my teeth as Andrea or Fran had taken the piss out of some hapless, useless, illiterate get they were assigned to; being funny at the expense of their stupidity, their complete inability to deal with straight society. Sure, I knew it was partly a defence mechanism; they did it because it was laugh or scream, and we were always told it wasn't good to let the clients get too close. But all too often - not always, but enough times to make me seethe with irritation - there was an ingrained, self-serving elitism in there too. Who'd see it better than me? They sealed them-selves up in their white-collar world like chrysalides and waited for some kind of reward for being good girls and boys, for playing the game, being a bit of a cut above the messy rest - a reward that didn't exist, would never come and that they would only realise was a lie when it was far too late.

Now I would be one of the Others, the clients, the ones who stood outside in the cold and, shivering, looked in at the lighted windows of reason and middle-class re-spectability. I would be another colossal fuck-up, another dinner party story. But my sin was all the greater because I'd wilfully defected from the right side to the hopelessly, eternally wrong side. I was not only a screw-up, I was a traitor.

They'd distance themselves as fast as they possibly could. Was Piff doing that?

I realised she was talking. Numbly, I tried to grasp what she was saying.

' . . . not saying it's not admirable, sugar, it's good of you to even think about carin' as much as you obviously do, but it's no good, you got to see that, really, just think about it. You can't get too close to the clients, get emotionally involved, you just can't. First rule, you know that, I know you know that. Look, I expect you're worried about work, I can understand that alright, Bob's been a complete wanker but that's nothin' new, we can sort him. You must be exhausted, baby, done in. That's why this is getting to you so much. Why don't you have a holiday? Somewhere easy, warm, relaxin'. You know, the Greek islands, or Spain or something. Nothing strenuous, just chill out. You'd enjoy it. Not like me an' my fancy fuck up - that's what it was, if I'm honest, still never mind, eh? Nothin' I can do about it now. Annie? Annie, did you hear any of that, baby? You miles away. You look so tired, I know you must. . .'

Nothing she said seemed to make sense to me. A holiday? Greece? Work? What did all that matter now? Oh, Piff, Piff - why couldn't you see? Why couldn't you just be my friend, be loyal?

'Yes, yes, I know, I know all that, I know - of course I'm tired, I - OK, it does sound mad, I know it does but - but I don't understand why you can't - why you can't be on my side. That's what I don't get, Piff. If it was you, I - there'd be no problem. For fuck's sake, I don't say anything when . . .'

The insane polyphonic burbling of Piff's phone playing 'You Sexy Thing' nearly made me jump out of my skin. Piff fumbled it out of her bag and answered. I think I knew then, that it wasn't going to be how I'd hoped, wasn't going to be all right. She'd never cut me off to answer her phone before. She said it was rude. People can wait for you to ring back, she said. They wouldn't like it if you left *them* sitting there like a lemon while you wittered on to someone on your phone, ignoring them as if they weren't worth your attention. The height of modern non-manners, she called it; she prided herself on her courtesy. She was worse than Hannibal Lecter for etiquette, she always joked. Now she half turned away and clutched her girlie pink Samsung like it was a lifeline thrown to a drowning man.

'Um, yeah, yeah, OK, no problem, yeah, on my way, won't be - oh, sure, I'll stop at the garage on - yeah, yeah, Well I - still if you're going out, I don't - no, there's nothing wrong, no - OK, I'll . . .'. She stopped speaking and, taking a visible breath, turned to me. You could almost see the web of our friendship being cut and I realised, with a painful clarity, that I had always thought more of her than she had of me. I'd always depended on her more than she would have ever thought of doing on me. Of course she liked me. Probably a lot. But in the end, she had Lina. She had her own beloved. I was just her friend. With women, the lover always comes first, protest as they may. I understood, but that didn't stop it hurting. One more hurt to add to all the rest. When this was over, I'd get back with Piff, sure, because even if she couldn't be on my side one hundred percent she was a good, kind, loving woman, nothing altered that fact. But our friendship would never be quite the same again.

I knew what Piff was thinking in the back of her mind; probably I'd think similar thoughts in a similar situation. I could drag her down into a mess of trouble if she wasn't careful. She wasn't being cruel, she was surviving, as she always had. Without doubt she felt it was better she got some distance because then she could see the problem clearly, help more efficiently when I'd calmed down a bit. That would be like her; reason was everything - when it didn't concern Lina. I looked out of the window. The storm was pitch black. It was coming, like it or not, and it would be better to have shelter when it broke. You wouldn't want to be out in it. You wouldn't want to be caught unprotected in that chaos.

Piff got up and started bustling around, stowing her things away in her over-size bag. She wouldn't look at me directly. 'Well, gotta go, darlin'. Lina wants to do dinner, do a stir-fry before she goes to this gig at The Big Bean, just an acoustic thing, you know, local stuff, but her friend Leanne is on and - I'm gonna call every day, Annie. We can get this sorted, we can. OK?'

I knew I should say something. I should respond. Cheerfully. You know, appropriately. I should say something like *oh, OK, super, well have a nice dinner and I hope Lina enjoys the gig. See you soon and I'll make that appointment with Jackie. You're right, it's the stress.*

But nothing came out of my mouth. I watched my friend gather up her shawl, her bag, her umbrella. I watched her still not really looking at me. I felt her kiss on my cheek, barely grazing my flesh. I watched her go out the door. I didn't say anything.

What was there to say?

What the fuck was there to say?

Twenty-two

Tragic Jakey's Mum In Drugs OD.
Baby Jakey's Mum ODs In Niteclub. Pics Exclusive.
Little Jakey's Mum Says Social Workers Let Her Down.
They Killed My Kiddie Says Jakey's Mum.
Were Social Workers To Blame For Tragic Toddler's Death?
My Girl No Angel Says Jakey's Psychic Gran.

I'd got the papers when I went for breakfast milk to the corner shop by the Drunk Bloke statue. I'm sure it isn't actually called that, probably it's Reclining Cubist Concrete Giant, or something but everyone calls it the Drunk Bloke. It's hideous, and that's not just my opinion. It's half of Bradford's. There weren't anything like as many reporters outside the flats and with a woolly hat and scarf and my reading specs on I strolled out the garage entrance unmolested and back in the same way. I dumped the papers on the breakfast bar and drank my morning coffee. Then I saw the headlines.

They'd taken Sam half-dead out of a club, where she'd collapsed in the toilets, full of heroin. Her latest addiction, the culmination of her long search for oblivion. Just before she collapsed, she'd rung me, that night, from the club toilets where she was having sex with a stranger whose phone she'd used. She had my number written on her purse, from when I'd been able to look after her. She'd said that would be the thing she'd be least likely to lose, so she'd scribbled it on the greasy canvas with a biro. She'd made the man punch the numbers for her as she was too smashed to do it herself.

I Rang Social Worker While I Tried To Die Says Jakey's Mum.
I Want To Help Tragic Sam Says Ex-Addict Supermodel Lainey
Jakey's Mum's Mystery Love Rat Tells All Exclusive
Jakey's Gran: My Daughter's Drug Hell

Sam was recuperating at the Infirmary. According to the papers (my only source of information, as Bob's *no contact* rule was still in place, or it was while I nominally still had a job) 'vowed' to go into rehab for the sake of her remaining children. I couldn't imagine Sam 'vowing' anything, I doubt if anyone used that word in real life. De-tox, eh. Where? Hardly The Priory or The Cedars for Sam. She didn't have that kind of cash, so it would be the grimy subsistence of the NHS. The smarmy countenance of her erstwhile squeeze from the club bog smirked forth from the inside spread of *The News Of The Screws* as he detailed his 'espresso sex' encounter with 'troubled mum' Sam, whom he recognised from her 'profile' in the media and had been only too happy to shag in a doorless cubicle in one of Bradford's salubrious city centre niteries. Of course, he knew nothing about the heroin that had been sliding through Sam's system like a mendacious promise of sanctuary from her aching brain. Oh no. He never touched anything like that. The manager of the club, Winston's, also expressed horror and amazement that drugs had been used on his premises.

180

He had, apparently without any sense of irony, offered 'celeb' Sam free drinks - including Winston's famous cocktails! - for a month when she 'recovered from her ordeal'. Alcohol, as my dear old Dad would have said, is a decent person's drug. Not of course that he'd have used the word 'drug', that being reserved for other, illegal intoxicants. Anyhow, it seemed the love rat, Darren Prentice, was hoping for a chance with male strip revue The Romeoz, but given his incipient beer gut and slightly melted-looking features I couldn't see his dream job becoming reality.

I stared at the grainy pictures of Sam, her hair scraggled into a pony tail, fag in her mouth, baby Brittany on her hip, caught by the camera as she flicked a V at the reporters. She was a modern tragedy, a walking disaster, the twenty-first century's perfect moral outrage; an ignorant, un-educated, drug-addicted, drunken, neglectful underclass mother of offspring sired by unknown fathers, whose response to the terrible death of her son was to get high and fuck a stranger in public. It had been in public, too, the pictures from a dozen of Darren's mates' mobiles had joined the vet's assistant's photos on various internet sites, where illiterate text-speak messages condemning Sam as a 'hoer' and a 'rotin junky bitch yeah' accumulated like curdled vomit.

Jo-Jo had done well though. There was rumour of her getting her own psychic show on cable, which she wanted to call *Angels Are For Everyone* and which would specialise in family problems. I nearly spat my coffee out over that one. What could she tell the troubled souls who came on her programme to spill their guts? Ignore your kids then make money as quick as you could out of their despair and degradation? Knowing Jo-Jo she'd do just that and manage to make it sound perfectly reasonable; the hypnotic cadences of that beautiful voice soothing the audience into a compliant trance before they had time to digest the appalling nature of what she'd actually said.

I nearly dropped my coffee when my phone rang. One minute I was chuntering out loud about the state of things, the world, humanity in general, the next I was rummaging through my coat pockets like a mad bag-lady going through posh trash. Piff, I thought, it'll be Piff, she's thought about it and wants to . . .

'Annie, is that you? It's Gordon, I saw all the missed calls, I thought I'd give you a bell. Are you . . .'

'Oh - oh, yeah, I'm fine, I'm fine - are you OK?' Without thinking, I checked myself in the kitchen mirror. Why did I do that? It wasn't a video phone, for God's sake. Vanity, it gets you every time.

The phone line burbled slightly in the way that always gave me the impression of laser-like signals bouncing off spiky satellites floating in the vast black cold of space; they turn a little sideways and your voice is morphed to Donald Duck's. I was inordinately pleased to hear Gordon's non-duck-like voice. Very pleased indeed.

He laughed. 'Best as can be expected. I'm in Portugal, that's why I didn't call you back straight off, I'd turned that phone off, it's my work phone. Bloody reporters kept ringin' it non-stop. How's it been for you? They're all mad, they are, stark mad.'

'Portugal? Why . .'

'What? Signal's not that good here, but I wanted to see if you were alright, like. I took leave, took my holidays. Boss said it was best thing, said he could issue a statement, I'd be best off out of it. I weren't keen, but . . . well, I've seen the English papers, I reckon he was right. My partner's mother retired out here, runs a little B&B, it's very nice. Weather's not bad, not boiling but better than home, eh?'

'Your - your partner? I didn't . . .' I could see myself in the bloody mirror; crossly I turned away from that foolish, disappointed face.

'Well, fiancée I should say now, I suppose - we've been together for two year now, but out here, we decided to get wed - did I never mention her? She's always goin' on about that, saying I never introduce her to folk. Emma, her name's Emma, Em, she has two little 'uns from her last fella, useless bugger he were, anyhow, they're our lasses now, eh? So you're OK, yeah? Proper bad do that were, Em got really shook up when she saw that photograph of the - the lad, the creature, whatever it were. She had nightmares, like, thinkin' what could've happened to me, you know. That's partly why we came, she's a bit nervy, high-strung, delicate like. Needs a bit of lookin' after sometimes, you know. Look, I've gotta go, we're takin' the kiddies ter the waterpark - I'll ring yer when we get back, see what's what, mebbe it'll all have blown over by then - *yeah Em, it's Annie Wynter, the lass - yeah, yeah she's fine, yeah, I will* - Em says hi and she says hopes you're alright an' everything. OK, I won't keep yer, you tek care now, see yer.'

'Gordon - thank you, I just want to thank . . .'

But the phone went dead. A lump of plastic and metal in my hand. Jeez, everyone seemed to be going away and coming back from interesting places. Piff went to Goa. Gordon to Portugal. Me? I never left Bradford. Never. Worse than an estate shut-in. Worse than - a partner? Emma? Two little girls? Oh, I see. No, Gordon, I had no idea you were spoken for, as they say.

I felt irrationally pissed off. There was absolutely no reason why Gor should have told me he was taken. Like so many men, if he didn't see a woman as potential totty, he didn't feel any need to apprise said woman of his relationship status. Sometimes blokes didn't bother elaborating on their personal life even if they'd been married for ten years and had six kids, for God's sake. I'd been propositioned by enough roving husbands in my time, men whose partners apparently didn't understand them - which in real terms meant their missus had stopped giving them blow-jobs after the first kiddie came along, and looking at them - crumpled, predatory, half-cut, stinking of fags - I could see why; I wouldn't, either.

And to be fair, I had left Bradford, been on holidays, of course I had. I'd had ten days in Hawaii a couple of years ago, much to the envy of the whole office - especially after I described the lomu-lomu massage I had in glowing, lingering detail. Or what about the weekend in Venice on that £1.50 air ticket offer? I was just being moody. I cracked the living-room window open and lit a Sobranie. I had a rule about not smoking in the flat - no point buying expensive scented candles if all they did was mingle organic ylang-ylang with fag smoke. Still, rules were meant to be broken, especially by me and especially when I made them. I contemplated rolling a spliff from my emergency store of weed but realised I was all out. Niccy-rush it was then. I inhaled deeply and felt the bite in my lungs. Must give up. One day.

It was a bright, sharp day. Bradford sat in a bowl of golden light as if it had been immersed in honey. I was going to Bankcrest later, to see my boy, but in the meantime, I could do anything I wanted. Housework. Laundry. Nip to Tesco's. The world was my lobster now I was 'resting', as it were. I could go to Costa's, have coffee, eat cake. I could go to Cartwright Hall, look at the art then walk round the boating lake, or sit in Centenary Square and watch the poor little hoodie kids trying to offend people by wearing black and snogging each other. Oh yes, I could do anything. Anything at all. Whatever the fuck I liked, in fact. I was a free woman. Fabulous.

I smoked meditatively. Of course I was annoyed about Gordon. No woman, and no man either for that matter, likes to think they're not attractive to someone they fancy, even if they don't fancy them all that much. We all prefer to think the world sees us as desirable, rather than otherwise. I hadn't actually fancied Gor so much as enjoyed his company because he was so practical and pleasant, so - undemanding. Hardly deathless romance, but then, I'd had that and look what it had got me. This.

A cold draught snaked in at the window, hazing the smoke from my cigarette round my face. I coughed and flapped my hand to clear the fumes. My great love. Oh Johnny. Even if I said your name, even after all this time, I still felt that splinter of glass push a little deeper into my heart. Romantic? Oh yes. But if I actually thought about it, almost as destructive as it was glorious.

I wasn't blind to what my passion had brought me; a solitary life, a hermit's existence high on a lonely mountain, wrapped in a devotee's icy robes, my sky-coloured eyes fading as the years went by and the blinding light of my faith burned cold into my vision. What if Johnny and I had stayed together? What if he'd never gone to America for that tour, got those all-important supports with the Chilli Peppers and then the spot at Big Green Dream Festival in Oregon, where the Shank were filmed as part of the documentary that got shown all over the world to rave reviews and a prize at Sundance - Johnny, what a star, my love, what a star you were. That mesmerising performance, you dressed in nothing but a pair of skin-tight metallic pewter jeans and vintage cowboy boots, a heavy Mexican silver rosary bouncing off your perfect brown chest as you threw yourself round the stage

185

like a shaman possessed by a spirit-tiger and the crowd screamed along to 'Black Mirror White Lines'. The furore in the American press about drug references, the cover of *Rolling Stone* with you naked to the waist and maybe beyond, your head thrown back, a look of dreamy ecstasy on your face. The rumours you were being blown by Lainey Stone in the photo and the resultant internet frenzy for the 'uncut' picture. You becoming the hottest of all the young rock-gods, famous beyond your wildest dreams. The dreams I did my best to help you get. That cost me everything.

What if none of that had happened? What if the band had just been moderately successful in Europe, a second-stringer, never really getting to the top for no real reason other than it just happened that way in the business sometimes? What if we'd stayed together for years, despite the age-gap?

What if you hadn't died?

Programmed as I was to the self-abnegation of faith, the nuns, the Virgin, the Sorrowful Heart pierced with swords of pain, the Pieta, the state of Grace and the droning of the priest handing us the white body of the dead son, and His blood in the graven chalice, when the time came and I lost you forever I fell into the arms of devotion to your memory like a drowned swimmer falling through blue water to the silent abyss. I knew what to do. I wanted it. Fight against my religion as I had, deny the experience of my childhood and my youth, when the cool dark called me, I walked in at the gate without question, locking it behind me and renouncing the world without a qualm for the sake of my ghost-bridegroom.

The purity of my love was preserved by its not being touched by the dull hands of habit, worries, treachery or boredom. It was as perfectly preserved as a fly in amber, a rose blooming forever in a crystal ball. Oh, sure, many people would think me mad for living as I did - but I didn't give a shit what anyone thought. My life. My faith. My love. I did it, as the song goes, my way. Who said people were straightforward, logical or simple? Only fools, that's for sure. If I couldn't have my perfect love, couldn't have been my Johnny's age and had that wild ride with him, then I'd have what I wanted - Rapture.

I stubbed the cig out and shut the window. It didn't matter now, anyhow. I could what-if and philosophise all I liked. The past was a far country and a done deal. What was, was. Nothing mattered except Adam. He was my reason for living now, just as Johnny was my reason for dying. The sheer injustice of what was going to be done to my boy made a lump of rage knot in my chest. I might not be able to stop them taking him, but by God, I'd see to it they had me to contend with. Yeah, I bet they thought they had an uncontested fight, that no-one could possibly care what happened to a creature so vilified in the media and loathed by the public at large, who loved - in their ignorance - to hate what they were told to hate without question, thought or pause. Well, sorry, but they'd have a furious bitch to deal with, and nowhere on earth is there anything more single-minded or determined than a woman with a cause. A woman with nothing else in her life but the fight. A woman with a child to defend. What do they call it? Emotionally invested. I was emotionally invested. All my destroyed childhood, my driven youth, my anchorite womanhood was invested in seeing that poor, abandoned child got some kind of justice.

I couldn't change the whole world, re-make it into something kinder, something fairer, something better, but I could do this for one destroyed scrap of humanity.

Put it on my gravestone: *At Least She Bloody Well Had A Go.*

I'd laugh, y'know, if it were funny.

Twenty-three

I turned left at an unmarked, unmade side-road half a mile before the entrance to Bankcrest and drove into the soft grey light of the woods. I had a moment or two's worry that I'd got the wrong road as the jeep bounced on stones and ruts, but the Director's directions had been very specific. In view of the press congregating round the main entrance, it was better I used the old service road and came in the back near The Little House Annexe, where Adam was now housed. The Director would meet me and let me in the service gate, I just had to ring him when I got there, he'd be waiting along with Adam's carers.

The good news was that Adam was doing as well as could be expected, it seemed. He'd eaten at last, some raw minced steak and eggs mashed up together with vitamin powder and his crushed-up meds. His health was good. He seemed to enjoy the chance to be outside in his run, despite the recent rain, though it was proving impossible to get him to wear clothes as yet. He was apparently impervious to the weather and preferred night to day. He slept most of the day. Bit of a rock 'n' roller, then, my boy. Also, forensics had come back with the news that there was nothing in their samples to link Jakey to Adam. Nothing. They tended to the opinion the dog-pack had attacked Jakey and killed him and that Adam may, or may not, have been part of that attack. They couldn't say. However, you couldn't try a dog pack, and even if you could, they'd been shot and disposed of - there was now no way to prove forensically that the dogs had killed and mutilated Jakey. There was only Adam left to blame, only Adam left to punish and - the Director sighed - the public and the media wanted someone to blame. They were insisting someone was to blame.

That was bad enough, but more pressingly, The Director had just been informed that the team from Whitecliffe were due to collect Adam in a fortnight when his quarters there were fully finished and secured. They wanted to meet with me as soon as possible though, as they had been somewhat dismayed to find Adam had a Special Guardian. They hoped, the Director had said, that I was fully aware of my role? He had assured them I was, but they were not convinced and had started looking into ways to void the guardianship. The Director asked I keep this last bit of information confidential. He shouldn't really have told me, but to be frank, he didn't much care for the Whitecliffe team's approach. If I understood him.

I was pretty sure I did, from his tone of voice; I imagine they'd been arrogant and dismissive to someone they considered the janitor of a provincial holding pen for weird trash. They themselves were scientists, researchers, not jailors. Quite a different thing. Oh yes. Still, not that clever at people, it would seem. Everyone has their pride, their bit of vanity, and they'd obviously ruffled the Director's feathers. You catch more wasps with honey than you do with vinegar, as they say. I'd always had trouble with that one myself, but I knew it was true and my training in rock 'n' roll had served to hammer the veracity of that old saw home often enough. Pity scientists, academics and such didn't have to do a couple of months on the road working in some suitably humbling capacity - say tour manager's assistant or a T-shirt seller, living in a fourteen-berth tour bus with a rock band - as opposed to a girl-group or boy-band. Don't ask me to explain the abyssal difference between the two types of outfit, suffice to say one sort behaves like monsters - drugs, drink, temper tantrums, shagging, fisticuffs, cancellations, the lot, while the other works its arse off in a professional, go-get-'em kind of way and does all the drugs and drink and shagging bits as well. Guess which are the monsters?

Working on the road would serve as an excellent short course for anyone who wanted to learn how to get on with other people - in fact, it ought to be mandatory for everyone aged eighteen. Sod wasting your time at a crap Uni. It'd be a sort of Alternative National Service. Perhaps I could write a book called *The Rock N' Roll Life Guide*. Lesson Number One: How To Deal With An Egomaniac Singer On Bathtub Black Speed Who Hasn't Slept For Four Nights And Wants To Cancel The Entire Tour Because He Thinks A Roadie Looked At Him Funny And Is Locked In The Bogs Screaming Blue Murder And Threatening Suicide. That'd be Ultimate Angel, that one, the infamous Köln E-Werk *Carcinomicon Tour* show. Great gig, in the end, mind you, really jumping. In more ways than one, as it goes. I reckon it might give people a few insights into - what do they call it? Oh yeah, conflict management. Hey, maybe I could have a best seller. Go on *Richard and Judy*. Make a million - why not? I'd read some of those big self-help books and all them said the same things, but dressed up in various stupid disguises - you know, do as you would be done by. Shit happens. Stop beating yourself up about stuff in the past. Eat proper food and get off your lardy fat arse sometimes and go for a walk. Don't go out with wankers and expect them to be knights in shining armour. Women Are From Harrogate, Men Are From Barnsley. Like, whatever.

I laughed in my head at the thought of my potential fame and fortune as best-selling author as the unmade road bumped round a slight curve and began to run parallel to the twenty-foot wire perimeter fence surrounding the facility.

191

There were occasional 'Private: Keep Out' signs but on the whole, the shrubs and outbuildings placed near the fence tended to obscure the view of what seemed, if you didn't know better, to be a boarding school, or perhaps a minimum-security prison. Security might seem lax, but then, not many people wanted to spring a ten-year-old rapist-arsonist. They were in there because no-one wanted them anywhere near where they could do again whatever it was that got them in there in the first place. They weren't exactly career criminals with a stash of stolen diamonds, a dodgy porn star bird and a villa in Spain to run to.

I saw the Little House Annexe and pulled up. I was about to ring when I saw the Director waving from the chain-link gate to the side of the compound so I got out and went over.

'He's napping at present, but come in. Welcome - you found the road OK? It's a bit tucked away in the trees there.' The Director spoke through the mesh and smiled, teeth white and even in his pepper-and-salt beard. Normally, I'm not gone on beards but in this case, it reinforced the sturdy, decent-bloke-ishness of the Director. Mark. Mark Albright. I must remember to call him Mark. Must remember he was on my side, as best as he could be. Must keep calm.

'Oh yeah, no problem - I didn't realise it was so, you know, *forest-y* round here, you'd never guess from the front entrance.'

The Director pressed a code into the keypad and opened the gate, handing me a Visitor pass. It all seemed pretty casual, but I knew CCTV was everywhere and no doubt we were being watched. You'd need to be the Human Fly to scale the fence, but I imagine some inmates had tried - human nature, to try and get out of confinement, even if you're twelve. Especially if you're twelve, probably.

The Director smiled again. '*Forest-y*'s the right word actually, some of this wood is classified as actual Ancient Forest, untouched primitive woodland. I like it myself, but some people do say it's a bit claustrophobic, even spooky. Still, each to their own. I don't like beaches and that kind of thing and it is useful having a bit of space between us and the world, as it were. It's all private, no trespassers etc so it does give us some space. I don't suppose many folk round here know what kind of facility we are. Probably best that way - um, look, I'm - well, I'm babbling a bit. Annie, I'm sorry - there's a representative from Whitecliffe here. They sent her up without a prior, just expected to be given free rein. She was told you were expected, she wants to see you. Imogen Cole - Doctor Imogen Cole, I should say. I realise it's short notice - will you see her? While Adam is napping? I have to tell you, I'm sorry, but they're very keen on overturning the Special Guardianship.'

I looked at the small unassuming cottage, apparently so normal, like a gatehouse, yet in reality a high-security holding cell - and the tiny garden where my boy watched the moon or tried to smell the sleeping, silvery world of his little night-time freedom. He'd have none of that at White-cliffe. Just the tests, the procedures, the pain, the fear. I sighed. Perhaps I was being melodramatic. Maybe it wouldn't be so bad. They'd take care of him, he'd be protected. Then I thought about how it would be from his point of view; I thought about how as he had no language, no socialisation, no-one could explain what was happening to him and why it was painful and frightening. How it was no good him getting attached to any of the people he came into contact with because they were scientists, not foster-parents. How they'd move on to other projects, be replaced by new personnel. How eventually, they'd have learnt all they could from Adam and the funding would stop. How he'd end up in a long-term institution for the criminally insane because what foster home would take him and if they did, what would he be? The tame dog-boy, the never quite trustable animal. How he was a strong, healthy young teenager. He could live until he was eighty. He could be alone, treated like mad scum, bullied, abused, tormented and hurt until he was eighty.

'No problem, Mark. I'd be happy to meet with Dr. Cole.' I was very calm.

The Director looked at me closely and smiled the sort of smile that has nothing to do with happiness and everything to do with caution and wariness. 'Good. Good. We'll go up to my office then.'

The Director's office was a masterpiece of beige and khaki, decorated with more of the inmates' artworks blu-tacked to the walls and a pin-board of notices, leaflets, holiday postcards and birthday and Christmas cards. Endearingly misshapen thumbpots and other mystery clay objects were scattered round and a yellow hand-made plate painted wonkily with the name MARK in blue was on the low coffee table opposite his cluttered desk. The plate was filled with paper clips, push pins and the usual office de-tritus. In one of the synthetic bobble-fabric chairs grouped round the table sat a woman, reading some papers. She got up when I came in and The Director introduced us. She didn't smile. I had the distinct feeling that smiling willy-nilly at strangers - anyone - wasn't her forté. The Director introduced us manfully.

Doctor Cole was a short, slightly built woman of about thirty-five with a mass of wiry, matte black hair twisted into a knot and held in place with a brown velvet scrunchie. She was wearing jeans tucked into brown squashy boots and a brown V-neck sweater. Her complexion was olive, Mediterranean, and she wore no make-up or jewellery.

Behind rectangular tortoiseshell frame glasses her eyes were as near to black as eyes get. Not Greek descent, I thought, not Spanish - Portuguese? Brown didn't suit her, made her look sallow. And her scent was a vibrant, chemical citrus; I bet she thought it was modern, fresh, but it was sharp and cloying at the same time. High street. Cheap.

She didn't so much look at me, as study me. I thought about all the interviews I'd done in my life, the hysterical record company executives, agents, musicians, drug addicts and alkies I'd worked for and with, the coke-head paranoiacs and twitchy stoners I'd dealt with. She didn't look so much. I returned her gaze steadily.

She consulted her notes. 'Ah - Mark, I'd like a few moments alone with Ms. Wynter, if that's OK.' Dismissing him, dissing him, a pissing contest. Not talking to me yet. Did she learn all this jockeying for position, establishing dominance crap from a manual? Must put a chapter about it in my book, ha ha. I smiled slightly.

'I'd prefer that Dr. Albright stayed, if that's alright, Dr. Cole.'

That annoyed her, and she didn't realise her square jaw tensed - but I did.

'Ah - well, of course. As you wish. Now, Ms. Wynter...'

'Oh, call me Annie, please, everyone does.' Strike two. I didn't give a shit about status, and given the tight-arsed, hypocritical, oh-so-polite, desperate cut-throat jock-eying for position which was the backbone of any type of academia, that must be a minor headfuck for our Doc C. I watched, dying for a fag but not showing it as the papers were shuffled unnecessarily, the glasses adjusted involuntarily.

Dr. Cole smiled tightly. 'Annie, then. Now, I see you've obtained Special Guardianship for - er, for Adam. My colleagues and I are . . .'

'What are you a doctor of exactly?'

'I'm sorry?'

'What are you a doctor of? Linguistics? Psychology? Medicine - what?'

She looked confused, then pulled herself together. 'I - er, psychology. Abnormal psychology actually. That's really why I'm here, to evaluate the sub - um, Adam, to find out how we can help him, see what damage has been done, if it's repairable. Look, er, Annie - we all want to help Adam, we don't judge him, we're not the police, the courts. He's a remarkable individual, what he's been through, it's . . .'

'Invaluable to your research. You don't get many genuine feral children, do you? And you can't subject a normal child to the years of neglect and lack of human contact that would replicate his circumstances, can you? Wouldn't be allowed. He's a gift from God, isn't he? Your team must be ecstatic.'

The room was stuffy, overheated. Typical council-run, government-run thing - the heating is regulated, never mind if it turns unseasonably sunny, or there's a summer cold snap, you can't change the temperature. A fine sweat glistened on Dr. Cole's upper lip. She should think about waxing that 'tache, I thought. Really. Bet she regretted the chunky knit. I was so angry I felt ice-white and completely calm. I'd jumped past the desire to shout, to get hot and cross, and gone straight onto cold fury. I think it was the patronage inherent in every word she spoke, the *we-know-best-dear* tone and especially, the clumsy manoeuvring at the start of the meeting - that sort of tosh always pissed me off. At GMC, they sent execs on weekend courses to learn stuff like that - the over-hard handshake followed by a slight pulling of the other person towards you to establish control, standing up to take an important phone call, sitting with the light behind you to back-foot people - all that

196

rubbish. Vinny always tried to practice on me. I used to laugh. I wanted to now.

'Annie, please. I'm sure Mark will agree, we all want the best for Adam. I won't deny it's a brilliant chance for science, for furthering our understanding of the human mind, the capabilities of the physical self and . . .'

'Have you met Adam yet?'

Try as she might she couldn't stop a shadow passing over her face. What did my naughty boy do, I wondered? Piss on her boot? 'Oh, er, yes, yes indeed. Of course, as yet he's unused to strangers, as it were, so . . .'

The Director leant forward. 'Adam was very disruptive I'm afraid, Annie. The presence of Dr. Cole seemed to disturb him a great deal. He became quite aggressive. We think that's why he's sleeping now, it seemed to exhaust him.'

Dr. Cole shot him a venomous look. If she'd been from Bradford she'd have been bridling fit to bust.

I looked out of the window. You could see the front gate. Not a journalist in sight. Where were they? Never mind. I sighed again. 'It's your perfume, I expect. Dogs hate citrus smells. He'll have smelt it, it upset him. What is it? Something by Calvin Klein?'

'Calvin . . . I don't . . . No, it's a cologne, I don't know, a Christmas gift from - are you serious?'

I looked away. How could she be so clever, so highly qualified in the study of the human mind, and so thick all at the same time? 'Quite serious, Dr. Cole. Adam has a wild animal's sense of smell. For example, I think that the perfume I was wearing the day I found Adam affected him in some way, was one of the things that prevented him from attacking me. Your scent is - well, it's too harsh for an animal, or for Adam. It would be like you being forced to breathe in the fumes of neat bleach, something like that. It'd be painful, distressing. You see, you want to take him

197

away from here and subject him to all kinds of invasive tests, scare the shit out of him on a daily basis and you don't even think about how he'll perceive you on your first meeting. Can you see why I'm bothered?'

'Ms. Wynter, I'm a psychologist, I specialise in subjects like this - I hardly think some scent would cause the reaction you suggest. Really, it's obvious that Adam lacks all socialisation, is an extremely aggressive. . .'

'He's got a great deal of socialisation, when it comes to dogs. It's humans he can't do. Personally I've got considerable sympathy with him on that score. Oh, let's cut the crap, eh? I'm his guardian. You can try and get rid of me but I intend fighting you. And trust me, Doctor Cole, I'm a good soldier.'

The Director coughed. I'm fairly sure he wasn't covering a laugh. Fairly. The sound dropped into the frozen silence like a gunshot. I nearly had a cardiac but managed not to jump. Doctor Cole on the other hand flinched and dropped her pen. As she bent to pick it up I saw her hand was shaking - slightly, almost imperceptibly, but shaking. Then it struck me. She was afraid, of me and more so of Adam. He scared the shit out of her. She was terrified of him. This whole *Miss In-Control* act was a cover for her fear. How embarrassing for her, how unprofessional. She, who'd probably interviewed mass murderers, rapists, and villains of all stripes was afraid of a teenage boy. But the criminals she'd dealt with were adult men, normal enough apart from their terrible crimes. They could hold a conversation, even if wasn't about anything you'd want to talk about, they could move in society, go to the supermarket, drink in a pub, buy a whore. You could strike deals with them. Trade-off good behaviour for small prison privileges. At all times, she would have been surrounded by security systems, guards, fellow scientists.

What could she trade off with Adam? A doggie chew? A pat on the head and a *good boy, good boy*? Adam was a creature made of iron and blood, a child in a demon's altered body with the power and reflexes of a wolf and the random mind of an infant. You couldn't bribe or cajole him. You couldn't barter with him or promise him goodies in return for co-operation because he literally didn't understand or care about a single fucking thing the Doctor Coles of this world could offer him. He was wild, savage and untameable; like the moorlands or the great crags, like nature itself. He just - *was*.

And that meant our good doctor had no power. No control over him. All she could do was torture him into a cringing submission that cloaked his desire to rip her throat out the first chance he got.

Fear? She stank of it, yellow and sour under her nasty cologne.

She was frightened of me, too. Not like she was of my boy, but still, she was unnerved. People always said I was too direct, too intense even, especially when I'm angry. Piff always used to joke that if I was cross, you could almost see my spine turn into a ramrod, she said I was too skinny to hide it. The phrase 'rigid with tension' could have been coined especially for me. Doctor Cole came from a world where everything was negotiable, where she believed she and her peers were inherently superior, and the likes of me should be a humble supplicant approaching the priestess, not a bony witch glaring at her with icy blue eyes, the static fairly sparking from my twisted braid. She had expected maybe a bored social worker all too willing to offload an onerous task, or even a misguided hand-wringing do-gooder she could patronise and browbeat. She hadn't expected a mother defending her child; she hadn't expected my love for Adam because she couldn't imagine anyone loving the Monster, the Cannibal, the bloody-handed savage.

She hid behind the cold mask her kind wear so well, it was her only defence; her voice was a flat masterpiece of petty triumph. 'Well, Ms. Wynter, I'm very sorry indeed you feel so conflictual about this. Unfortunately, we will be taking Adam to Whitecliffe within the next ten days. I believe we arranged for his transfer on Monday the 12th, Mark? Yes, so, I'm afraid whilst of course we sympathise with your attachment to Adam, given your, er, statements in regard to the guardianship and Adam's care at our facility, I must inform you that we will do what is necessary to ensure Adam has the best care possible and a safe, controlled environment. With us. At Whitecliffe. So, I'm sorry to say, you will be hearing from our law department.'

The big stick. If she could have thumbed her nose at me and gone *yah*, she would have. I'd blown it, of course. I should have wheedled and begged and grovelled for visiting rights, for progress reports. Just to be allowed to see my boy once a month for an hour. To watch him forget me, to watch him diminish, dwindle, become a panting, hollow-eyed shadow. Now she'd do her best to get her revenge on me for challenging her. Not that she'd ever admit that, people like that never do. If you suggest it they raise their eyebrows and smirk. They say you're being a bit paranoid, surely, not to mention a touch egomaniacal? They had far, far better things to think about than you, or vulgar things like petty revenges. Lies, of course. We're all human, wherever we're from, be it Buckingham Palace or the worst run-down slum estate. We all feel what we feel and find ways to assuage our hurt pride. Being superior about it doesn't alter the fact. Doctor Cole would shaft me if she could - in a genteel, middle-class way of course - but she'd do it, right enough.

I nodded and got up. 'Fine. Whatever. Mark, I'd like to see my - to see Adam now, please.'

I turned on my heel and walked out the door.

In my head, something hard and cold clicked and I felt again that strange sensation of being pulled partly into another world, somewhere beyond the reality around me. I smelt the sweet amber and musk of my own perfume, Adam's favourite as I now thought of it, and his face coalesced in my mind's eye, swarming out of a million golden specks - then through it, through it, formed another face; it was speaking but I couldn't hear the words, it was shouting, desperate, but there was no sound. It was Johnny.

I put my hand out and steadied myself against the corridor wall.

'Annie, Annie - are you alright?' The Director's voice pulled me back and I shook my head; why did he have to speak? I'd lost the vision, the - why did he have to speak?

'Oh, yeah - just got up too quickly, I think. Sorry. I'm OK now, really. Sorry.'

He nodded and walked on. I followed.

I knew now, with complete clarity, what I had to do.

Book Four

Azrael

'Love. Of course, love. Flames for a year, ashes for thirty.'

Guiseppe di Lampedusa.

Twenty-four

'Well, I dunno. There's a funny knocking noise from the gear box and y'know, it's seen better days - if you want a straight exchange, it depends on what you're after to be honest.'

I pointed at the battered blue van with the stub of an air vent on top, that I'd spotted in the roadside garage used car lot. 'The old Berlingo. The one with the ventilator.'

'Oh, that - ar, yes. Used to be an RSPCA van that. You got animals, then?'

I smiled. 'Hmm. Yeah. Big dogs. Sick of them messin' up my good vehicle. Thought I'd swap this one for summat more practical, if you see what I mean.'

The mechanic folded his arms and sucked his teeth, then lifting his greasy baseball cap, scratched his scalp with black, broken nails. Across the obstacle course of the yard, the other blokes were buying tea and bacon butties from *Mr. Sandwich's* travelling buttie van. The smell of frying bacon was indescribably delicious. My stomach rumbled, reminding me it had been more than a day since I'd last eaten. The mechanic followed my gaze.

'Well, that's do-able. I'd be a liar if I didn't say yours is worth more than the van - sure you want a swap?'

He wanted his dinner; it was written all over him. Hunger makes people careless. That's why they tell you never to go food shopping on an empty stomach, you'll buy anything, supermarkets count on it. In this case, I counted on a quick deal - and by the way he was ogling the garage lad's fabulously oozing egg and ketchup sarnie, I'd get it.

'Oh - I don't mind, to be honest. Just need the van. You

know - soon as, really. Today, if possible. Gotta take those big boys off on their hols you see.'

'Ah - Alsatians are they? Or Rotties? I do like Rotties, me, had one meself once. Tyson I called 'im on account of him bein' a right scrapper, geddit? Yeah, but anyroad, the Missus didn't get on wi' him, had ter get rid. Got a Jack Russell instead. Bites worse than Tyson, but there we are, she don't see it that way. That van's ideal, though, got the vent, plenty of air, the silverin' on the back windows is a bit iffy but it'll last a while an' there's a grille and board between front an' back - don't want them fellas jumpin' in yer lap halfway down the motorway, do we? Got yer paperwork? If not, I can hold on until . . .'

I pulled the plastic folder out of my bag. 'No, it's all here. We can do it now - or if you want yer snap . . .?'

He smiled. He had a nice smile, it lit his homely face up. Dirt granulated in the crows feet by his soft brown eyes. I wondered if he'd be smiling so warmly if he knew what I was going to do with the tatty little van. Maybe not. But he didn't know and we did the business double quick, rung the insurance, all that bollocks and I drove off in the Berlingo, catching a last glimpse of the mechanic snaffling a sarnie the garage's lad had got for him. He looked like he was enjoying it.

I wasn't enjoying the Berlingo which handled like a dead pig on a skateboard, but my vehicular preferences didn't matter. The van was a tool. Same as the cottage in Wales, near Snowden, I'd rented via the blessed internet. I'd made a few personal changes, too, just to get the whole thing going - I'd started wearing my trendy little square black-framed specs which normally I didn't bother with unless I was tired, and cut six inches off my hair. I put a hazel-brown semi-permanent on it, then put it up in a loose twist with a nippy-clip rather than my doing my usual braid so the rather uneven ends resulting from my home barbering didn't show. I banged on a spot of red lipstick, too, which normally I never wore, and dug out an old red pashmina scarf that had been lying at the bottom of a drawer for years, knotting it at my neck in that pull-through-the-loop way Tamsyn always favoured.

You'd be surprised how different all those little changes made me look. It doesn't take much to alter the way you appear, much less than folk think. A make-up artist I knew told me, she said people always went too far, made themselves look false with bad wigs and weird clothes they'd never normally wear. You had to work with what you'd got, so you felt natural, but as if you'd decided to a bit of a make-over on your existing wardrobe and look. She was so enthusiastic on the subject I began to wonder if she were planning a bank job, but it turned out she worked for one of those agencies that help big celebrities get around unnoticed.

I'd sorted a few other bits too, like setting up an email account in the name of Anne Eliot, and I booked the rent-a-cottage through it. The owner, Evan, took cash, which made life much easier. He was new at the holiday home game and didn't ask for a credit card number for security. If he had, I was going to say Wynter was my married name and look tragic, like I didn't want to talk about it. I hinted at a recent divorce to set the scene but he never said a dickybird about a card when he had a nice, tidy stack of twenties in his hand. Let him think my finances were a bit irregular after my recent break-up. Whatever. I took a wodge of readies out of my account in three goes, too, just in case. You never know when you'll need actual money, instead of virtual plastic wonga.

I'd been down to the cottage at the weekend, in my new persona, to put down the deposit and two weeks in advance with Evan and get the key. I made myself appear suitably interested when he discussed his plans to do up the tumble-down outbuildings into flats and secretly rejoiced he wasn't intending to start work on them until next autumn. It was perfect as it was - for my purposes. Stuck on a hillside, over two miles from the one-street village, the main little farmhouse converted into a 'remote and peaceful' holiday let. It would have been my idea of an anti-vacation, normally, given I'm a sun, sea and slingbacks type of girl in regard to holidays. A wet winter in Wales miles from anywhere would not exactly have been my ideal destination. I'd be lucky if I saw the sun for five seconds at a time. The cottage was snug enough though; uneven floors, plank doors with forged iron latches, low beamed ceilings, rough-plastered walls. It could have been very bijoux but the décor was a miasma of cheap yellow varnished pine and a clashing mélange of bloated florals that rioted unchecked on every loose-cover, frill, flounce, valance, ruched cushion and dainty tie-back like Laura Ashley on acid. But it had central heating and a big old telly and DVD player. What more could I want?

'A bit lonely out here,' Evan had said as he locked up after our brief tour. He had big, square red hands and wore a padded check shirt and an elderly green body-warmer. In his Landie, his lurcher stared morosely at the rain-soaked hillside, desperate to go rabbiting. 'Sure you won't mind?'

'Oh - no, no, not at all. I'm looking for total peace, you know complete quiet so - so I can finish my, er, book. You know how it is, deadlines.' I laughed casually, like a sophisticated yet professional writer-type. Citified. Arty. Bit dizzy but pleasant enough. The sort of person they do Hollywood rom-coms for the older set about, starring Michelle Pfeiffer and that dreadful smirker George Cluny.

'Ah, writer are you? Should I have heard of you, then?'

I simpered. Yes, I did. I'm not proud but I did. I was well into the part at that point, almost believed it myself. 'No - no. Just a hack writer really, I do - er - self-help books, stuff like that. For a company that churns out that kind of thing. Boring really. Still pays the rent, better than a proper job, eh?'

He smiled. 'Yeah. Well, you'll get all the quiet you'll need out here. This was my gran's place, I had to do somethin' with it, the farmin's gone you know. Williams has a few sheep over the hill, but it's not enough these days. Still, I didn't want to let it go. Sentimental, I s'pose. I hope you'll enjoy it anyway. You need anythin', just give me a ring, no problem. Let's hope you get nice weather, well, not that you'll be bothered about that but at least you'd be able to get some walks. Have a break, you know, from the writing.'

'Walks - yeah, that'd be great. Well, I'll bring some things over then I have to pop back again for a quick - um - progress meeting in London with my editor, you know, then I'll be back to settle in properly. Can't wait, lovely here, really.'

I'd waved at him cheerily as I drove off down the bumpy road; Min Y Mynydd, the House At The Foot Of A Mountain the cottage was called, according to the website. 'Mountain' was pushing it in regard to the black hill that sloped away into the fells, the cottage crouching at its foot like a lost child taking shelter from the wind that unceasingly blew the scents of wet earth and stone in cold, fluttering ribbons down from the distant valleys. God alone knew how to pronounce Min Y Thingie. *Minny Minið?* Didn't matter. I wasn't intending talking to anyone if I could avoid it.

So I'd swapped the jeep and filled the van with necessities. The black cashmere wrap. Johnny's framed photograph and the Memory Box. Candles, face grease and two bottles of Ambre Passion - Adam's Favourite. My laptop. Phone charger. Food. Ten packs of Black Sobranie. The pink wellies. My knackered old black festivals and open-air gigs industry standard North Face waterproof and the matching down jacket, now extruding feathers like a dying duck. My I-Pod and I-Trip, the good American one not the crappy Euro version. An assortment of books and DVDs, including the Big Green Dream Festival documentary. A thick, furry leopard-print Minky blanket of the sort you can only ever get in Bradford and that's the most comforting thing in the world, and a big box of those painkillers with the muscle relaxants. And my stash. I couldn't see myself scoring much weed in the village post office. Mind you, shouldn't assume - you do hear about Women's Institute stoners, maybe they did a wicked hash-fudge along with the usual vanilla and chocolate kind in the Spar. I could live in hope.

It seemed further on the second trip to the cottage than it had on the first, not that I minded and, probably, it was the van's fault, it not being exactly nippy. It was about seven when I finally coaxed the poor old motor up the lane and parked up. I got out and lit a black fag as a kind of reward for my patience with the slug-van. The hillside, knotted with outcrops of lichen-splotched greenish rock, swept up behind the little cottage like a rising wave into an evening sky netted with stars - you could see them all in the deep blue, it was so far away from the city's light pollution. It was beautiful, still and clear, laced with a sheen of ice, almost silent except for the soughing wind and the far-off stuttering cough of a fox. It was perfect. Sweet. The air was like country wine, all frost-rimed bracken and old apples. I wondered how long I'd be able to stay before I had to move on.

On the way back, with the Pod shuffling through my music like a tiny demented DJ, I was almost content. I only had to pull into the services once to cry, when 'Missing You (It's Gone)' came on. What a great voice my Johnny had. I mean it, fantastic, what a showman. Like I always said to him - you know - *just sing the fuckin' song, baby, if the work's good enough, that's all you need to do - no tricks, no lies, no clever-clever dickery. Just sing.* And he did, he sung his heart and soul out, proper, no holding back. He'd have understood what I had to do, he'd have known that sometimes, you had to break rules in a good cause. To do the right thing. People didn't realise how much Johnny felt things, how sensitive he was. OK, he wasn't political, I mean, who is these days, given that all the politicians are complete wankers more corrupt even than record company execs - that old hippie saw about it not mattering who you voted for because the government always got in had finally come true after all. But Johnny hated injustice, the system grinding people to a bloody mush, the straight world's petty tyranny. He would have been on my side, helped me. I know he would. He would.

Because I had no choice, no choice at all. I had to do it. It was the only possible way.

I had to get my son out of prison.

211

Twenty-five

The hardest thing to organise was the thing I'd thought would be the simplest - getting a decent pair of bolt-croppers. I'd driven up to B&Q assuming I'd be able to get some easily, but no - it seemed you had to go to a specialist supplier, and try your hardest not to look like a vandal or a robber. After I'd fiddled with a lock of hair artfully escaping from my new twist and pursed my red lips - not too tightly at my age, mind you, after all, I was aiming for vaguely pouty not old drawstring shoe-bag - whilst sighing that silly hubbie had sent me on an errand and, *oh dear, what was I to do?* The assistant I'd accosted gave me the name of a firm he'd got stuff from when he'd worked in the building trade. What a gent.

At least I wasn't worried about the media for a bit. I could have walked in my building carrying a loaded Kalashnikov unnoticed these days. The hack-pack had moved off to fresh pickings in the form of a scandal involving that poor old pop-tart Teena B. Aged and hor-rifically surgically-enhanced though she might be, she was eight-months gone with the crack baby of her new - and now ex - squeeze, waster indie-rock drug-celeb Mick Bran-nigan. At one and the same time, Brannigan's secret affair with the wild-child daughter of the Senior Minister For Health was outed (to the general public), when said daughter was caught on film by a pal with the ubiquitous mobile, cheating on her Man United striker fiancé with Brannigan and smoking crack whilst bent over the minister's very recognisable red velvet Eduardo Mendes sofa. She was clad in nothing but a rather nice pair of green silk tie-side Agent Provocateur knickers and Brannigan was doing to her from behind what boys like that will do to girls in pants like that. Or indeed, dogs, sheep or melons in pants like that. The video was a huge hit on Youtube, naturally. The whole thing threatened to bring down the government, as the Minister was notoriously outspoken in his views about the evils of drugs and our decadent society and this was a sleazy final straw that might break the ruling camel's back. If the press knew that the politician I'd once seen eating an interesting entrée whilst coked off his man-jugs was now the Senior Health Minister in question - a fact which had always made me laugh a great deal - the government wouldn't so much come down, as implode. I filed that thought away for just-in-case purposes. Sadly, mobiles didn't come with video in those days, what a shame.

But there we are. I'd known the media would move on to pastures new eventually, their appetite is only stimulated by what reeks of fresh blood. I knew if I kept my head down and said nowt, sooner or later they'd be off and sure enough, there wasn't a whisper of a journo anywhere. I was relieved, to say the least, given what I intended. It was Sam and Jo-Jo who'd feel betrayed and violated as the lovely, lovely people with their sympathetic expressions and soft, caring voices dropped them like tainted carrion and tore off to seek out trout-pouty, bazooka-bosomed Teena and her scandalous chums - the whole thing was completely brilliant for all their careers, of course, and they were moaning like mad about media intrusion, but they were pros, they knew how to play the game. The press must have been howling with joy when the various publicists released that farrago.

Anyhow, all that aside, the bloody bolt-croppers held me up somewhat, but while I waited and searched around for them, I'd got some thick sheets of foam rubber from the place in town that cut it to size for you and glued it - wonkily, it must be said - to the van's interior walls and floor. Then I'd thrown in a cheap mattress, four market-stall heavyweight quilts and a few old pillows from my bed. Hopefully the smell of me would linger on them. I sprayed a bit of Adam's Favourite around too, which I thought might help. Then I made a doctor's appointment. Given that it normally took ten days to get seen, I had to pray for a cancellation and ring up at some ungodly hour in the morning; fortunately, my luck was in and I saw the quack straightaway.

I was having trouble sleeping, I said to the harried-looking locum, assuming a pious expression. Work was stressing me out something terrible and my partner - well. Run away with a younger woman, the bastard. It was very upsetting (not too upsetting though, I didn't want her putting me on suicide watch). I just needed something to, you know, start my sleep rhythm again. Nothing major - some sort of Valium thing? I tried not to seem too knowing about drugs, doctors hate that, nor did I fidget as she stifled a yawn and wrote the script for a dozen tablets of ten meg Temazepam. I also managed not to smile when I left the depressing grubby pastel shed housing the practice; I was supposed to be suffering, after all.

Oddly, I wasn't. Suffering, that is. Far from it, in fact. If anything I felt weirdly liberated and calm. I slept - in reality - like a child and woke with a smile. It was as if a great weight had been lifted from me. I'd made a decision, and now things would turn out how they did. It was fate; what would be, would be. I wouldn't have to grovel to Bob for my job back, or wrestle with the bureaucracy that tied social work up in a throttling gag of paperwork and jargon. I knew my little adventure wouldn't last, it was mostly a gesture of defiance, but I was making the gesture, I was running the show, I wasn't being pilloried for trying to help someone in need like when I did my best for Sam, or patronised and dismissed by the powers that be. I was free, I was giving twos-up to the establishment and I was giving my son one last chance to be free, before they nabbed us both.

Oh sure, I could understand many people would be horrified by what I was doing. Of course they would. A lot of them would simply think I was stark mad and belonged in an asylum. We were bound to be caught, bound to be slammed in jail quicker than a breath, so what was I ruining my life for? I could hear Piff in my mind running through the pros and cons in her logical way and not actually coming up with any pros whatsoever. But I didn't care, I really didn't. I accepted my fate, embraced it, even. It felt like the first blissful rush of cocaine, but much, much better; it was the pure, blinding exhilaration of jumping off the cliff into the arms of God, into the hands of something greater than your petty, squirming, spineless, scrabbling, soft ordinary little self. It was Glory.

If I was mad, well, so be it. But it was insanity that sparked and ignited in my heart like the fire of angels, the flame of grace. If you've never felt it, you can't believe how beautifully crazy it is. And it filled my head with energy - and ideas.

For one - I'd had a bit of a brainwave after my chat with Evan. On the way home, I'd thought - why not write a book? Like I'd thought before when I'd toyed with the idea of writing my memoirs - only really actually do it? I mean, obviously, I wasn't actually a writer but I reckon anyone who reads a bit and can string a sentence together grammatically could write a book. You just had to be determined, stick at it. Look how many dreadful, leaden bestsellers with cardboard characters, predictably twisty plots and laughable prose I'd ploughed through, or thrown across the beach in disgust. The people who churned them out made millions - reached millions of readers, and they were peddling rubbish. Well, if they reckoned *they* could write a book, God, I knew *I* could. I'd write the story of my life and Adam's. But - here's the cunning bit - I'd write it in a funky, really modern kind of way, as if it were a sort of off-the-wall self-help book, not a straight-forward account of what I was about to do. Make it more interesting, more - literary, if you know what I mean. Not cheesy. That would get the London arty crowd interested and people like that are well useful if you want to have something taken seriously - they do fancy themselves the arbiters of taste and intellectual merit, above petty bourgeois concerns about morality and decency. If they're with you, it's *Newsnight Review* and monochrome serious photo inter-views in *The Guardian Supplement*. If not, you're lost in the artistic wasteland of the tabloids.

I thought about it quite deeply. It was fun running scenarios in my head then discarding them, rehearsing what I'd say in interviews, stuff like that. It had to be real, though, I certainly didn't want the book to come out like yet another ghost-written *True Crime*, or pathetic-victim-tells-all. Or worse still, like a glamour-model-weather-girl-failed-celeb autobiography-style whinging self-justification. It had to be done properly. Be cool. I'd start it like it was a handbook for how to survive in rock 'n' roll, just as I'd first imagined, mix it up with all the great stories I knew about the industry, and our own tale, too. And Johnny's. I'd tell his true, proper story as well. A kind of Rock 'N' Roll Magic Realism. It'd go like hot cakes when all the publicity hit, about me getting Adam out and why I did it. And yeah, it'd show how Jakey had really died and how Sam was condemned out of hand without a hearing and how the likes of Jo-Jo, the vet's bastard assistant and even the stupid delivery boy from the Co-op - whose appalling metal band Dogs Of Death had been booked for Download Festival on the strength of the publicity he'd got, according to the *Bradford Telegraph & Argus* music column - benefited from everyone else's misery and pain.

Then, you see, no-one could secret Adam away somewhere, and torture him covertly in the name of science. He'd have a profile, he'd be Someone, not just a nameless monster gawped at then forgotten by the public. He'd be famous - or infamous, more like, but in this day and age the two were interchangeable. If I managed it well, got a good agent and everything, there'd not only be the book in the UK, it'd all go international. There'd be films, documentaries, questions asked. The media spotlight would illuminate not just us, but those people who thought of Adam as just an expendable lab rat. He'd be safe, or as safe as I could make him. Safe in that terrible, searching light, not forgotten in the shadowy corners of some institute half-life. I'd use the press as they'd used us. Yeah - yeah - dangerous - but it was a weapon I knew, albeit an unstable one.

And truthfully? It was the only thing I could think of to do for him. I wasn't wealthy or connected. I wasn't powerful. I didn't have publicists and media handlers, expensive lawyers and global corporate backers. I was just an unemployed middle-aged woman from the frozen fucking Northlands. But I had something all those people in power feared. I had nothing left to lose. Nothing.

That's always scary for the people you're fighting; how can they threaten you if you have nothing they can destroy? How can they strip you of what you don't have? How can they bribe you if you don't want what they're offering? How can they shut you up if you keep on shouting no matter what?

They can kill you.

Maybe they'd try. But if I had our stories in print first, well, that wouldn't matter to me, not anymore.

Wild Thing, oh, Wild Thing - my Wild Things, how I love you both, but - you know what? How could they kill me, Johnny, when you'd already done that?

Twenty-six

The moon was a sickle of ice in the cloudless indigo night sky; it barely showed any light and when I turned the van's lights off as I coasted along the slight incline of the forest road at the back of the facility, I was momentarily blind until my eyes re-adjusted. The faint glow from the perimeter lights gave enough illumination for me to guide the free-wheeling van bumpily towards Adam's enclosure, but I stopped just on the curve before the gate so, hopefully, no-one would notice the dark-coloured vehicle or its number plates - fake ones, I might add; I had two pairs, one set for now, one set for later, both done for me amazingly cheaply by an obliging chap on the Leeds Road - obscured with mud, parked close up against the trees. It was my biggest worry, being seen before I could get sorted - well, not true really, it was my second biggest worry. My worst fear was about to be put to the test.

Creeping out of the van, dressed as a sort of Women's Auxiliary SAS nutter in black everything, including a black headscarf wrapped around my head like a faux-Ninja, I felt reflexively for the doped meatballs stashed in my pockets. There was enough Valium in the four patties of raw mince to fell a horse; I only hoped it would work quickly. I eased the bolt-croppers - bloody things, cost an arm and a leg - from out of the back and left the doors open. I couldn't chance fiddling with them and at three in the morning it was fairly unlikely that anyone else would be around to nosey then raise the alarm. But speed was of the essence. I had to be quick and not fuck up. Everything depended on me not fucking up. It was amazing how my heart was pounding; *bang bang bang* in my bony chest; I thought it would knock right out of me. I could see the tremor of it through my hoodie - it made me grin mirthlessly; just like the good old days and one line too many, eh? My God, if Vinny and the girls at GMC could see me now - they'd shit themselves. If Piff - well, Piff would just call the coppers without question. Things like this didn't happen in Piff's logical world. Or so she thought. She didn't count Lina of course. We are all blind in love, me included. Me more than most, I suppose. Oh well.

Finally I stood in the scrubby undergrowth opposite Adam's yard. Tomorrow, they'd take him to Hell. The extremity of the whole situation now seemed perfectly normal; it's amazing how making a decision clears the mind and steadies the nerves. I imagine suicide bombers feel the same. Once you step over that line, it's a done deal. It's shilly-shallying and faffing that gives you stress. I wasn't stressed. Scared shitless I'll give you, but stressed as in *oh, will I meet that deadline or will the boss shout at me?* No. My spirit moved in me like the wings of grace, it was better than any drug I've ever taken and I couldn't shift that rictus grin off my face.

Mind you, my legs were shaking with adrenalin, my guts were churning and my mouth felt as if it had been swabbed dry with cotton-wool. I clutched the bolt-croppers to me as if they were a comfort blanket not a big, heavy, awkward lump of steel. My mind was dinning warnings, too, of course - I'm only human. The echo and re-echo of my thoughts were reduced to one phrase; *go now and save your-self.* I could. I could just go, forget everything, run. Forget Adam. Forget Bradford. Make a new life abroad - I might be OK, I might even be happy, in time. I might . . .

In the yard, a dark figure loped silent as an owl flying up to the fence and sniffed the air, phosphorescent disks gleaming briefly in the moonlight. He smelt me. I knew he smelt me. I froze, and after a minute Adam moved off towards the cottage, a shadow amongst shadows, the dim moonlight sliding over him like metallised water. He didn't go far, just hunkered down on his haunches, as if he were waiting. I couldn't see for certain but I felt with every pore of my body that he was watching me - not in a malevolent way, but just watching. He definitely knew I was there, not just any human, but me. He knew me and he was waiting to see what I'd do.

Which was my biggest fear. I was afraid of him and I don't mind admitting it. He wasn't predictable like normal, tame people. I couldn't be sure what he'd do, what he was thinking or indeed if he even thought like the rest of us. I'd once seen an artist's impression of the way a fox might see and interpret the data it got from its senses; did Adam see that strange, surreal chaos and make his choices based on it? No doubt of it, I was proper afraid of him, as anyone would be of a half-grown tiger or a wolf. It was the natural fear of the predator, but I couldn't give in to it, I had to master it and him, for his own good. But - as much as I felt that fear I was attracted to the power of it. You hear about people who are drawn towards wild animals, men who go off for months to live with bears or wolves, or women who prefer to live around gorillas, and often they pay the price because fascinated as we might be, when it comes to it, that beautiful, huge, amazing polar bear would just as soon eat your head as not. They aren't fucking poodles or teddies, they aren't cute and safe; like a fella I saw on a wildlife documentary said about stupid people who try to keep wolves as pets because they're caught up in that Wild And Free Warrior nonsense - don't have them round your kids because sooner or later that toddler will be your lovely pet wolf's dinner.

221

Was that what happened to Jakey? The forensics people had said there was no actual proof, but - did Adam? I couldn't think about that, I couldn't. I couldn't blame him if he had - done that. It wasn't like he knew any better, none of our conditioning; the building blocks of our so-called civilisation weren't even in his head. If he had done what everyone said he'd done, it would have been no more to him than bringing down a stray lamb. The pack must eat.

I shook my head as the thoughts I couldn't prevent swarmed round me like biting insects. Of course I loved Adam, that was a given. If I didn't, I wouldn't be here, *going equipped* as they say, in the middle of the bloody night outside the back of a secure facility, trying to spring an inmate, my whole life as a respectable citizen hanging by a frayed thread. Love, sure. No problem. But the object of my love was a feral creature stronger and faster than any attack dog going, with no language, no socialisation and very few human attributes whatever - what if he attacked me? What if he was spooked and just bolted? In other words, how much, if any, control did I have over him?

I didn't have the answers to any of those questions, just as I'd had no time to get Adam accustomed to me or familiarise him with basic commands - all that stuff they do on those *Train Your Dog* programmes that are in fact, train the owner shows. I wasn't this wild boy's owner, I was his mother. He'd chosen me, but would that be enough?

I stood shivering. Then it occurred to me. It was go-time. Either I did this and took the consequences, or left. Walk the walk or fuck off with my tail between my legs and pretend I'd never been here.

I walked over to the fence and started cropping. Ping, ping, ping. The chain-link gave like butter in the jaws of the heavy-duty cropper.

I supposed it took a couple of minutes, no more, but it

felt, as they say, like fucking hours. The croppers were heavy and difficult for someone not used to them, but in my favour there was only one layer of interlock fencing because as I said, no-one wanted these kids out, not even their families. High the fence might be, but it wasn't that thick and I cut a ragged flap, then pulled the drugged meat from my pocket and held it out.

He came, moving smooth and fast. In a blink he was at the fence, head on one side, sniffing the meat-scent, eyeing the hole in the barrier.

I sang, in a whisper shaky with terror. *Wild Thing, you make my heart sing you make . . .*

He pushed through the flap, taking the meat from my hand with his mouth before I'd quite registered what he was doing. I felt his breath hot in my palm, like a kiss. He butted me with his head, and I rubbed his scalp with my knuckles, like you do a pony. He grunted and I walked towards the van a few steps my heart in my mouth. He followed. I gave him another patty. There was no going back. My son was free.

Power radiated from him like a fume; a sheer physical strength that rippled through his frame in tight webs of muscle layered sheet over sheet to form configurations of flesh that warped him out of humanity into some other, older place. I could feel the heat of him, his normally elevated temperature notching up with adrenalin. He paused, snuffing up the damp earthy smell of the woods at night, the patchouli odour of leaf mould, the bite of pine needles' dark essential green.

And through it all was the sweet aromatic of that most archaic of scents, amber, laced through and lifted with musk and vanilla, his favourite perfume as I thought of it, overlaying the smell of me, of his chosen, of his Ma. He turned and looked back at his prison then followed me, close at my heels as I walked to the open doors of the van.

His proximity was a thing so exciting, so magical, that I felt half faint with it. He was a creature from another world, a being out of some primitive cul-de-sac of the human species; what we could have been, what we sold for a mess of pottage. Again he butted my hand and I laid it on his rough head, the hair beginning to spiral again from the crop that had sheared his crazy locks, not wiry or coarse but thick and soft; you could feel the mass of shining ringlets he would have if he was cared for, if I could care for him.

I paused at the open doors. This was the vital moment. I lobbed a patty into the van and patted the mattress on the metal floor.

'Baby, come on, come on sugar, in you go, go on darlin' go on, go on - *wild thing, I think I love you* - come on, Adam, please please get . . .'

He sprang up into the van, quicker than I could take a breath. For a heart-stopping moment, his beautiful, weird face was on a level with mine. He cocked his head again and rubbed his cheek against mine. He smelt of wildness; a thick funk of unwashedness and heated flesh. His breath was sweet and musky, hot as blood against my ear.

'Maa, Ma . . .'

Then he was snuffling amongst the quilts for the last patty and I shut the doors, locking them with hands that shook like a palsied gimmer's and I drove away, away, away fast as the crappy old vehicle would go. The whole thing had taken less than ten minutes but my life had changed forever.

My son was safe. We were together. I'd never let them take him without a fight the like of which they could only dream of. I would die for him. I would . . .

And in my head black wings beat like sheets of iron clashing together while a face coalesced out of the rain that started to bead the windscreen, dark eyes fixed on mine, a face full of sorrow and terrible regret that opened its beautiful, familiar lips, lips I'd kissed a thousand times, and cried my name and I thought *Johnny, Johnny, soon, my love, soon* and I didn't give a flying fuck about the world, the law or the stupid sad and shameful hypocrisy of the Judas straight world anymore.

All I cared about was love.

Twenty-seven

At first I was so busy concentrating on getting out of the woods along the bumpy track that I didn't register Adam was howling like a demented banshee and throwing himself round in the back. The van rocked and I grew shit-scared he'd break the back doors open and leg it into the night. For a moment I considered stopping and checking on him as he thrashed about, but it would be pointless. In a way, he was set on a path now too, and he would have to accept it. Also, the drug would kick in eventually, before he wore himself out and got overly distressed. Better to crack on, better to run far and fast before the alarm was raised, which wouldn't take long, if it wasn't already in progress. I had a momentary twinge of guilt when I thought about the facility Director - he was a very decent bloke and if I stretched a point I could imagine he'd tacitly approve of what I'd done. If I stretched a point, that is, like, to infinity. He might not want Adam to go to Whitecliffe, but he'd never have consented to this. No-one in their right mind would.

As I drove and the banging and noise in the back faltered and died out to a heavy snoring, the phrase *in their right mind* repeated over and over in my head. Was I in fact, mad? Properly mad as in, you know, insane? After all, mad people supposedly didn't realise they were mad. Were my visions of Johnny the harbingers of insanity? Was what I'd done the product of massive and destructive delusions? I didn't feel mad, but what did mad feel like? I could justify what I'd done, but so could demented serial killers if the true-crime type films were anything to go by. I'd always known some people would think I was completely off my head and should be locked up, of course I had. But it had been a passing thought, not something I'd dwelt on. But - I mean - what if - you know, I was actually bonkers? Would I suddenly start losing the plot and wobble out of control, just sit in the van weeping and gibbering until some copper found us and carted Adam off to Whitecliffe and me to Broadmoor to be locked up forever with the paedos, rippers, and cackling fire-setters? Would the asylum that many would think I really belonged in become a reality? Would I end up wrapped in a chemical straitjacket, drooling and lobotomised, trying to make thumb-pots in Art Therapy with no memory of myself left, no memories of Johnny, of Adam, of freedom until I died alone and in terror in my institutional bed, locked down, locked up and royally screwed?

I knew the reality of long-term institutions, I'd been a fucking social worker, I'd dealt with it all, been sickened and made furious by it. I knew what happened to the inmates. The things no one wanted to talk about, the things that had always gone on since Bedlam and before and always would. The late abortions performed on wholly catatonic women who couldn't possibly, despite the claims of the staff, have initiated sex. The black bruises wrapping unloved old people from neck to toes that could not have been caused by them 'falling out of bed', like, in any way unless they'd fallen from the roof, rolled down a hill and been caught up in a thresher. Human beings left to sit in their own piss for hours and days. People terrified beyond comprehension, tormented, and abused. If you were sane when you went in, a fortnight on the drugs they shelled out like sweeties guaranteed you'd never be right again, even if you managed to get out alive. No-one wanted the inmates of those places, no-one. They were the warped and shredded living dead, the mottled carcasses of the previously real

227

who jerked spasmodically into a yawning void of terminal unreality. No-one wanted to think about how they were treated. The best you could do was hope to God you never got put in there with the poor bastards.

As I drove along the motorway, the rain closed in around the van in unfolding sheets of black pearl, the shimmering iridescence of oil sheening the snaking tarmac. I found myself looking for the first time properly at a fate so awful only death was preferable. Sure, I'd known if it went tits up it'd be bad, but I hadn't really allowed myself to dwell on the details. Now in the dark, on the road, with the deed done and spark out in the back of the van, it began to hit me. Honest to God, if it was prison, maybe, *maybe* I could hack it. Prison was an excruciating limbo of boredom and constraint but it was human. Asylums were the portals of unimaginable horrors that made Hell look like a Halloween theme park. Death was most certainly - most abso-fucking-lutely certainly and completely preferable.

At first I thought that dramatically, in a kind of *Death Or Glory* tattoo way. Then, as the miles passed, I began to realise I meant it. Oh, everyone in the West was so afraid of death, it was another thing - yet another thing - no one wanted to deal with. Yet, we all die. No one lives forever, just as no one's young forever. The universal truths that everyone seems to want to avoid loom up despite our cowardice like the sunrise and the sunset. Inevitable and always freshly shocking. It will happen. You will die. I will die. Adam will die. Johnny - well. Yeah. It wasn't so bad, I thought. I'd lived a life. I'd done stuff. Lots of stuff. I'd had the kind of life many people can only dream of and I knew it was a media-manufactured sham, a shill, a joke. That the in-crowd parties were just parties, no better in reality than your twenty-first at the Liberal Club, the people dressed in no better taste, their behaviour no better and no different from you catching your bird/fella getting hot 'n' heavy with someone else in the toilets or your cousin having a punch-up with a schoolyard rival. Everyone takes cocaine now if they can get it, and they can. Everyone drinks themselves stupid and shows their arse for the camera and usually, the world-wide-web. There are no 'betters', no higher end of society, no moral examples, no boundaries. No God, no Devil, no hellfire - and no heaven. Just some folk who can afford expensive things and some who can't; some who drink Cristal, some who neck Morrison's own-brand fizzy white. This is the West. We have everything.

Except courage. We don't have that. We can't bear to face the realities of our lives, we can't die.

But I could. And given the alternative, if it all went horribly wrong, if I couldn't draw the media with my book, if I couldn't save Adam, then better death than - than - the other thing.

So I was pretty cheery as I thundered towards the cottage - it was the adrenalin leaving my system, the release of a tension I hadn't properly appreciated that had been shrink-wrapping me in invisible, ever-tightening bonds. Then a wave of drenching depression, grey as drainwater, flooded through me bringing the jittery flotsam of uncertainty and regret knocking against my mind like the pallid, gormless corpses of the drowned. Sod it, I had to stop and have a fag and coffee break, so despite my misgivings I pulled into the services and parked bang in the middle of the car park because if Adam did something bonkers it wouldn't make any difference if I was skulking in the truck park or not, frankly.

The telly was on in the café, and I scanned it anxiously for news, but it only showed the lead stories of the day - some American hotel heiress's latest sex scandal and the recent anti-gay arson attack on that big nightclub in Leeds.

229

Sex and death, dontcha just love it? Nothing sells better. Still, there was nothing about us. Yet. I toyed with the idea no one had noticed Adam was missing as I chewed my waxy concrete-hard Danish and sipped the machine coffee. But I didn't really kid myself. They knew, they'd have known minutes after it happened. The only reason I'd managed to do it at all was because it was utterly unthinkable. That meant it hadn't been anticipated. If it had been, I couldn't have got within a mile of Adam. But the things I'd thought as I was driving, about society not wanting to deal with stuff, had given me a loophole to crawl through; nobody, but nobody wanted the kids in the facility out in the general population. To Mr. and Mrs. Average UK they were tainted, ruined, repulsive, terrifying. Therefore, no one thought anyone might actually spring one, least of all, the Cannibal Killer, the Beast Boy, the freak of freaks.

It put me in mind of a conversation I'd once had with Johnny. I'd asked him how he got away from the life that had been so fully mapped out for him. The good, steady job. Marriage to the pretty, sensible girl in the family church with dear old Father O'Shea officiating. Babies. Holidays in Spain, family parties at Christmas and dinner at Mum and Dad's once a month, regular as clockwork. Johnny's family was a huge, loving, warm, clinging and suffocating morass - how had he got away? He'd laughed and said he'd just thought the unthinkable, then done it. It had been the only way, or he'd be manager of that fucking Townie shoe shop he'd worked in before the band took off, and married to Leanne, his ex, with a kiddie or two, no doubt. So he'd unzipped it all like an outgrown cocoon and spread his great wings in the sun. *Carpe diem*, an' all that. You know.

I knew alright. Hadn't I done the same? We'd giggled like kids at the idea of Johnny with a family, living straight life. But he'd been right. Think the unthinkable - then do it. No ifs and buts, no hesitations, no regrets. I'd done it, done it often. And this time, done it colossally.

I gulped the tepid coffee and left half the disgusting pastry. It took another two hours driving, then just before dawn, I finally got up the track to the cottage.

Twenty-eight

I pulled into the yard, did a brainless ninety-point turn and reversed the van in, stopping just short of the ruined outbuildings. I was exhausted, mind-numbingly knackered, as if I'd done a triathlon in concrete wellies. The hill loomed in front of me, a dark shape cut out of the faint light-haze beginning to grey the night sky. I slumped back in the seat, too tired to even get out of the van and crawl into the cottage. I caught sight of myself reflected briefly in the windscreen; I know it wasn't time for vanity, but Jesus Christ, I looked like shit. Siberian Ice Mummies buried thousands of years in the glacier looked fresher and more alive than I did. Groaning, I unbuckled and unfolded myself creakily out of the van, dragging my bag with me as if it weighed a ton, which in fact it pretty well did, I could never travel light.

Staggering to the front door I unlocked it and dumped the bag then went to the fridge and got a plastic mixing-bowl full of chopped steak from the fridge. I half-filled a bucket with water and took it all back to the yard. I put the meat and water in the corner of the outbuilding, the bowl of steak on an old bench pushed against the wall. Save it from the rats and mice, or feral sheep or whatever. I kicked a heap of straw and a ragged horse-blanket I'd chucked in there previously further into the corner of the walls, in the dark at the back of the shell, where a bit of roof still remained. Cosy. Returning to the van, I cautiously laid my ear to the back door. All I could hear was faint snoring. As quietly as possible I unlocked the doors and opened them.

232

The quilts were raggled into a nest and bits of stuffing foamed like a maelstrom where he'd ripped at everything in his panic. The whole interior stank of piss and shit and the yellow funk of fear. Adam lay braced against one side, a white curd of spittle crusting his open mouth and his eyelids fluttering as he dreamed and twitched.

I could have cried, he was so beautiful. So beautiful. I know it sounds as if he was disgusting but he wasn't, not to me. Ask any mother - is your child revolting just because they're ill, or have dirty nappies or have sicked up their dinner in the car out of nerves? You might be momentarily irritated but if anyone suggested you thought your kid was gross or you didn't love them, you'd take that person's face off. Adam was beautiful to me, even in this mess. I touched his cheek with my fingertip. The feel of his skin, flushed and moist, was like warm, honeyed silk. Again, I thought about the youth he would have been had he not suffered the fate he had. Tall, strong, handsome, intelligent - any mother's joy, any girl's desire. Who would love him now, if I did not? Who would care for him, fight for him, protect him? Poor boy, poor boy.

The open doors of the van faced the outbuildings. Scuffing round I found a bit of wood and wedged one of them half open. When he woke, he'd be free. He could run and never come back, but I hoped he'd have at least one bolt-hole here, in these ruined buildings that so resembled his old lair at the farm. Then I'd see him sometimes. That was all I wanted. Just to catch a glimpse of him, in the half-light of dawn or dusk, a shadow moving, a vanishing sinuosity. Eventually, they'd get us both, but I had to give him this for however long it lasted, and I had to try and ensure the Whitecliffe bastards didn't have him, secret and sacrificial, in their torture chambers, like some kind of modern day Inquisition, ecstatic to have got hold of a real devil, at last.

So tired, so tired. I leant forward to kiss him and as I did he turned slightly and I kissed his parted lips instead of his cheek. His breath was rank but sweet, and hot. A shiver ran through my body as if my blood had reversed momentarily in its flow, as if a ghost had passed through me, as if the dawn was dusk and day, night. His lips were like, like - I shook myself. Like nothing. Like no one. Like my son's innocent lips, his mouth the soft mouth of a sleeping child. I was tired, that was all, bone-tired and stressed, naturally enough, if anything about this was natural. But then, unnatural or natural, it was a done deal, choose how.

I stood back. Had I believed in, or cared for, the stern, distant daddy-God of my childhood or his sad son, I would have prayed to them, but instead, only images of Mother Mary slid into my mind - her statues - anodyne, passive, invincible in her sacrifice and unstinting love. Protect my boy, Holy Queen, I asked in the extremity of my exhaustion, protect him because he's one of your children, like us all. Like me. Protect me too. And Johnny, and Jakey, and Sam and Piff and all of us, protect all of us, wrap us in the piercing tender blue of your cloak, kiss our closing eyes, dry our tears and keep us safe from the brutalities of the world. We are lost, we are lost and only the ineffable kindness of your mother-love can keep the nightmare and the snake-bite shakes at bay.

I don't remember getting into the cold, squashy bed, or falling asleep; only that for one moment I poised like a diver on the high board above a great dark well, the next I was waking with a crashing headache to the daylight streaming silvery through the deep-set little windows of my new bedroom.

It was raining. Welcome to Wales, I thought blearily, struggling into my enormous grey-marl fleece dressing gown and stuffing my bony, freezing feet into black sheep-

234

skin mules. A vision in monochrome, I thought, a symphony in shades of grey to match the morning. Lady Grey Day. Even my nasty, sleep-wrinkly dehydrated face was grey. I looked at my tongue. Grey. A sudden revulsion of feeling beat through me in time with my throbbing head - stuck out here, miles from bloody nowhere, nothing to bloody do, no-one to . . .

I stuck my horrid tongue out at my reflection. Stop whining. Who did you see socially anyway, aside from Piff? - and that increasingly sporadically since Lina, getting older and more desperate, took up more and more of her time and energy. That's what happened when your mates got partners, especially if those partners were - what's the euphemism for arseholes? Oh yes, 'difficult'. Your friend's whole life turns inwards, slowly but surely, like blind eyes with the light fading, as all they can see is the beloved and all their time is spent explaining why Bob/Jane is behaving like a spoilt toddler, explaining how it's not their fault, they have problems. *'He's got a heart of gold really - no honestly, he has, he's so nice when we're alone but - he doesn't mean to be - to be annoying, he's just crap at people, but if you knew him like I do . . .'* Yadda yadda, bing bang bong. On and on, the old excuses limp along like lame horses dragging to the knacker's yard.

Done it myself many times. Probably, I thought morosely, still doing it. Sighing heavily I didn't even get round to brushing my (grey) teeth. Why bother?

I ate a scratch breakfast without milk or bread and realised I'd have to drive to the village for supplies and at some point, go to the nearest town and a supermarket, because I couldn't keep on buying big quantities of raw meat without attracting suspicion. The day yawned out in front of me singing with tension and jittery with worry. I have to take it hour by hour, I thought, a step at a time or

235

I'd go mad. Ha bloody ha. Madder, then, or what I thought of as mad and I couldn't do that, because there was the boy to think of.

Scrambling into trackie-bottoms and a hoodie I stuck my shiveringly bare feet into my pink paisley wellies and went to go out - but I paused at the door. Again the fear of Adam shivered through me. If he was still in the van and half-awake, in his groggy state he could - he could - yes, say it, he could attack. I had to come to terms with the fear and deal with it. If I didn't, I'd be trapped in the cottage until the police finally got here and that would help no-one. I pulled myself up straight and re-twisted and re-clipped my hair. There was another mirror by the door - I'd have to dye my hair again soon, the colour was returning to my natural straw silver-yellow; also, glasses on and lippie applied, mustn't forget, must be nice Anne Eliot, the slightly flaky but sweet writer woman holed up for some much-needed peace and quiet to finish her book. Right. I opened the door and went out.

In a quick-change so rapid a burlesque dancer would have been startled, the rain had receded leaving a pale, ethereal sun lighting the damp hillside into a carpet of diamonds, illuminating the lichen on the rocky outcrops and filling the air with that wonderful earth-after-rain smell. I could hear the fat trilling of the little beck and even a bird, running through its repertoire. But nothing else. No traffic hum, no sirens, no dim buzz of city life, no car alarms, no shouting or horns blaring. Nothing. Just nature. The air was clean and seemed extra full of oxygen, the day mild for the time of year. I felt roses trying feebly to bloom in my cheeks and I was almost light-headed with the raw loveliness of it. The van door was still propped open OK, so I went over to it, slowly and deliberately, making a bit of noise but not too much, enough to warn him someone was coming but not enough to startle him.

I needn't have bothered, he wasn't there. I looked in the barn hesitantly but it was empty too. The meat was gone though, and the bucket of water knocked over. I picked it up and refilled it from the outside tap. I felt suddenly weak and tears prickled behind my eyes. He'd gone, maybe forever. I'd wanted to see him, maybe rub his head with my knuckles again, maybe - what? Take him walkies? Have him curl up on the rug in front of the fire and lick my foot gratefully? No - he was free, that was all that mattered. I had to accept that, and again, take it day by day.

In a frenzy I ripped all the soiled and torn crap out of the back of the van, bin-bagged it and decided to drive the long way round to the village, dumping the bags on the way. Then I thought I'd just go to the nearest town and that supermarket, because the less I was in the village, the better.

I drove for an hour, only stopping to throw the bags in a roadside skip, until I found a small out-of-town shopping park with the obligatory Tesco. I went round like a whirlwind filling my trolley with food, including as much fresh and frozen meat as I thought the fridge-freezer would hold. Then I went into the café for a cup of coffee and a sandwich. As I hurriedly ate my prawn mayo on sliced white, I watched the TV which - as in the service station the previous night - burbled in the corner, this time viewed desultorily by me, a couple of genuinely desperate young housewives and a gnarled knot of wool-wrapped pensioners mumbling through their discounted lunches.

I was just finishing my sarnie when the news came on. The doll-faced presenter - her straightened shoulder-length bob unmoving, clipping her words out as if the sheer fact her lovely self was saying them made them a thousand times more valuable - announced that there was a nation-wide manhunt in operation and that the public were warned in the strongest terms possible not to approach - me. Or Adam, who was referred to as the 'escaped inmate'.

A hot sweat swept over me, followed by the cold shakes. I dabbed my upper lip and forehead with the slippy paper napkin, hoping I just looked like a menopausal woman having a hot flush, not a wanted felon feeling guilty. I fought the impulse to run; I forced myself to breathe slowly and watch the TV. I glanced round furtively, but of course no one was looking at me, why would they? The picture the police were using was an old one, a straight-on head and shoulders. I was smiling slightly, no specs, long yellow braid flipped forward over my shoulder, my Navajo squash-blossom necklace glinting. It must have been six or seven years old - I recognised the top I was wearing, I'd thrown it away when I spilled bleach on it cleaning up after - after - my birthday dinner. Oh God. Piff. Piff had given them the picture. She'd taken it to mark my birthday, to show me, she said, how great I looked for my age, to stop me moaning about getting older. I remembered her doing it, against the living room wall. We'd joked that it would look like a *Wanted* poster. Piff gave them my picture.

Piff betrayed me. For the second time that day, tears prickled in my eyes. And again, I pulled myself up hard. Of course she helped the police. What else could she do? Lose everything by fighting a lost battle for something she thought was completely insane anyway? No doubt, know-ing her cool, logical mind she thought she would better help me when I'd been caught and brought to my senses. Organise a lawyer, get me counselling, a psychiatrist. If she hadn't washed her hands of me that is. I thought about phoning her from a pay-phone - she couldn't ring me, my mobile was in a rubbish bin by my flat. I'd stamped on it first, then bought a cheap pay-as-you-go for emergencies.

Anyway, I realised I didn't know her number, it had been in my old phone's memory, I'd never written it down, who does these days? You just go to Names and press the green icon. Easy - until you lose or knacker the phone. Anyway, if I did ring her somehow, what would I say? *'Hi Piff, I'm fine, yes, everything's going to plan - lovely cottage, very peaceful. Adam, oh, very well thank you, just running wild. Boys, you know...'* Inappropriate hysterics bubbled up inside me. My instinct always had been to laugh when things got dark, now I wanted to cackle until I cried myself sick - this wasn't dark, it was fucking midnight in a cellar during an eclipse.

A copper came on the telly, serious-faced, scrubbed. He repeated the warning about not approaching us then said they had good evidence to suggest where we were. Hundreds of people had rung the help-line already with sightings from as far away as mainland France and the Shetland Islands. He had no doubt we would be apprehended shortly. Then a TV psychiatrist, a nice woman, came on and spoke calmly about my mental health issues. If I gave myself up, I'd get the help I so desperately needed, as would Adam, who was extremely vulnerable and very dangerous. In her opinion, this was a case of a misguided and ill-informed individual thinking they could help someone they thought was being unfairly persecuted - a sentimental, emotional delusion common amongst lonely, older women - which in this case had unfortunately resulted in the sorry old cow (well, OK, she didn't actually say that bit) taking the law into her own hands instead of trusting the experts to help Adam. She was very sympathetic. I hated her, the smug bitch. Not that it was her fault, she was just doing her job, being a talking head. She wasn't the worst, though, by any manner of means.

Frozen, I watched as pundit after pundit pontificated on my obvious insanity and the danger Adam presented to the nation's children. In their view we were a *folie à deux:* a deranged anti-social woman and a ravening predatory child-killer harnessed in a devil's pact to cause as much mayhem, terror and violence as we could. Not one of them actually mentioned Adam's upbringing or his feral child-hood, instead they dwelled on poor Jakey's death. None of them whispered a word about the fact that no forensic evidence linked Adam to Jakey, but that in fact, it had begun to seem more likely the dogs had bought the poor baby down. They showed a five second clip, heavily edited, of the Director, looking exhausted and worried - which made me feel vilely guilty - trying to explain Adam's actual condition, but he came across as wishy-washy and apologist. The rest of the talking heads seemed to agree, without actually saying it, that we'd be better off being brought down by police marksmen. Just like the dogs had been.

I saw the pattern emerging. The dull, un-sexy fact that a feral dog pack had killed a child in a dreadful stroke of fate that could only be called an Act of God just wasn't interesting. That was boring. But a Cannibal Killer, a Monster, a child-murdering, ripper Beast who could be touted as the horrific epitome of Stranger Danger to a drooling, hysterical public - now, that was sex, ladies and gentlemen. That was news, baby.

I carefully gathered up my bag and walked out, trundling my trolley to the van, resisting the urge to put on my outsized black sunglasses. I was in Wales, not L.A. They would have made me look twice as conspicuous, how-ever comforting they might be. Tuning in the radio as I drove, I heard more of the same. I knew I had to get rid of the van, false plates and all. I'd be OK for a day or two, but then I'd have to drive it somewhere like Scotland, burn it out and get the train back.

240

I couldn't risk moving Adam again, though. I'd have to leave him to run the hills for as long as he could. We were on the edge of Snowdonia, the area was a vast mystery of folding valleys and craggy nooks and crannies. He'd have as good a chance here as anywhere. Without me, though. Pain sawed through me like a cold knife.

Suddenly I felt overwhelmingly shaky. I pulled over into a lay-by and sat shivering, staring at the trees and the fields beyond. I don't know what I'd thought - that miraculously, Adam and I would be together, albeit on the run, forever? But it had come so fast, so fast. I had to set him free, let him go. I could run, but he couldn't. I had to evade capture so I could get our story written, get the book done at least enough so it would be taken seriously. I felt so lonely I started crying, just crying, sitting there, all alone in the middle of nowhere.

When the copper knocked on the window I nearly died on the spot of shock.

Twenty-nine

'Everything all right, Miss?'

She was a young, rather stocky woman with a plain, kindly face. I stared at her as if she were queen of the flesh-eating zombies. Fumbling with the window like an alkie on a five-day bender, I tried to look calm as I stared up at her, bereft of speech. I could smell her; tired, day-old shirt, generic deodorant. There was a plain gold band on her wedding finger. The air through the open window was cold and laced with exhaust fumes. It brought me to myself a little.

'Anything wrong with the vehicle? Do you need help?' She looked concerned. I felt paralysed with shock. What in the name of God could I tell her? I searched my rag-bag head for something that might sound plausible.

'I - er - no, no, nothing, no. I just - I just - look, to be honest? I'm having a bit of trouble with - with *the change*, you know, all a bit grim. Got one of those bloody hot flushes, felt a bit dizzy, so I just pulled over for a sec to get myself sorted. I didn't mean to . . .'

The copper sighed and made an *oh-dear* face. 'Oh, well, yes. My mum, she's havin' a terrible time with it. Look, you get on when you feel like it, get your old man to pamper you a bit - blokes, eh? Don't know how easy they got it, right?'

I smiled. My mouth felt like over-stretched elastic. 'Oh, yeah - you're right there. Sorry to have . . .'

'Oh, no worries, I was only checkin'. Woman alone, see. There's a new push on to be more sensitive, more aware, like. Sounds silly, but it's a good idea if it gets some of my male colleagues to sharpen their ideas up, yeah?'

Her radio burbled and she pulled it up to her mouth and spoke briefly and monosyllabically into it, then turned back to me. 'OK, take care now and safe drive home.'

And with that she trotted off back to her car and drove off, oblivious to the fact she'd just let Britain's Most Wanted Woman get away scot free and shaking like a leaf in a hurricane.

The drive back was horrendous. I got totally lost and was far too scared to ask the way, so I ended up driving for two hours solid until I got signs for the village. As I drove through it, dusk was falling and the windows of the pub glowed a welcoming gold, and outside I noticed Evan's Landie. A mad urge to go in and offer to buy him a drink washed over me. To sit in a warm corner, amongst normal people talking all the familiar nonsense, gossip and hilarity that people do, drinking a glass of - well, whatever they had. Vodka. Bell's. Wine if they did it, even if it came out of a box and had the sharp-sour flavour of petrol mixed with nail polish. I didn't care. Just to be with people. Evan was nice, he'd chat to the poor lonely writer-woman. Who cared if he was dull, or went on about sheep or whatever? He was real. He was alive.

The dead were with me too much. As I'd driven, crying, round the lanes looking for home, the faces of those lost boys gazed at me from tree shadows and leaf dapple, turned in hedgerows and bloomed in the deep recesses of my mind like black roses; Johnny and Jakey. Hand in hand. Johnny bending down to whisper in Jakey's ear while he smiled at me, his eyes holes letting onto infinity, his face an ivory mask. Holding Jakey's hand. Like he was his Dadda. Like he would have held our son's hand. The terrible ache that sat in my womb, that void, that echoing place that had held my child clamoured and resonated like a sea-cave scoured by the rising tide.

I found myself saying *I love you I love you* over and over under my breath as I passed the pub, the Post Office, the Spar. But who did I love? Who?

All of them, I loved all of them. I loved them like breathing, it was all I had now.

When I pulled in at the cottage, I turned the headlights off and sat for a moment, numb. I'd left the front room light on. You know, the old joke - saves the burglars tripping up over stuff. It shone faintly onto the yard. As I sat there, the shadows round the outbuilding thickened and coiled into a shape. It was Adam.

My breath caught in my throat as he looked straight at me, head on one side, half crouching, a dead rabbit dangling bloody from his hand. He snuffed at the air, the faint light of the front room causing the phosphorescent disks in his eyes to flare briefly. Then he loped forward and dropped the rabbit by the cottage door. Though he wasn't looking at me directly, I knew he was aware of exactly what I was doing. I felt my heart physically pounding in my chest, banging the blood through me like breaking waves.

Then turning with a powerful, economic fluidity which only highlighted his un-humanness, he looked at me again and I saw his lips move. I couldn't hear him but I knew what he was saying.

Ma.

Then he was gone. Totally gone, vanished. It was as if the night had eaten him in a gulp. I strained to see him but all I saw was a glimpse, a shadow moving over the hill, a deeper darkness in the shape of a wolf, or a man. Or both.

It took me forever to get the shopping into the house. My hands shook, I dropped things, I stumbled on the doorstep, and knocked my elbow painfully on the door frame. Finally, having stowed everything away, I sat on the sofa and rolled a spliff from my stash even though I'd sworn only to do it in emergencies. The rabbit was in the bin. Lovely gift, but I passed on skinning it for my tea. When I saw its oozing purple guts cased in a bloody membrane and its neck flopping limply where Adam had broken it, I threw up my prawn sandwich in the kitchen sink. I needed that joint, and a vegetarian supper. What a child of the urban world I was: meat came on polystyrene trays wrapped in clingfilm and milk was bottled cow-juice. The countryside was another planet, really.

As I inhaled the sweet hash, and felt its warm tingle start to frizzle at the edges of my Inner Hippie, I thought about the nature of fear. I was afraid of Adam. There was no point denying it and in many ways it was the only sensible re-action to him. He could dispatch me in much the same way he'd killed the rabbit, at any time. I didn't think he would. In fact I was sure he wouldn't ever harm me knowingly, but still. He was what he was and I'd be a complete idiot not to be - shall we say - wary around him. What mattered was that he didn't find out. He must only ever see me calm, controlled - dominant. Adam was a pack animal; he needed to know I was pack leader. Or at least, Alpha Female.

Feeling peckish, I floated to the kitchen and heated up a carton of soup. Then I set up my laptop on the kitchen table. Time to start on the book. Yeah. I opened Word and - drew a complete blank. How did you start a book? *Once upon a time? Call me Ishmael?* I cast my mind back to my first University course. The creative writing module I'd taken for one term, led by a bloke whose novel had won some prize or other. What had he said? I'd been so busy copping off with one of my fellow students - pretty face, disappointing body, even more disappointing shag - I'd barely paid atten-tion. *Start at the beginning and don't stop until you get to the end.* That was it. Everyone had laughed and groaned at the old cliché but the writer guy had repeated it - it was the only

way, he'd said. The world was full of people calling themselves writers whose only actual output was in their bar-
room boasts. If you wanted to do it, do it. Otherwise, be a
plumber. The pay was better.

Right. OK. I could do this. I thought about everything
I'd read. It was no use. I couldn't do either the kind of
coolly detached, awfully clever stuff the English favoured
or the tough-guy histrionics of the Americans. I wasn't a
real writer, a professional a - but I could do what I did. I
could be me and it was so important, so . . . No. Couldn't
think that way, I'd freeze. OK. I took another toke. Like
the song says, Annie girl, you gotta do it your way. I began.

The Low-Down and Dirty 100% Authentic I-Kid-You-Not Guide to surviving a Life in Rock n' Roll & In This Case, Way Way Beyond, Baby.

Parental Advisory: lots of swearing and talking about weird stuff. Certificate 18. At least.

Part 1. On The Road, or, Don't Forget The Con-
doms And Remember You Can Never Have Enough
Clean Socks.

This Guide is brought to you by **ANNIE WYNTER**,
who lived the Life, loved the Life and gave it all up for
another Life and is very, very tired. So will you be.

OK, here goes: first off, you think because this
Guide has a funny intro and looks kinda hippie-fied
that you don't have to read it properly or pay any *real*
attention to the advice given or pay any actual attention to the stories, histories and magic herein. Either
you think the likes of me couldn't possibly enlighten

the likes of you or, man, you don't like reading anyway, and hey, what can some, like, weird old woman
who worked with, duh, *ancient* bands you don't have
any interest in - if you've even heard of them, heh heh
heh - tell *you*, a young, cool hipster/intellectual/fully-
paid-up suburbanite/university lecturer/librarian/di-
vorcee with two kids/pub bloke/football fan/Bridget
Jones wannabe/girl-about-
Town/student/fashionista/teacher/tattooist/bookseller/j
ournalist/artist/writer/archaeologist/doctor/
Computer freak/bank clerk/shop assistant/chef *anyway?*

**YOU JUST MADE YOUR FIRST MISTAKE,
BUBBA.**

**IT COULD BE THE BIGGEST ONE YOU'LL EVER
MAKE.**

Oh, you're pissed off now, aren't you? You *so* don't
like being told what to do, especially by a Weird Person and worse, a Weird *Old* Person - but get this,
sugar, taking advantage of someone else's hard-won
experience, hearing their war-stories and learning
from the mistakes they made so you don't make them
yourself will GET YOU WHAT YOU WANT - FAME,
GLORY, DRUGS, SEX & RESPECT. Yes, it will, because **REPUTATION IS EVERYTHING IN ROCK 'N'
ROLL** and this Guide will teach you how to maximise
your rep potential both in *the* Life and in *your* life. Do
you want to be known as a decent, sorted person
everyone likes and wants to do well, or a complete
wanker everyone despises - and therefore, won't
bother to help on the way up and - much, much more

importantly - on the way *back* up? Exactly. Easy, eh? Read This Guide. Others will fail, but you will succeed because you will be armed with **KNOWLEDGE.** And, baby, knowledge, is **Power** and in Rock 'N' Roll, as in every other walk of life, only the strong and powerful survive. Even if you want the punters to think you're a sensitive, kitten-cute, doe-eyed singer-songwriter type with 'fey' written right through you like Blackpool rock. Don't be fooled. *No-one* survives this life without balls (or ovaries) of solid titanium and the will power to match. Power - hmmm, dontcha just love it? Baby, you're gonna.

Now, I'm going to tell you how to *Do It* like a rock 'n' roll band. I'm going to tell you how the greatest and most beautiful rock star that ever lived and died did it. I'm going to show you the secret serpent's path to everlasting glory and I'm going to tell you about what I did and why, who did what and how and who they did it with. I'm going to tell you about my great escape and **why** my son, who everyone thinks is a monster, isn't. The truth. The complete, unvarnished and actual truth. Cross my heart and hope to die. I'm going to do this, darlin', because the truth, as they say, will set us free. You don't get much truth in these days of spin, hype and hullabaloo - you get sold lies. Well, for once in your soon-to-be-glorious life, you're going to read the real and actual unvarnished truth and that, my friend, will wipe the shill and scum from the mirror of your heart and you will know the what, wherefore and why of everything.

Or you can put this book back on the shelf with a little quiver of fear in your guts because you'd rather have you nice little boat un-rock 'n' rolled.

Your call.

So, what's it going to be?

You in or out?

Right! Let's go then. Buckle up, baby, it's going to be a bumpy ride. From now on, whatever age, sex or denomination you are, you're a young and hopeful rock-star, and Nanny Mambo here is about to give the whole low-down-and-dirty voodoo hoodoo. Just remember; where it says 'musician' it means *you*, whatever you do because the first secret is - we're all rock 'n' rollers, sugar.

Lesson 1.

On The Road:

Supporting A Bigger Band or, your big break.

At some point in your career you will get the support slot with another, bigger band. They might be of your generation, or older musicians with a long history giving you, a young outfit, a break. In other walks of life you may be starting a new job, having a tricky interview, going to university, meeting your squeeze's friends/family for the first time, it doesn't matter, it's all a gig.

And how you behave can make - or break you. Reputations are made or ruined in the blink of an eye. And I don't mean just onstage. The Star I'm going to use as an example in this little cosmic cartograph of the heart, is the one and only Johnny X - yes, him - my lover, my beloved, my friend and my Muse in this Grimoire as I was his Muse in life; because first confession - I am *The Blonde.* As in 'My Beautiful (thank you, baby) Blonde', 'Breathe', 'Lovesugar Queen', 'Sweet Sun Sister' etc etc. Me. That was - is - me. Annie Wynter. And if you don't believe me, ha ha, I have the photographs to prove it. Well, my Johnny never, ever forgot that a Star is a Star is a Star. In the street, on the road, in a bar, in bed or out of his head. *Be what you want to be and be it 100%* was his motto, which is why he was the flamin' ace meteor boy he was. And I know whereof I speak. So:

1)   Do not forget one simple rule: From the moment you get into that venue/meeting/bar/seminar/in-laws-house/interview until the moment you leave, you are being watched and judged. Stop moaning about that not being fair etc., it's the way it is. You do it to others. How many times have you said that so-and-so is a complete tosser? Many, many times. Johnny knew it because he couldn't take a leak without someone trying to catch him on their mobile with his pants unzipped but he bore it like a Prince because he knew Fame is the price you pay for art. It is, baby, trust me. It's not the re-ward, it's the price. Now, if you want to be a success at anything, have anything, be everything you want to be, stick a rod up your spine and never, never whine. Only losers whine - like it or not, it's how it is and accepting what's real-real and not what's wannabe-real is the first big step for personkind, sugar. Here's a little story to il-lustrate what I'm on about.

The Support Band Blues, or a Study In Indigo Of How To Be An Arse.

Over the years, Velvet Shank, like every other band in the world, had support bands. When they'd achieved fame and fortune, bands paid to support them because it exposed them to a whole different, bigger audience. That's standard practice and as big bands go, The Shank were decent to their supports giving them proper sound and lights and being pleasant to them, as opposed to say, Ultimate Angel who were notorious for screwing their paying supports over, refusing to give them more than a quarter of the lights and often, rigging their sound so while they thought it sounded great onstage through the monitors, the out-front was a feeble whisper. But aging rockers Angel had a lot to lose from being blown off by some young contenders and their insecurity was as legendary as their amphetamine intake and of course, completely related to it. Not so The Shank, who were true Kings of Rock 'N' Roll and therefore, generous and open-handed to a fault because they were sure of what they were doing.

Now, you'd think supporting a bigger band on whatever level (just think of it as getting the big boss's personal mentorship and guidance, or similar), would be a good thing for which any sane person would be grateful. But no. Some support bands went hysterical with the kind of idiot, egomaniacal *Pop Idol, X-Factor* competitive stupidity that only exists in telly-world and does not translate into actual rock 'n' roll.

One such merrie band of tossers always stuck in my mind because they were concentrated essence of arsehole. It was when The Shank were playing medium-sized venues and about (though we didn't know it at the time) to go massive with 'My Beautiful Blonde'. The support in question had won the gig in a dire *Battle Of The Bands* contest. Naturally, the contest was won by the band that sounded as much like the year before last's pop-rock sensation as was humanly possible.

So, in swaggered the winners of this lame nonsense with a colossal heap of brand-new, the-music-shop-saw-them-coming gear, all sign-written with their name, which I shall never forget due to its extreme cheesiness: The Joe Kerrs. Geddit? Right. From the off, they complained about everything, and I mean everything, including the sandwiches (had they never seen *Spinal Tap*?). They told The Shank's soundguy, Gunnar, to fuck off, their cousin Dave was doing sound, he had a recording studio and they knew the type of games London bastards got up to. No-one was gonna get one over on The Joe Kerrs. The bass-player remarked long and loud that he was a proper showman, a real performer, him, and everything of his had to be turned up to eleven. Dave obliged. It sounded like a blender full of nuts and bolts.

Everyone shook their heads and sighed. Been there before. Even had the leathery, orange mum with the raffia razor-cut screaming at The Shank's tour manager - me, at that time - that I was out to do her boys down, I was, after I asked them not to kick the monitors into position and stop having a beer fight onstage during the soundcheck. But the icing on the tedious cake came when the bass player and his gormless, spineless cohorts slouched into The Shank's dressing room without asking (a rock 'n' roll no-no of the first water, please note) and started playing pool, drinking The Shank's beer and - horrors - picking up Rick, the Shank's guitarist's precious vintage Gibson to *'see what this old*

crap's like, man'. I asked them to leave. They got mul-
ish. Lips were stuck out, brows lowered. The bass
player informed everyone loudly that they could buy
and sell us ten times over 'cos their drummer was shagging a rich bird whose dad owned a meat factory and
who'd given them the gear, the gig (courtesy of a few
well-placed back-handers) and five grand in the bank
so they could make it huge. I squashed the impulse to
tell the drummer that the aspiring rock-chick whose
daddy had bought her this bunch of losers for a toy had
already tried to get off with Johnny to the point of giving
him a damp beer-mat scrawled with the immortal line;
*'I wanna suk yr cok yr so hot txt me I kno u want it Jenni
07986 125437'*. I had said beer mat in my pocket,
where it hummed gently, like an unexploded bomb.

By the end of the gig, everyone in the venue: the security guards, the bar staff, the tech crew, the promoter,
the other musicians, like, *everyone,* loathed The Joe
Kerrs like the plague. No-one did anything; no-one
rowed with them, no-one shouted at them or their ob-
noxious entourage, no-one said a dickey-bird to them.
They were so full of themselves they didn't see the ex-
pressionless faces surrounding them, the doors not
opened for them, the gear not packed for them, the
hands unshaken, the compliments on the band unpaid.
But I saw it, and I saw their future, a future twisted
through with bitterness, failure and humiliation, when
the rock-chick scored elsewhere or got tired of her toy
and the lippy bass-man talked his way into a dead-end
having fucked off one promoter too many, one record
exec too many, while never having the slightest idea he
was doing it. Then it would be the call centre/the hotel/the
IT/the accountancy job for the lads and none of them
ever having any real idea why they hadn't made it.

253

So, draw your own conclusions - do you want to be a fatuous, stupid Joe Kerr, or a true contender? If the latter, remember, you are being watched and judged; do not be found wanting. Do not be a fool.

So, moving along, my little rock bunnies, to another

I stopped typing and rubbed my temples with my fingers. I wasn't sure if this was how to do it, but I'd started at least, that was something. As long as I didn't give up I could hone the stuff and polish it up as it went along. Maybe I'd look up hints on writing on the internet, that might help. Jeez, I'd forgotten about that bloody awful support band until now - what had happened to them I wondered, or that plump, silly girl with her tacky clothes and serum-greasy straightened hair? She probably had two kids by now and a posh house. I wondered if I should change the names in the book, in case I got sued. No. I was going to write what really happened and if anyone sued - great, more publicity for Adam's cause.

I shivered, it was draughty. Outside the wind was getting up and I could hear it soughing round the eaves. Solitude filled the brightly-lit kitchen with a dense fug of silence, broken only by the ratchet of the old clock on the dresser ticking. I stared into the black of the window that looked out onto the hill. Was Adam out there, loping through the hills, every part of his body alive and tingling with freedom and the cold wrapping his hardened flesh in a shattered cloak of invisibility? No-one would go out in the wild in this weather at this time of night. No one would see him. The fells were his kingdom, just as the stage had been Johnny's. Both of them were princes, both lived at night, both were strong and proud past reason; pack leaders. But Johnny died. Why? Other people lived with broken hearts

- he was young, beautiful, famous, and brilliant. He had everything anyone could have wanted. Why would giving up a woman like me, certainly no prize in the world's eyes, be such a killing blow?

I wondered how many people would simply not believe I was Johnny X's Blonde. Whole articles had been written about his 'mystery woman' likening her to Shakespeare's *Dark Lady*. Some even said, as they did about Shakespeare, that Johnny was secretly gay and the Blonde was a Blond. A whole swathe of lovely girls were perused, poked at, fingered and dismissed - in a literary sense of course - as contenders, but no-one ever looked at me. But I was there, all the time. I was even in some of the press shots. If you look at the famous picture of him onstage at Glastonbury, the shot where he's got his shirt off, eyes closed and arms outstretched like a crucified angel, in the crowd side-stage all applauding like crazy, in the middle, that's me. Not clapping. Just watching, quiet, like always. But no one thought of me because I wasn't a model or a starlet or even young. I was just someone who looked after him. But he loved me. I think he loved me as I loved him.

He panicked, that was it. He panicked because the thing he wanted so much took up so much of his heart he thought he couldn't spare any of it for anyone else. He cut me loose so he wouldn't have to think about me, to look after me, to give me time he thought he'd need to be the thing he was. And then like many another before him, he realised that having the prize without your love beside you is a hollow, hurtful thing indeed. It put him off-kilter, it unbalanced him, it ripped at his guts like a rat in a trap rips at its own leg to get free.

So why not just call me, email me, have me back?

Because it all goes so fast in the Life when you get on that road. Faster than anything you could ever imagine.

And you have no peace, no time, not even a moment to yourself, literally. No chance get your courage up and say *'come to me, I need you, I was wrong'*. And then there's the free drugs, the free oblivion, the pretty, dead-eyed women eager to piggy-back your rising fame and the blank-eyed cameras clicking your spirit away in flickering instants. And the road unrolling like a devil beckoning ever onwards. Another gig, another twenty-four hours on two hours sleep and innumerable big fat white lines, another gig and a flight, a five-hour drive, and a sea of faces, smudged and featureless with gaping mouths open, hands grabbing at you like deep-sea creatures that never know the light and it's roaring in your ears like the tsunami coming but you love it - oh God, oh Jesus, how you love it - and you can't resist it and you want to throw yourself into those vast black waters blind and insane and be obliterated and deified and cleansed by it more than - anything.

Until it stops. And then you sit in a bleach-clean hotel room so blindingly anonymous it hurts your tired eyes and all the cells in your wasted body are screaming with fatigue but you cannot, cannot sleep and all you want is that voice, those arms, those kisses that tell you *It's OK, baby, it's OK. I love you, I forgive you, oh, baby, I understand.*

And I did understand.

Maybe - maybe if he hadn't taken that last shot, if he'd had some time off the wheel, he'd have made that call and even if we couldn't have been lovers again, I could have been his friend, been his comfort, been his old, dear love. I could have saved him.

And I hunched over the shiny yellow pine table in the old cottage high in the hills lost in a no-place of exhaustion and a distant drumming of old heartache as the rain spat and the wind knifed through the cracks under the wonky doors, braceletting my ankles in icy shackles. And out on

256

the tops my son put back his brutal face and howled at the waxing moon, the thick cords in his neck bracing against a sound no human had made since before time began.

Thirty

I was so busy writing the story about Johnny refusing to do a fatuous duet like a good little boy with a very patronising Bono at the Earthday Party, the one where Madonna's heel broke mid-song catapulting her into her dancers and showing a couple of million world-wide viewers her naked arse (not that we all hadn't seen it before, mind you, but a girl likes to pick the times she shows it rather than have it beamed round the globe inadvertently while you flail around on your belly like an ageing crab), that I didn't hear Evan's Landie and nearly had a cardiac when he knocked.

I staggered to the door, quickly putting on the specs and lippie and re-twisting my hair. My legs had gone numb from typing hour after hour without moving from the chair and I realised I was incredibly thirsty. It was cold, too; even my thick black Aran sweater and black trackie bottoms couldn't keep out the winter nip. I could smell the sweet, seductive scent of Adam's Favourite, which I'd sprayed on my hair and neck last night after my bath. At least I smelled nice. I don't know why that comforted me, but it did. I wanted comfort after last night.

I'd sat with the lights off for hours, gazing out at the hillside, hoping to catch a glimpse of my boy as I did every minute I could, day or night. The clock had ticked, the roof creaked and I could hear the wind in the eaves. It was like being in a sailing ship at sea, or what I imagined that would be like. Then, in the early hours of the morning, I'd seen him, moving down the slope, moving smooth as water flowing in a brown beck, a creature made out of layers and shards of darkness, only visible as a shape thicker than the shadows as he went into the outbuilding.

I'd drawn back from the window, not wanting to spook him, just pleased he was all right, that he seemed his strong and natural self again. The drugs that I'd had to give him were well out of his system now, along with the others that had been used to keep him in check at the facility. He was himself again, and it made me hug myself with a strange thrill of pleasure to know it, to glimpse him moving in the world and to know he had come back, if only for a little while. Then the realisation came on me that soon I'd have to leave him and run, draw the hunt away from him and, probably, I'd never be allowed to see him again. For a few thudding moments, all I'd won, risked, seemed completely pointless. That depression engulfed me again, pushing me down into icy depths of total bloody misery. I hadn't seemed to be able to get warm again after that and when I'd finally made a hot water bottle and crawled into bed, it had taken ages to fall asleep because I kept crying, and shaking like a sick dog, and when sleep came it was broken and twisted with nightmares.

Johnny standing backstage at the Astoria, the old Astoria, standing in the filthy black piss-stinking stairwell by the side-stage that led out to the loading alley. He looked up at me, an expression of terrible yearning and love on his face. In his arms was a baby, wrapped in a tattered cream crocheted shawl, fine and ruined as an afternoon spider's web, like my old christening shawl that I'd had to play dolls with. Holding his hand was Jakey, scared by the unfamiliar surroundings, the noise of the gig being broken down, the dark narrow place. I ran towards them, starting down the stairs; really, Johnny should know better, bringing children to such a place, with used syringes and broken glass littering the alley and . . . I reached out my hands for the baby and he passed the bundle to me. I looked into the wrappings as it lay in the crook of my arm. To my

*thrashing, strangling horror, it was the mangled dead rabbit Adam
had brought me, its shiny skinned head and bulging blue-bruised
ruptured eyes a mockery of a child's face. Didn't you know, Johnny
whispered, didn't you know our little one was dead? And Jakey, eyes
like saucers, started crying, crying as if his heart was breaking . . .*

And so it had gone on, all night. I'd eventually got up at
dawn, and made tea. But I couldn't shake the suffocating
atmosphere of the dream, try as I might.

Now I had a visitor - someone from the real world, an
actual living person. Freaky. Shaking myself out of my
reverie, I pasted a welcoming smile on and unlocked the
door - it was one of those stable doors, in two halves top
and bottom and by accident I only opened the top half,
which hadn't been bolted to the bottom.

Evan smiled back at me as I fumbled with the door trying to open the bottom half so he could come in. It seemed
to take an age. I felt silly and useless and barely resisted the
urge to kick the fucking thing and scream.

'Oh - God, sorry, I'm not used to - there we go, please,
come in - tea? Coffee?' I sounded flustered and ditzy, but
probably that was a good thing. In keeping with my
role as the recently divorced arty type, getting menopausal
probably, but game in a fey kind of way. I should get an
Oscar for this, I thought - and then realised that from some
angles, that actually *was* me. Or a part of me. I took a breath
and increased the wattage of my smile.

'Coffee would be great, thank you.' Evan smiled back.
'Just thought I'd pop round, see everything was OK. You
got enough oil for the heating, have you? I'll check in a bit.
Everything working?'

I indicated a chair by the table and he sat down as I
filled the kettle with shaking hands - the outbuildings -
oh fuck, fuck - what if Adam was still in there asleep and
Evan wanted to go in, get something, check something -

Jesus. I forced myself calm and spooned coffee into the cafetière.

'Um, do you like it strong? I'm afraid I always drink it like tar. Bad, I know - oh, milk? Sugar?'

He smiled again and rubbed his forehead at the hairline with the palm of his hand like a schoolboy. Again I thought he looked a nice bloke, a decent bloke, not unlike Gordon in many ways though they weren't alike physically - Evan was tall, well-built, very dark, with unruly black curls cut badly into a workaday crop and dark blue eyes. His face and neck were ruddy with the outdoor life he led but I suspected his skin, past the V of his open shirt was milky white. I bet he never got a full tan. Hardly the type to laze out on the patio in Los Gigantos wearing red Speedos, Ray-Bans and smothered in Ambre Solaire, our Evan.

'I'll take it black, if that's alright. No sugar, don't have a sweet tooth, me, never did.'

'Oh, me neither. Just as well really - I don't appear to actually have any sugar. Sorry.' I settled into my Annie Eliot persona and gave that quirky, eyebrows raised, eyes wide, mouth closed smile thing dizzy chicks always do.

He nodded at the laptop. 'Book going OK? Am I allowed to ask that? I don't want to put you off, or anything, you know, interrupt you. It's just that - well, we got a bit of a problem. Some bloody fool of a tourist - I don't mean, I'm sorry I . . .' He reddened even more, the embarrassed flush turning his cheeks a dull brick colour.

I shifted in my chair, half looking out of the window, praying Adam had gone. 'Oh, please - I don't mind being a tourist. I mean I am one, aren't I? But it must be - you know - difficult, some people, well . . .'

'I'm sorry, I didn't mean to be rude, but see, some - someone must have left, or abandoned a dog round here, or up Snowdon and it's come down round here. It must be

261

a big one, too. Maybe a Rottweiler or an Alsatian. It's started taking sheep, so it must be a good-sized beast. Took one of Williams' ewes last night, ripped it to bits, very nasty. So, really, apart from wondering if everything was OK with you, I just wanted to warn you to keep a bit of a lookout, be a bit careful if you go walking.'

It was my turn to go red. I felt sweat trickle down my back under the thick jumper. 'Oh - God, er - horrible. Um, right - right, well, I certainly will keep an eye out. I've your mobile number, I'll just ring, you know, if I see anything, anything at all, anything - suspicious.' What a lying bitch I was. Still, nothing else for it.

He smiled again. We were smiling a lot. His teeth were very square and white with a big gap between the front ones. Nice. A nice man. With nice, square, dirty calloused hands. For a mad moment, I wanted nothing more than to fling myself into his arms and weep, while he stroked my hair and told me in his lovely Welsh accent that everything would be alright, that he'd fix everything, that . . . Yeah, right.

He sipped his coffee and glanced again at the laptop. 'So, everything going alright, then? The old place giving you some inspiration? What is it exactly you're writing about - you said it was some sort of self-help book?'

'Oh - yes, mmm, God, lot of nonsense really, you know the kind of thing.' I did that fey smiley thing again and hooked my feet behind the rung of the chair, hunching my shoulders and cradling my mug in both hands.

'Me? No - no, never time to read, me. I think the last thing I read was a manual for my phone, bloody thing, you need a degree to work it out. My wife reads, mind you - loads of stuff. Thrillers, that kind of thing. I'm surprised she sleeps at night, if the stuff on the covers is anything to go by. So, this one?'

I sensed a woman's hand behind his keenness to know what I was writing about. I could almost hear his wife going 'ask her what she's writing then, you great fool, she could be famous, you know, I could have read one of her things, oh, don't be such a baby, Evan, ask her . . .'

If I said nothing, it would look even more suspicious than if I didn't. I coughed as if my coffee had gone down the wrong way to buy a moment. 'Ah, oh, sorry, the book? Oh, it's - you know - um, for older women. What to do if you have to start a new life, after a divorce - well, a bit of a manual, really, like your phone thing, in a lot of ways. Men don't buy this kind of thing much so we go for the women's market. Put a pink cover on it, that kind of stuff. It's partly practical - the law, how to sort things out, and partly to make them feel a bit better about themselves, that they're not on the shelf, that kind of thing. Not totally rejected, you know, give them a bit of hope they can find someone else. It's not easy, splitting up mid-life, not easy at all, I like to think I've helped someone a bit, you never know.' I smiled. He looked uncomfortable. Women's things. You could see he thought I'd written it from experience. You could also see he thought it best not to continue down that road in case I turned out to be a right bunny-boiler and threw my knickers at him. My desire to hug him evaporated like the foggy, foggy dew-oh.

'Ah - OK, yes. Well, I hope it goes alright. Like I said, call me if . . .' At that moment, his phone burst into a rousing chorus of Queen's 'We Are The Champions'. I definitely wouldn't be hugging him now. He made an *excuse-me* face and I smiled yet again.

'Oh, hello love - I - what? Say again, signal's terrible, you're breaking up - oh, OK, I'll get some - have you rung the Vet about Shan's paw? What did she - oh, right-oh. I'm on my way, bye.'

'My wife. Needs a loaf from the shop. Don't know what we did before mobile phones, eh? So, you let me know if you want anything and, er, mind out for the Beast Of Black Hill - oh, sorry, village joke. Still, just be a bit careful, you never know, an animal like that. Can be nasty if you corner them or something. I reckon Williams'll get it soon, anyway. A dead shot he is, and . . .'

My guts turned. 'A - he'll shoot it? But . . .'

Evan nodded grimly. 'Oh yes, it's his right. Can't have it taking his beasts, like. I give you ten to one it's a city animal, some bloody chav dumped it because it outgrew its welcome or whatever. Not the dog's fault, you can only blame the owner, but - got no choice, I'm afraid. Bad business all round. Still, don't you get nightmares or anything, it'll all get sorted shortly I don't doubt. No, don't worry, I'll see myself out, you get on, I didn't want to disturb you.'

And he left, the muffled roar of the Landie fading into the damp air as it rattled down the lane. I barely heard it. I was so grateful he hadn't gone into the outbuilding, so grateful he hadn't . . .

Williams would shoot it? Shoot 'The Beast Of Black Hill'? Oh, for fuck's sake. Jesus Christ Almighty. Not only was the whole of the British Plodderie after us, now we had a sharp-shooting Welsh farmer on our case, trusty shotgun to the fore, thinking he was about to blast a starving Rottie and save Snowdon from the detritus of the urban hordes.

I sat shakily and stared at the computer. The words on the screen danced irritating little jigs as that bloody tune started to jerk and stutter in my head. Randomly I re-membered the old film of The Troggs doing 'Wild Thing', dressed in candy-striped suits, following some girl with a baby-doll zig-zag pattern frock and back-combed flick-up hair through a door and out of the studio directly into a crowded railway station. Surreal and oddly sinister. Every-

264

one in the station totally ignored them as they jiggled through the song - *'you make my heart sing, you make everything . . . groovy'*. It was meant to be psychedelic but it came across as unnervingly dream-like.

I felt like that. As If I'd open a door in my flat and stepped out into a screaming whirligig of horror. Guns, eviscerated bloody rabbits, coppers mouthing on the telly and my son, the werewolf. Because that's what he was. The werewolf. Not the silly Hollywood bloke-in-hairy-mask, or the modern horror-film staple where a nice American boy turns bodily into an animal, courtesy of special effects. Adam was the thing that had shaped the legend to start with, the legend that was now a corrupted and semi-comical melodrama. Adam was the beast that lives in all our hearts, in our brains, the primitive creature we distanced ourselves from in order to be civilised, to eat pallid, cold meat we buy in Sainsbury's, to go through ridiculous mating rituals and get married dressed in ludicrous outfits, to kill our enemies at a safe distance by pushing buttons and raining hell down on them from a satellite. We didn't eat raw, steaming meat straight from the kill, fuck anything we could catch, fight hand-to-hand or stink of our unreasonable selves anymore. We were nice. We were proper little ladies and gents. Weren't we?

Adam was the man-beast, the loup-garou, the Wendigo, Skin-walker, Bruxsa, Tlahuelpuchi, Vlkodlak, Henge, Li-cantropo, Ihmissusi, Rakshasa. Skin-side inside, fur-side outside. Beware the man whose eyebrows meet in the middle - he'll do more than break your heart, he'll eat it. The *loco lobisón* that is a shapeshifting terror red in tooth and claw, the mark of the beast burning in his hands plain as the carnage he leaves in his howling wake. The most primeval of demons, the most feared of all the echoes of our long crawl into the light. He must be eradicated, or we

265

acknowledge where we came from, which would never do. They wouldn't spare him if they caught him. And me? Oh, my God - they'd throw away the key.

I was a traitor, the wilful betrayer of civilisation; the anti-mother, the False Maria.

Anathema.

Thirty-one

I sat for a long time after Evan had gone, immobilised with despair, unmoving, not even really thinking, just numb. It was so quiet and still in the cottage, so completely isolated. Only the wind blowing outside and the patter of a brief rain shower that had the slushy edge of water about to turn to ice hitting the windows disturbed the clock-ticked minutes. The sounds of the conversation seemed to echo round the room, coming back in strange random phrases from the walls or ceiling, looming unconnected to anything in the darkening day.

I'd known it wouldn't last - that eventually I'd have to leave Adam to his fate. I'd thought at least, you know, he'd have a slight chance of freedom in the hills. I'd known I'd be caught and punished. Of course I had. But again, with the spotlight on us and the nature of the modern media, I'd at least hoped to be heard before being banged up. But that was all fantasy, it was, it really was. A fucking fantasy. Madness. The reality, the brutal, inescapable reality was that I was thoroughly stuffed, kippered and stitched up by my own, rather shaky, hands. It lay on me, that raw, aching burden like the crushing weight of the night-hag crouching on your chest, breathing into your mouth, foul as vomit.

I can bet that many folk would just nod smugly and go - *serve her right, stupid bitch, she brought it on herself.* Of course I had, I knew that. But I had known - and I mean, proper known - there was nothing else I could have done to save my boy, my son. But that didn't mean I was Rambo, for fuck's sake. It didn't mean I was strong and gung-ho 24/7. Doubt and fear, those nasty hand-in-hand twins, jeered at me and shouted the truth of what was to come in coarse, cruel voices that dinned and echoed round and round until my guts twisted like a nest of snakes and adrenalin spurted through my system randomly, jerking and twisting me, hook in mouth, spine juddering. I would have cried, but no tears came. I would have screamed, but no one would have heard. And if they did, they wouldn't have cared, I knew it.

Eventually, at tea-time - tea-time, Jesus, get out the Royal Doulton, Mother, we've got company - I set the kettle on and managed to chew a bit of bread and butter. Time was like beads on a bit of worn elastic - one minute it was two o'clock the next it had snapped into six and I had no recollection of where the hours had gone. Or five minutes stretched and stretched in a glowing filament that made me feel like I was looking down the wrong end of a kaleidoscope. But a plan was formulating in my aching head. I'd drive to the village and tell Evan I'd been called away unexpectedly, my mother had been taken ill down south. It wasn't serious as such, but I and my family - that was good, *family*, people understood family - felt I should be there, etcetera - I'd be back shortly and not to worry, here was another fortnight's rent. He'd accept that and not question it until the money ran out and there was no sign of me returning. After seeing him, I'd come straight back, pack the van, change the plates to the remaining false set again and leg it pronto to France via ferry. The risk was that they might flag my passport and detain me at the port, but I had to try. If I got through, I'd somehow get another identity and go and work at a recording studio like I'd thought. Vanish, in fact.

Yeah, yeah - it was a good plan, simple, it might work it might be - my head hurt so much. It was as if a red-hot iron band was tightening in my skull, I could hardly think for the pain. I staggered to the sink and necked two aspirins, I was out of iboprufen. I had a sudden feeling I'd done the same thing an hour or so ago, or was it ten minutes? Well, never mind, it was only aspirin, not cocaine - though if I'd had that to hand it would have been straight up my nose in a fucking shot. I'd have a bath, that'd relax me, help me think, help me screw up the courage to go. I'd have a bath and pack.

Adam, Adam I have to go baby boy I have to leave you I don't want to Wild Thing I don't want to God I don't I don't Ma loves you darlin' but I have to for your sake I'll always always love you I'll never forget you never I love you Johnny I love you I love I . . .

I stripped off my clammy, sweat-soaked jumper and trackies and wrapped up in my big old fleece dressing gown. So cold, so cold. I ran the bath, pouring six drops of organic lavender, six of rose attar into the water, watching with brainless fascination as the oil bloomed on the tumbling surface, until I realised the hot water wasn't coming through. I felt the bathroom radiator - stone cold. The heating wasn't working. Evan - the oil, the - he meant to - never mind, never mind.

I staggered downstairs, the fleece wrapped tightly round my bony, yellow body. Suddenly, the heating oil made me think of the van - I must check the oil and water, see to it. Yes, that was a good thing to do. That was organised, efficient. Pausing to slip on my wellies I stumbled into the yard and got in the van. I started it, like they say to do before you check the oil. At least, I put the key in and tried, but nothing happened. The fucking, fucking battery was flat. I must have left the side-lights on or something, something stupid like that. I pounded the steering wheel in impotent rage, tears hot on my icy cheeks. Oh fuck it, fuck it. Oh shit, bastard . . .Wiping the snot off my nose I thought what to do. OK, right. I'd ring Evan, beg for help. Ditzy, silly

269

Annie Eliot - he'd roll his eyes at his wife but he'd come, he would - he'd feel guilty about not checking the heating anyway, that would bring him.

I trudged painfully back to the cottage, my wellies slipping on the wet ground that was rapidly icing into sheet glass and fumbled with the phone. Nothing. No signal. I tried again. No signal, no signal, no - OK, OK, don't panic, don't . . . I'd walk to the village, it wasn't more than a mile or so. I'd walked further than that in worse weather before now.

The wind was getting up again, the temperature had dropped, and it had gone dry and icy, frost-roses were blooming on the windows. I thought of the yard, like a skating rink already. And it was getting darker by the second. So cold. Maybe I'd go tomorrow. I'd go tomorrow, definitely. That'd give me time to get myself together, sort my head out. Meantime, I'd boil kettles, fill a hot water bottle, wrap up in my leopard-print blanket and the cashmere shawl. Be as snug as a bug in a rug. A right little snug-bug. Who used to say that? Oh yes, Johnny's nana, he told me, she used to call him her little snug-bug when she read to him at bedtime. I had been jealous of that, of his big, warm family, of the love showered on him as a child. Jealous because of the arid white stretches of my own childhood nights, lying there, listening to the bile and poison spewing from my father's twisted mouth, hearing the dull, muffled thuds and my mother's passive, hopeless weeping limping on and on until he beat her silent. A snug-bug. I wish I'd been snugged up with a loving grandmother, the coal-fire flickering as she read *The Wind In The Willows*, giggling together over silly Toad, being a proper kid.

I'd watch Johnny's DVD again. That would make me feel better. *The Big Green Dream Festival* - he'd been on top form, truly brilliant. Better lock up first though, better snug-bug the cottage up as best I could.

I shuffled towards the front door, still in my wellies. A cold draught hit me, the top half of the door banged open in the cutting wind. Bloody thing. Bloody countryside, rustic bollocks.

I caught hold of the door. As I did, I looked out into the endlessness of the thick, roiling night. I thought I saw - I thought a shape - it moved . . .

It was Wild Thing.

He was out there. On the frost-silvered black hillside. I knew what he looked like; I'd watched him so many times before. He was a dark shape cut out of the icy ground and the sharp diamond glitter of the freezing stars; sinuous, silent, full of power; a shadow moving this way like thunder creeping over the horizon. You'd never spot him if you didn't know how to look for him. But I know. I know. I . . .

He was up on the bottom half of the door before I finished thinking, crouched for an instant framed in the black terrible night, his eyes catching the light in an opal blaze, his naked body wet and reddened with cold, the smell of him rank and feral, twisted through with a rising twist of musk, the smell of . . . A filament of spit spidered from his partly-opened mouth as he lunged forward, crying like a lost child, *Ma Ma Ma* . . .

As he jumped down from the door frame towards me and I instinctively backed away, slipping in my silly boots, slipping on the wet flags, on the cold Welsh slates, I knew what he wanted and I saw in that second the human and the animal merge in his face; a man and a wolf, a son and a predator. He wanted me.

He loves me.

He . . .

i cant type so good want to tell piff tell everyone sorry so sorry i think wrist broken nose too in pain awful he bit me my neck the side of my neck its theres a big hole tore at me hes so strong so ive got a towel on it but fuck its bleeding bleeding everywhere all over the keyboard what a mess oh god i didnt think i never thought never thought what he would want what he thought he jumped me i fell face forward hit my face my nose couldnt breathe my wrist went crack as i tried to stop myself falling thats why its broken i think swollen up cant move my hand my fingers i cant stop shivering cant stop he fucked me over and over licking my face saying ma ma ma then hed do it again biting at my neck holding me down tearing me, so much pain white and sharp i dont remember everything i dont i never thought christ forgive me i never thought of it but he wanted his mate its logical it is of course but he was my son is my son and im his ma but im his female too the only female he knows and our morals our codes mean nothing to him he doesnt even know they exist dont blame him dont he doesnt know he doesnt im going to walk to the village now im going to try and give myself up i cant do this now i cant do it anymore it was oh god oh god mother mary it was terrible terrible so terrible the pain and the unnatural i cant go through it again no but he ll come back he will i know he will hes hunting now out in the dark on that bloody black hill but he will come back to me and i cant im sorry piff im sorry please dont hate me please its dark out there but theres a bit of moonlight i ll be ok, i will i cant stay here im going to go to the village now im so sorry

he loves me dont hurt him he meant no harm he just followed his nature our nature im going to leave the laptop plugged in and open so whoever reads this whoever reads this dont hurt him dont hurt him please please

272

he loves me

he loves me

i love him

im sorry

johnny

johnny im coming wait

Epilogue

Azrael

BBC NEWS

The body of a woman discovered on a remote Welsh hillside on Friday afternoon was identified today as that of Anne Louise Wynter, the 'Most Wanted Woman in the UK'.

Wynter hit the headlines after she freed killer Adam Bell 'The Cannibal' from a high-security juvenile detention facility and fled with him causing a nation-wide manhunt. Bell has not yet been apprehended and the public are warned under no circumstances to approach him as he is considered extremely dangerous.

Acting Det. Supt. Jim Goring said the terribly mutilated remains were discovered by the owner of the property Wynter had rented using the alias 'Anne Eliot' and posing as a writer seeking a retreat.

He said: 'We are definitely treating this as a case of foul play. Her accomplice, Adam Bell, is an extremely dangerous individual who is our primary suspect and we are doing our utmost to apprehend him. However, the weather and the mountainous terrain are hampering our efforts. I urge the public and the media in the strongest terms to avoid visiting this area either for recreation or any other reason if at all possible and would also ask they refrain from trying to visit the site as we must remind them this is a murder enquiry.'

He added that they expected to detain Bell at any time and anyone with information should contact their local police or ring the central helpline number.

The Sun

WYNTER NOT MY DAUGHTER SAYS MUM

The family of Anne Wynter today sensationally washed their hands of the Cannibal Killer's crazed accomplice. Through the family solicitor they announced that the blonde former junkie - groupie to tragic rocker Johnny Eliot among others - was 'not part of their lives in any way' and hadn't been for years. The family have asked the media to leave them alone as the shock of recent events is telling on the health of their elderly mother. 'She is not my daughter and she's a disgrace to the memory of her late father' were the words read out at the family's press conference, on behalf of frail mum Theresa. Meanwhile the Cannibal Killer still roams free in the Snowdon area terrorising surrounding villages. Police seem no nearer to apprehending the vicious killer as weather conditions worsen and fears are growing that the beast might strike again in a repeat of his shocking murder of little angel, Jakey Jagger.

I'M GLAD SHE'S DEAD SAYS LITTLE JAKEY'S MUM

BRING BACK THE NOOSE FOR CANNIBAL KILLER SAYS JAKEY'S MUM

JAKEY'S GRAN: MY FEARS FOR OTHER LITTLE ANGELS

EVIL WYNTER TRIED TO BED ME SAYS ARTY STUNNA LINA

The Independent

BODY FOUND IN SEARCH FOR BRITAIN'S MOST WANTED WOMAN

A body found on Friday has today been formally identified as that of Anne Louise Wynter, the woman responsible for freeing Adam Bell, the 'Cannibal Killer', from detention.

Wynter, a former drug-addict and record company secretary who worked latterly as a social worker for Bradford Social Services, discovered the notorious killer living rough whilst caring for his mother, now deceased. Wynter appointed herself Bell's guardian despite being involved with the family of tragic toddler Jakey Jagger, Bell's victim, and after suffering a psychotic breakdown over the death of her former boyfriend (the pop star Johnny Eliot) freed Bell from a high security juvenile detention facility. Sources close to the family of Johnny Eliot say the family strongly contest Wynter's claims to have been Eliot's long-term lover saying she was 'delusional' and no more to their son than a 'passing fling with an older woman'.

Today, white forensics tents are erected round the isolated Welsh farm cottage Wynter had rented posing as 'Anne Eliot' a journalist from London, and the lane leading to it, where her remains were found, is a hive of police activity.

Wynter's body was discovered by Evan Griffiths, a local farmer and owner of the holiday cottage. He said at a hastily convened press conference held in the village hall, that he had 'no idea' Eliot was in fact Anne Louise Wynter and that he had on one occasion joked with her about 'the Beast Of Black Hill' which the locals had thought was a wild dog but was, in fact, Adam Bell who is still at large. He also said the village was shocked and horrified to learn her identity and that a number of families with children were staying elsewhere with relatives until Bell was apprehended.

He said: 'We are a quiet community, this is devastating to us and our families. She seemed a nice, friendly person, not at all what you would imagine. She did not look like the photographs of her on the news and she certainly fooled me. We are all praying that the Cannibal is caught as fast as possible so we can rest easy in our beds and life can return to normal.'

Bradford Social Services today declined to comment other than to say the matter was under full internal investigation.

Wynter's only known friend, Ms. Epiphany Charlot, also a social worker, gave a statement to the press saying that she believed Wynter had not been in her right mind when she committed her crimes and that she could not be held wholly responsible for her actions. She further added that she had known Wynter to be 'a caring and responsible worker' and 'a true friend' until her final breakdown. She stated that while her every sympathy lay with the victims of Bell and Wynter, she was personally deeply saddened and distressed by Wynter's actions and her death.

Police have appealed to the public not to try and visit the cottage or the area and remind them that Adam Bell is highly dangerous and known to be extremely aggressive and they should not approach him under any circumstances.

Johnny X – The Journals (GMC Books) £20.00.
Reviewed by Naz Singh

The short lives and untimely deaths of rock 'n' rollers
are the stuff of pop-culture mythology - and the demise
of Johnny Eliot ('Johnny X') of chart-topping rock outfit
Velvet Shank apparently fits neatly into the stereotype,
allowing him to pass swiftly into legend alongside
Hendrix, Joplin and Cobain.

The publication in facsimile - a faux-distressed imitation
of one of Eliot's favourite black Moleskine notebooks -
of Johnny X's rambling *Journals* should both create yet
more wealth for mighty corporation GMC, of which
GMC Books is a subsidiary, and enhance Eliot's status
as a beautiful loser. The speed with which GMC
produced post-mortem 'Best Of' albums, downloads,
ringtones and tribute CDs was breathtaking even in an
industry not known for its empathy or tact. This repro-
duction of Eliot's personal *Journals* would seem to be
yet another cash-in on a dead cash-cow.

However, Eliot turns out to be somewhat more than
merely another stoner rock star. His lyrics are often
genuine poetry - darkly tender and unexpectedly
romantic. His observations of the roller-coaster world of
music are, when he was wasn't high, wry, intelligent and
very funny. The contradiction of Eliot's short life would
seem to be that he was aware of the superficiality and
avarice of his world, but he genuinely loved music and

showmanship. He knew fame is a tainted gift, but he couldn't resist it.

But aside from Eliot's thoughts on his industry, what grabs the attention most - and has produced a tabloid feeding frenzy - are his relationships. Naturally, his on-off partnership with supermodel Lainey Stone comes in for considerable scrutiny. Eliot gives the lie to Stone's much-vaunted claims he wooed her relentlessly until she reluctantly succumbed - in his version she dropped Bob Deichmann of The Data Slaves (her fiancé of the moment) to pursue him relentlessly across the USA on his infamous *White Lines* tour. Eventually, he 'gave in to Lainey, like everyone does in the end, man she just won't f*****g let go.' Stone is reportedly furious at the publication of Eliot's *Journals* and has stated she will be giving her side of events in her forthcoming celebiography, *Lainey - Gathering No Moss* (Brown & Witfield). Stone is now engaged to Dave Shaunessy of the Polar Chimps and expecting her first child.

But it is the stunning revelation that Eliot's famously anonymous lover 'My Lady' was none other than the notorious Annie Wynter, the woman who freed from prison one of the most terrifying and dangerous killers of modern times, that gives a breathtaking immediacy and tragic dimension to Eliot's writings. Given all the notoriety and hype, you might be forgiven for dismissing the *Journals* as mere car-crash voyeurism. This would be an error - as the true cause of Eliot's personal agony is both poignant and genuinely affecting. Eliot, it seems, was passionately in love with Wynter - not with the fragrant Ms. Stone, but with this older, unstable woman he abandoned to chase his dreams of stardom. The loss of Wynter seems to have driven Johnny Eliot to dangerous, and finally fatal, extremes in order to assuage his heartbreak and emotional pain. Knowing that he himself had ended their affair and broken her heart only made things worse and there are innumerable love-letters, poems and lyrics addressing Wynter as 'My Lady' that are agonised confessions of regret and tender evocations of their lost love.

Almost a modern day Romeo And Juliet - except Wynter, from his descriptions, was far from an innocent maiden. Instead she comes across as bright, bold and full of energy with a genuine and empathic understanding of the artist's soul. The perfect Muse, in fact. Also, the perfect mystery. How could such an apparently intelligent woman have committed such a bizarre and insane act? Did Eliot sense her madness, become infected with it? Eliot's family have denied publicly and at length that Wynter is 'My Lady', obviously not wishing to associate their son with Wynter's infamy, and a number of other sources have poured scorn on the idea that Eliot could have been referring to Wynter as 'My Lady', despite the photographic evidence of their affair found at Wynter's welsh bolt-hole after her death. It is a mystery that will doubtless never find a solution, now the two main protagonists are no longer here to speak for themselves.

Johnny X – The Journals are more than a maudlin piece of memorabilia of interest only to Velvet Shank fans, but instead, they are a fascinating insight into the mind of a young and talented artist who chose to burn out rather than fade away and who left in the lingering embers of his destruction the story of an enduring, scandalous and ruined love.

Buy *Johnny X – The Journals* at a special C2 reader's discount price of £15.00 (inc. P&P) from C2booksonline@theclarion.co.uk

Forum @ wordfeastforwordbeasts.com

Subject: The Annie Wynter Story (SingerJackson)

Bubbadee: its bollox im telling you she never was johnny xs squeeze shes lying why would he want an old slappa like that when he had all those hot models on tap. I think its crap anyway I read half of it and chucked it in the bin I don't believe she knew anything about music either she was too old

Dantegirl: I don't think it's fair to slag off a dead woman and I don't see what her age has to do with it. Lots of guys like older women, maybe he did. I don't understand why you think she didn't know anything about rock music, she did work for GMC, that's a fact. I liked the writing, it was contemporary and immediate. I'm only sorry she didn't live to finish it because I don't like the end bit where some corporate editor has put that annoying epilogue.

Bubbadee: you an old chick then dantegirl I bet you are that's why youre sticking up for the fool lol I'm in a band 'the original mind screw' and theres no way id listen to anything from an old woman about the industry anyway she was only a secretary what do they know its complete crapola and she was totally mad

Citizenx: I've read reviews where they say this is the book of the year because it's so raw and powerful and cutting edge. The Times said 'this book changes the face of modern literature forever' and somewhere else I can't remember where said it was the quintessential 21st century novel but I'm not sure it should be classed as a novel, or what it should be classed as. I did enjoy it but I agree with Dantegirl about the add-on bit being rubbish. I wish they'd just stopped it where she stopped, that would have been more poignant I think. Still it's an international best seller so what do we know?

Dantegirl: It's up for the Orange and the Booker and they say it will win. Maybe it should, but I don't know if I count it as true fiction because it's supposedly her memoirs or her journal, or something in between, but who knows? It might all have been made up, or half-made up or anything. We'll see if it wins anything but my vote for the Orange would go to Julia Allston's 'Living Half A Life' it's a beautiful and delicate story about a young woman's coming of age in Venice and OK it's gentle but it's strong too in its way.

Bubbadee: still bollox you lot are just trying to be clever that book is pathetic its all hype and don't forget she was a crim and only got off with it all by getting herself killed by that cannibal nutter if she hadn't no one would have given a s**t about her stoopid book. if you want a good read and a winner for sure try dave allburns 'crux-i-fiction' it's the dogs bollox proper hardcore

Black Glass White Lines
© 2008 Velvet Shank:
Eliot/Graves/De Souza/Peters/Jackson

Black glass white lines why do you try to stop me all the time
Black glass white lines I get the feeling you don't love me at all

The night comes with old tales red smiles and black nails
The liquor pours from diamond rings I am alive I am free

Black glass white lines why do you try to stop me all the time
Black glass white lines I get the feeling you don't love me at all

He room spins through opal eyes blood shot black and white
Her blue eyes meet mine and turn into blood red sugar
and silver white

Still don't know how I came here it doesn't feel like a dream
I said I don't know how I came here it doesn't feel like a dream

Black glass white lines why do you try to stop me all the time
Black glass white lines I get the feeling you don't love me at all

May the Lord my God greet my soul as a friend but remember
Please remember remember I'm not here I'm not here for love

Black glass white lines why do you try to stop me all the time -
no more
Black glass white lines why do you try to stop me all the time -
no more

Black glass white lines why do you try to stop me all the time -
no more
Black glass white lines why do you try to stop me all the time -
no more
No more no more no more no more no more no more no more -
no more

**CANNIBAL WOMAN'S BOOK WINS
TOP LIT PRIZE**

**CANNIBAL BOOK TOPS
BESTSELLER LIST**

**CANNIBAL BOOK TO BE FILMED
FAMILIES OBJECT**